Also by Christopher Dickey

Summer of Deliverance: A Memoir of Father and Son
Innocent Blood: A Novel
Expats: Travels in Arabia, from Tripoli to Tehran
With the Contras: A Reporter in the Wilds of Nicaragua

The Sleeper

A NOVEL

CHRISTOPHER DICKEY

SIMON & SCHUSTER
NEW YORK • LONDON • TORONTO • SYDNEY

SIMON & SCHUSTER
Rockefeller Center
1230 Avenue of the Americas
New York, NY 10020

For information about special discounts for bulk purchases, please contact Simon & Schuster Special Sales: 1-800-456-6798 or business@simonandschuster.com

Manufactured in the United States of America

10 9 8 7 6 5 4 3 2 1

Library of Congress Cataloging-in-Publication Data
Dickey, Christopher.
The sleeper: a novel/Christopher Dickey.
p. cm.
1. Terrorism—Fiction. I. Title
PS3554.I318S57 2004
813'.54—dc22 2004049153

ISBN 0-7432-5877-0

For Carol
Who is home

There is a land of the living and a land of the dead, and the bridge is love. The only survival, the only meaning.

—THORNTON WILDER

Kansas

SEPTEMBER 11–12, 2001

CHAPTER I

Sometimes, just to get my bearings, I think back on the sheer ordinariness of that morning in September. Betsy left before light to start her shift at the Jump Start Restaurant over on 70. I watched her moving through the bedroom, a familiar shadow in the familiar dark. She didn't need to turn on any lights to know where she was and didn't want to because she didn't want to wake me. My eyes were open, as they always were whenever she stirred, but my head was heavy in the pillow and I was as still as a stone in a churchyard. She leaned over and kissed me so lightly that I wasn't sure if I felt her lips or her breath, and she whispered to me, "Kurt, darling, don't let Miriam sleep too late." She stood up for a second, then leaned back down. "Love you, Baby," she said, and she was gone.

The first dim glow of dawn crept into the room about an hour later, and I watched the windows take shape as shadows on the opposite wall. But still, I didn't move. There was no work for me today, and I no longer had the energy or the will, or saw the purpose, of saying prayers. The idea passed through my mind, as ideas do in the early morning, that love had taken the place of faith. And if that was so, then so be it.

Miriam was in her room, too big for her baby bed now. Her Disney Pocahontas nightgown was all scrunched up around her, and her hair was damp. I like for us to sleep with the windows open and the night air moving through the screens. But last night was too hot for that, I thought. Too hot. And she was so peaceful in the dawn cool. She could sleep as long as she wanted. My baby here in my house in my old hometown in Kansas. Nobody and nothing was going to disturb her, not while Daddy was around.

The refrigerator door made a little noise when it opened. I drank the milk out of the carton, then poured myself some of the coffee that Betsy had brewed. The little countertop television was turned on without the sound. She'd just watched it for the time and the weather maps. She didn't care what anybody on it had to say. And now I watched it, too, silently. Smiling faces. Everyone so happy in the morning. So happy. I put a couple of Eggos in the old toaster. The smell of them warming filled the kitchen.

The faces on the television weren't smiling now. Katie Couric looked like something had gone really wrong with her day. And Matt, too. I'd never seen him so serious, unless it was when they were talking about colon cancer.

That's how ordinary the morning seemed. With the sound turned off, just watching their lips move, I thought they were talking about cancer. Or anorexia. Or maybe the death of somebody who worked at the network. And then they showed the New York skyline, and the World Trade Center towers. One of them was burning. Smoke was pouring out of it in every direction, worse than one of those hotel fires in Vegas, billowing up the sides of the building in gray waves of soot. A shape passed through the corner of the frame, and the second tower exploded.

It must have been thirty minutes later, maybe an hour, when Miriam came into the kitchen. She was headed for the refrigerator. She looked at the TV and paid it no attention. She pulled the milk carton off the shelf. She looked at me. She waited for me to say no, and when I didn't, she drank out of the carton, spilling a little on each side of her face. She put the milk back, clumsy and dainty at the same time, and she dragged her chair over to the counter, and climbed up to get a paper towel so she could wipe her face, then wipe up the floor, like Mommy taught her. In case I didn't notice, she held up the paper towel for me to see before she put it in the trash under the sink.

I remember all that now, but it was as if I didn't see Miriam when she was there in front of me. The first Trade Center tower had collapsed, and now the second one was coming down. Thousands would be dead. Maybe tens of thousands.

"Do you want to watch cartoons?" I said.

"Uh-hunh."

I surfed through the channels, but every one of them was showing the collapse of the towers. Finally I reached the Cartoon Network. "There you go, Sugar. Top Cat. I'm going to go out to the garage for a few minutes."

"Daddy?"

"What, Sugar?"

"Can I turn on the sound?"

"Loud as you want," I said. "Loud as you want."

The garage was my workshop. I had my bench and saws in there, and a lot of wood and veneer for the kitchens I install. Against one wall sat a big old lift-top freezer that looked like it might once have held Cokes and Yoo-Hoos in some out-of-the-way general store, which it had, but now there were metal straps on the top and the sides that were held together by a big padlock. If anybody asked, I told them that was so Miriam didn't think about playing in there, and everybody understood that.

I found the key where I had left it, under the bottom tray in my toolbox, and slipped it into the lock. It didn't budge. I turned it harder and felt the metal of the key start to give. Gentler now, I shook it in the lock, slid it a little out, a little in, the key quivering in my grip until the mechanism gave a click, and turned, and the lock sprung open. I felt a rush of satisfaction. "Still got a touch," I said out loud, and a low moan followed my voice out of my lungs until I was breathless.

Folks who go to the Jump Start for coffee in the morning feel kind of possessive about it, like only Westfielders would go there. It's not a franchise, not part of a chain. It's just part of our town. On days when I was working, I'd take Miriam over and drop her off about eight, just as the last customers were pulling out of the lot. But this morning, even at nine-thirty when we got there, the lot was full, and there was a crowd inside staring at the little television on the bracket above the counter.

"Oh, my Sugar! My Darling," said Betsy. I had Miriam in my arms and my wife threw her arms around both of us, stretching to pull us toward her like a woman who thought she'd lost her family forever. Tears were pouring down her cheeks. "This is the most horrible thing I ever imagined."

"It's like Judgment Day," I said.

"I hear you, Brother," came a voice that I didn't think I knew from among the television watchers.

"It's like Judgment Day for some people," I told Betsy, lowering my voice and passing our daughter over into her arms. "But not for us." Betsy rubbed her eyes. "You mind if I get a couple of Cokes out of the back?" I said.

"You have no shame," she said.

"I'm just thirsty."

"Well I don't want to know about it."

"I'll put them in here," I said, holding up my battered old JanSport daypack.

The freezer in the Jump Start is a big one. You can't exactly walk into it, but to get to some of the rear shelves you have to kind of squeeze in. The back corners of it, I'm sure, haven't been seen by any employee, much less any health inspector, since Kansas was Indian Territory. I pulled what looked like a small, red fire extinguisher bottle with no nozzle out of my pack and pushed it to the very back of the very top shelf, then shoved a bag of ice in front of it.

"You get what you wanted?" Betsy asked me when I came back out.

"Is a six-pack too much to take?"

"Baby, nobody's going to notice nothing like that missing today. And not for a long time to come."

On the morning of September 12, at a little after two, when even the neighbor's dog would usually be asleep, I heard the knock on the door that I'd been waiting for, heavy and insistent. Betsy shouted out in her dream, not sure if she'd heard the sound or imagined it.

"Don't you worry," I told her. "It's somebody I was expecting. I just thought they'd show up at a more civilized hour."

"Not some of your damn army buddies."

"Sort of," I said. "You get some sleep. I'll try to keep the noise down."

"You better not wake Miriam."

"Shhhhh," I said.

"Shhhh, yourself."

There were two men at the door, both of them wearing loosened ties and white shirts that looked slept in.

"Kurt Kurtovic?" said the older of the two, holding up his FBI credential.

"What can I do for you gentlemen?"

"Did you know a David Bigler?"

"My brother-in-law."

"He was killed in 1993."

I looked at these two under the porch light, one with his hair cut high and tight like a retired drill sergeant, the other younger and Mormonish, a missionary for the law. The moths and gnats hovered in the glare just above their heads.

"That's right—1993. God, that seems like—that *is* a long time ago. Got into some sort of trouble in Atlanta. I've asked Selma—you know, my sister, his wife—about it a million times, but she doesn't tell me anything. Why don't you ask Selma about it?"

"She said we should come talk to you."

I laughed. "Did she give you guys any coffee? I'll bet she didn't. Come on in."

The pot was already brewing. My Betsy must have started it, then gone back to the bedroom.

"You're not surprised to see us," said High-and-Tight.

"I'm glad to see you. After what happened this morning, I hope you pulled every card on every weird-ass case, every unsolved mystery—every X-file you've got. Dave fits all those categories as far as I can tell."

"What do you remember about the way he died?" asked the Missionary.

"Hell, I don't know. He and Duke Bolide, who used to work up at the cemetery, they got involved with some kind of crazy religious cult. I mean, even crazier than the ones we usually get around here. They went down to Atlanta. There was a shoot-up? Was that it? I don't remember. But Dave wound up dead in that big CNN building, and some Arab guy got hung from the rafters there. Did they ever find Duke? We'd have heard if they did, I guess."

The Feds didn't say anything.

"Is that about the way you've got it?"

"It's the 'Arab guy' we'd like to know more about," said High-and-Tight.

"Can't help you."

"Can't or won't?"

"Can't—and would like to. But I don't even know the name of the Arab guy. *Was* he an Arab guy?"

CHAPTER 2

I don't do my ten-mile run as much as I used to. But that morning after the agents left I thought there was nothing else I could do. I put on my old technical boots, laced them tight around my ankles, and set out for Crookleg Creek. In the first hint of dawn light, the trail was hard to see, and there were times when I had to run in the shallow edges of the water, half leaping from rock to rock. I bellied under fencing, vaulted posts. The sweat came fast, and with it the total concentration on breath, on the pain, on the path, on the nothingness that I was looking for until, three quarters of an hour later, the sun was a red dome on a horizon of tall green corn and the creek was just a trickle coming from a stand of cottonwoods in sight of the Route 70–Route 105 crossroad.

My lungs were burning like a furnace. I felt good. Real good. I entered the long shadow of the trees and followed the darkness in among them, tearing through thin branches of thorns that crossed the trail like tripwires. Near the center of the trees was a pile of rocks that hid the shallow source of the creek. Around them was a small clearing. A lot of trash was lying around, and it wasn't the kind of stuff you wanted to look at too closely. Beer cans, KFC containers, used rubbers. The rocks were scratched and battered and painted with names of high school students and Satanic rock bands. Some of the names I'd heard of, many I hadn't.

But it was the form of the rocks, not what was on them or around them, that interested me. I wondered if they'd been put here by men, and I believed they were, probably by Osage or Kaw. There was no way to be sure, because there was nothing written about this place in any of the books at the library, and everyone just called it "the Rocks" or "Jeffers' Rocks," because that was the family name of the people who used to own the land.

Ever since I was at Fort Benning, I'd been on the lookout for places like this, where a few men have come together to build with their own hands a house for their gods. There was a place like that on a back road at Benning, a rough one-room clapboard church with a sagging roof and flaking whitewash and torn plastic bags where the glass in the windows ought to be. There were two rough benches, and a table cobbled together from spare lumber, which would have been the altar, and behind that a cross that was nothing more, or less, than two boards nailed together on the wall. When I looked at it, I could see the hands of the men who'd made it, rough and cracked, with seams of raw pink in the black knuckles and torn calluses across the lightness of the palms as they gripped the splintering oak and drove home the nails.

There must be a time, I thought, when you're building the house of God, and you feel His presence.

That was what I had looked for in the pureness of faith and surrender to the One God, but I'd been wrong. I'd deceived myself into thinking man could kill for the sake of his God—and secretly I'd believed I could share in the power of that God. It took me a long time to realize that killing like that is for the sake of killing, nothing more. It is the builders who find their way to Paradise, if there is a Paradise.

The men who put these stones around this spring at Jeffers' Rocks, did they feel the presence of their gods? Did they leave their own spirits, and the spirits they summoned, somewhere hidden in these litter-filled crevices?

I couldn't know. Maybe they weren't Indians at all. Maybe

they were just homesteaders piling the stones that broke their plows. But it seemed to me there was a shape, an order, a purpose to the way the rocks were laid that went beyond that. There was something here, and one day at the end of a long hard run, I thought I would see it. Or feel it.

How do you make a home for God? I asked myself.

I headed back toward our house.

How do you make a home for yourself? What is the spirit that makes it happen—that makes one place comfort your soul, and another not?

I fell into an easy stride, somewhere between pain and meditation.

Betsy was the spirit that made our home. She's "just a little slip of a thing—a tadpole," her stepdad, Deputy Sheriff Bud Nichols, used to say, "but she's got more guts than a burglar." That wasn't quite right, I thought, but it was close. She sure wasn't tall. I was more than a foot bigger than she was. When we first started going out, one night I lifted her off the ground to kiss her good night and she froze in my arms. "That make you feel good?" she asked me, and I never did it again.

How tough was Betsy? I guess that depended on who you were. She was protective about her body. She wasn't easy to touch at first. And she was real protective about anybody else she loved because she didn't have that much loving herself as a kid. She never knew her father at all, and her mother brought her up alone the first eight years of her life, until Deputy Nichols, as he used to say, made an honest woman of her.

The deputy wished Betsy was a boy, and he wished Betsy was his own, and she didn't want to be either. She went kind of wild when she was fifteen, sixteen, I guess. A lot of boys, a lot of drinking, a lot of fuck-yous to the deputy. Then her mom died of breast cancer, and Betsy moved out of the house.

When I met her after my wars, in 1993, she was twenty-two and on her own and every bit a woman. She came up behind me in the Wal-Mart book section and the first thing she ever said to me was, "You gonna read one of those?" She was wearing shorts and flip-flops and a T-shirt that was a size too small, and the way she smiled I figured she was laughing at me inside.

"Why?" I asked.

"'Cause you been looking at the backs of those books so long, I wonder if you can read at all."

Not a great introduction, but things got better after that. I asked her out, and we dated about three months, and broke up about five times, before I asked her to marry me.

"Why?" she asked when I popped the question.

"To make a life," I said. And I guess it was the right answer, because that's what we'd been doing, or trying to do, ever since.

"What God hath joined together, let no man put asunder." I said the words out loud as I picked up the pace on that long run back to my wife and my baby and my home.

CHAPTER 3

The ringer on the phone in our bedroom didn't work anymore. It clicked and buzzed like a wounded robot, and I barely heard it when I got out of the shower. I thought Betsy's voice would be at the other end. It was her morning off, and she hadn't been at the house when I got back from my run. She usually left a note to say where she and Miriam had gone. But this time she hadn't.

"Salaam Aleikum." A man's voice.

"Aleikum salaam," I said, feeling a chill of recognition. "Griffin?"

"Hah! You remembered after all these years."

"I remembered."

"You been worried I'd call."

"Not until just now."

"I'm over at the Super 8."

"Yeah?"

"How about some breakfast?"

"Have we got something to talk about?"

"Just old times, that's all. Kuwait, Bosnia, New York, Atlanta. You know what I'm talking about."

"Let's meet at the Chuckwagon, it's down the road from the motel."

"I sort of like the Jump Start. You never know who you'll meet at the Jump Start."

"You want to see me? Meet me at the Chuckwagon."

I never liked Griffin, not since I first saw him during Ranger training at Dugway, praying secretly in the desert—the ritual prayers of a Muslim. He hated me before I hated him, and I always thought part of it was a race thing. My blond hair, my blue eyes: some African-Americans looked at me and saw someone perfect to hate. In the Georgia mountains during one of the Ranger exercises, Griffin turned the whole thing personal, and there were a couple of seconds when I thought he was going to kill me. Then, later, after I'd been with the mujahedin in Bosnia, I saw Griffin in New York on a Secret Service detail. I tried to call him from Atlanta when the moment came for the terror to begin—horror so vast that America might never recover. But Griffin didn't answer, and I had stopped the plague myself.

To hear from him now—and here, in Westfield—was bad news. Almost the worst news.

When I pulled the truck away from the house, the emptiness of the yard shook me a little. Where was Betsy's car? Where was *she*?

Griffin sat in a booth leafing through the newspaper. He looked at me, nodded, and waited for me to sit down. He folded the paper and looked again at the huge headline, holding it up for me to see: AMERICA UNDER ATTACK. "Good morning," he said, leaning forward slightly across the table. "Glad you could make it."

"What brings you here?"

Griffin looked into my eyes for a long time, waiting for me to fill the silence, but I just looked back. Last time I'd seen him he was part of Clinton's detail. He'd been steroid-hard, pumped up, like he ate and slept on the weight bench. Now his face was rounder, his shoulders not so square. I figured he had a desk job. "I came just to see you," he said.

"Ain't I lucky."

"Listen, Kurtovic, I know all about you."

"Uh-hunh." If he had, I wouldn't have been in Westfield, I'd have been in Leavenworth. Or dead.

"I know about you and the muj."

"Seems like a long time ago," I said. "I'm a carpenter these days."

"Yeah, I know that, too. Self-employed."

I shrugged. "What do you want, Griffin?"

"Kind of like Uncle Sam," he said. "I want you."

"Not interested."

He held up the paper so I could look at the picture of the Trade Center in flames. I nodded. "Nothing I can do about that," I said.

His eyes narrowed. "Hell, you say."

I smiled. "You ain't working for the Secret Service anymore, are you?"

"Changed agencies."

"I figured. And what you want—let me guess—what you want is for me to get in touch with some of my old buddies in the muj."

"That's about the size of it."

"Because you think they did this."

"We know they did this."

"Do you?"

"Yes."

"Bullshit. It's only been twenty-four hours since the attack, and now you know for sure who did it? If you know that much that quick, you *knew* enough to have stopped it. You don't know anything. You've got no idea and, you know what, me either. I got no idea what's going on. But I can tell you one thing, I don't have any old buddies in the muj. If I ever did, they're dead. You still pray?" Griffin made a motion with his hand like we were playing cards and he was telling the dealer he'd pass.

"No?" I said. "Did you let your bosses know how you prayed? I'll bet you didn't. But I'll bet you think you got great insights."

"Here's my insight. In 1992 you quit the Rangers. Seems you got religion, found Allah during the Gulf War or something. You went to Bosnia, where your father came from, and you joined the muj there. Then you came back to the States and landed a job Xeroxing stuff at the Council on Foreign Policy for a researcher named Chantal Richards, a middle-aged broad you were fucking. You were in contact with Rashid Yousufzai, who was at that time planning the first attack on the World Trade Center. His body was found in Atlanta, hung from the catwalk in the CNN center. Your brother-in-law's body was found there the same day. Also on the same day, we have video of you at the Atlanta airport. How's that for insight?"

"You guys don't share much with the FBI, do you?"

"We can if we need to."

"Y'all ready to order?" The waitress stood over us, and I had the weird sense she'd materialized out of nowhere.

"Just some more coffee," said Griffin.

"Ham and eggs. The eggs over easy," I said, "with hash browns." And she went away.

Griffin nodded and smiled. "Ham?"

"I'm dereligioned," I said. "I've got no use for preachers, no use for imams, and no use for holy warriors."

"So you're our man."

"No," I said. "I don't work for the USG. Not now. Not ever again."

"Don't say no," said Griffin. "Say you'll think about it."

"No," I said.

"You will think about it," he said. "You can't help thinking about it."

About that much he was absolutely right.

CHAPTER 4

Betsy's old Saturn was in front of the house, and I looked in it as I walked past just to make sure everything was the way it should be. Betsy and Miriam must have gone to Wendy's for a burger because there were some loose fries and a half-drunk shake in the back next to Miriam's car seat. In the front, the passenger side was piled with papers and a big loose-leaf notebook for the night class on Web design that Betsy was taking at South Kansas College. In front of the driver's seat the visor was turned down, and I figured Betsy had been looking at herself, and maybe brushing out her hair. She didn't wear much makeup. The checklist showed everything normal. A little messy, but normal.

I leaned in the car and picked up some of the trash, put up the visor, and cradled Betsy's books in my arm like I would have done if we'd been walking home from school together.

"Where'd you two go?" I shouted as I let the screen door slam behind me. But no one answered.

Fear ran under my skin like electricity. The kitchen was empty, and so was our little family room. I went down the hall. Miriam wasn't in her room. I listened. Nothing. The door to our bedroom was opened. Sheets were jumbled in a pile on the unmade bed.

I don't know what I saw at that moment. A kind of emptiness. As if the last five years had just disappeared and there was no history before this moment, and there wouldn't be any history after. Blank past, blank future, blank present, and the whole of me as hollow and weightless as a ghost.

Then the sheets moved.

"Well?" said Betsy. "You got something better to do?"

"Oh, Baby," I said, shaking my head to drive out the images that had just been there. I threw off my shirt and unbuttoned my jeans. "But where's Miriam?"

"Left her over at her Aunt Lea's. Thought we could use a little break to cheer us up." She looked me up and down. "I can see you're ready to cheer me up. Come here, darlin', put your arms around me like a circle round the sun."

She smelled like life, my Betsy. I held her close to me and breathed her in. We kissed so that our lips just touched, just barely, and passion moved between us like a spirit, through our mouths, through our eyes. Her breasts were small and round and as I ran my tongue over them in the mid-day brightness of the room she stopped me for a second. "Don't, baby, don't look at the stretch marks," she said. And all I could do was laugh. "Everything looks better than perfect to me," I said. There was no use telling her how much I loved every inch of her body, inside and out, including those tiny lines on the side of the breasts that had held the milk for my daughter. And those wonderful pink nipples, so hard against my fingertips and my tongue. Her stomach, just slightly rounded, and soft, and warm as the earth on a summer day. The light brown hair between her legs, glistening now, rich with the human-animal smells of love, her vagina tasting of salt and iron, like blood, like the world of the living. "Get your face back up here and do your duty," she said, and as I slid inside her, feeling her body slowly giving way to mine, there was no world but this one of the here, and of the now.

The Kansas sun coming through the little skylight in our roof made a shining square around us on the bed, forcing us to close our eyes as we lay in each other's arms. And in that enormous moment of peace I realized that I had never in my life been so happy, or so afraid.

"Let's talk," said Betsy.

"Let me listen to you breathe," I said. "Let's just let ourselves be."

It has seemed strange to me, always, that women want to talk about every single thing in life, while men just want to know that those things are there: love, family, home. Talking about them doesn't make them happen. They're worlds within worlds that you create by being together, by building together. And it's all so fragile, I thought, as I lay there with Betsy in our room in our house in the square light of the sun. You build and you share and you love and you dream—and you fight and you cry—and you build some more. And still people will come out of nowhere to take it all down, tear it all apart.

Griffin. He and I talked for ten minutes, maybe, and he threatened me ten times. He threatened me with the law, he threatened me through my family, he threatened me through my pride.

"Easy, Baby," said Betsy, running her finger along my jaw. "What's all this? You're so tense."

"What happened yesterday," I said. "It's left a kind of hole in me."

"Everybody feels like that, Darlin'. Everybody."

I kissed her. "Yeah." But I could not tell her what was closing in on us. I could not explain how much I knew about the terror, how much I had been a part of it.

I, Kurt Kurtovic, thirty-four years old, born in Kansas, have seen war and death and more than once have caught sight of the eternal hereafter. I have been a soldier of the American government, and of God Almighty. Righteousness followed me many days of my life, and there was a time when I believed that I, with the help of the Lord, could change the face of America and the world.

Killing was something I did well. I was trained as a U.S. Army Ranger, specialized in demolition. I first saw action in Panama, then the Gulf War. After that I embraced Islam, the unremembered religion of my immigrant father, and I went to Bosnia to find my family's roots and my self. But I found nothing except a new place to practice my skills at slaughter. Sickened to death by death, I wanted to find a way to stop the killing once and for all, and I let myself be persuaded that only by making the United States feel the pain of the rest of the world could there finally be peace and justice for all.

I have held in my hand a terror to end all terrors. And yet, I could not do the thing that I had prayed to do, could not bring myself to unleash a plague that would decimate the nation's children. And I had killed the man who would.

No one had known, I thought. No one had seen. I came home to the quiet unawareness of a Main Street where someone was always flying the American flag. Westfield, Kansas. I had left because I thought I had no roots here. When I came back I discovered this place was as close to me as the eye in my face. It was the lens through which I saw the world. And I had fallen in love with Betsy, who was a little girl I never had noticed when I left for the wars, and was a wonderful woman when I returned. We had built our life. We had conceived a future.

How do you protect such a thing, when you know firsthand the horrors that lie in wait?

"Betsy," I said, "I think I'm going back on active duty."

She was silent for a while.

I rolled over to look at her face and into her eyes. "I won't be gone long. A few weeks maybe. At most a few months. And we'll be getting a regular paycheck. That won't be so bad."

"Oh, God, Kurt." She turned her face away. "Oh, God. Don't—don't." She was quiet for a long time and I felt her body harden in my arms. "Just come back to me," she said. "Just come back to us."

"God himself couldn't keep me from doing that," I said.

"It's too early for a story, Daddy."

"You mean it's too early for you to go to sleep."

"Yes."

"How about a story now and sleep later?"

"Yes!"

"Once there was a mean old man—how mean was he?"

"Very, very mean."

"Very, very, very mean. And meaner than that."

"Ohhh, very mean."

"Yep. And the mean old man lived on a big old mountain. And you know what they called him?"

"The Old Man of the Mountain!"

"You've heard this story before."

"Go on, Daddy."

"And everybody around that mountain for miles and miles—thousands of miles—was scared of the Old Man. They knew he could turn boys and girls into birds."

"Big birds."

"Scary birds. With big claws. Who would swoop out of the sky and—"

"Don't tickle, Daddy. Don't!"

"And sometimes the birds would carry little children away and hide them in a cave deep in the mountain."

"Bad birds."

"Very bad. And sometimes the birds would poke holes in the clouds with their beaks, and make it rain when little kids wanted to go out to play. And sometimes they made big clouds of smoke that burned everybody's eyes. And sometimes they just pooped on everybody's head."

"Daddy!"

"Really! And then one day the birds made a big mistake. They picked up a princess who was, oh, just about your age, and they carried her away to the mountain and dropped her in the cave. And you know what her name was?"

"Miriam!"

"Yes it was. And Miriam was a very beautiful princess. She wore shoes just like yours, but made of jewels that sparkled like starlight. She wore a dress made of silk as blue as the sky.

And in her long blonde hair, which was almost as pretty as yours, she wore two golden barrettes as shiny as the sun. Princess Miriam took one look around that cave and she said, 'Hey, I'm not staying in this dump!' So she waited until she saw a ray of light coming down. It wasn't much. Just a thin, weak little light. But when she caught it with her golden barrette, it got stronger, and it started to light up the whole cave so that all the kids could see each other, and, even more important, they saw the ladder that was hidden all this time in the dark. One by one, with Princess Miriam leading the way, they all climbed out and . . . I'll tell you more next time."

"No! Now!"

"The Old Man used to eat his breakfast every morning at a big old table on top of the big old palace on top of the big old mountain so he could look out and see all the lands and all the people that were afraid of him. The little boys and girls he'd turned into birds were in cages and on perches all around and they made an awful lot of noise. So he didn't hear Miriam and the kids from the cave when they came tiptoeing, and sidestepping, and elbow-sliding through the hallways of his palace. They ran up behind him and pushed him so hard that the old chair, and the old table, and the Old Man fell off the mountain, down and down and down into a deep dark hole that sucked him in—pop!

"As soon as he was gone, the birds turned back into little boys and girls. The cave in the mountain suddenly became a sunlit garden. And everybody agreed that Miriam should be the queen of all the lands, and all the peoples, for a thousand miles around, for ever and ever. And so, Miriam, who was very happy, invited her daddy to come and drink milk with her every morning, sometimes out of the carton, and they lived happily every after."

Betsy stood in front of the bookshelf that took up one wall of our family room. She ran her fingers over the spines, many of them cracked and broken, touching them delicately, like she could learn something from their texture or their temperature. "You've been waiting a long time for this," she said.

A chill seeped into my gut. She could not know how right she was, how long I had waited for this time, and how afraid of it I was. She knew I'd been a Ranger. She knew I'd experimented with different religions and she knew I was "in a special counterterrorist task force." I'd told her all that when we were dating, and I wasn't even sure she believed me then. The stepdaughter of the deputy sheriff in Westfield was used to lawmen bullshitting her. But I didn't think I'd told her anything else. Not the whole truth, anyway.

"Look at all these books," she said. "There's hundreds of them." They were mostly histories and mostly in historical order, starting with my mother's Bible and my father's Qur'an. Karen Armstrong's *Holy War.* Amin Maalouf's *The Crusades Through Arab Eyes.* Bernard Lewis's little book *The Assassins,* which was the real story, I thought, of the Ismailis and the Old Man of the Mountain who led them nine hundred years ago. I was fascinated by the way violence and faith came together, and by all that they destroyed. And the books had helped me understand that world I touched and turned away from. They taught me about the difference between faith and fanaticism, between salvation and destruction.

"These books took you away from me," she said. "When you were reading them you were far, far away."

"They saved me," I said.

"Saved you from what?"

But that I could not tell her.

I looked out the window of the executive jet at splashes of light five miles beneath us. Small towns set among big farms. The heart of America in darkness.

"Do you think there's any chance it's over?" said Griffin.

"No," I said, "it's not over, and it didn't just begin. You

know that. I know that. The killers know it. The only people who didn't know this war was on were the people down there. And they still don't know what to make of it. They've spent their whole life in the eye of a hurricane. Death and destruction everywhere around them, but all they saw was blue skies."

"Didn't know you were such a bleeding heart," said Griffin.

"Now everybody bleeds," I said and looked away from America and into the face of this man from the Agency. "So, you tell me, Griffin. We've got a whole wide world of people who hate the U.S.A. And whatever it was that kept them off us, whatever that magic shield was, it's gone. How do you make it safe down there again?"

"You take out the bad guys," he said.

"Which ones?"

I leaned back and closed my eyes, trying to remember the touch, the smell, the taste of Betsy, and the deep honey color of her eyes before she began to cry.

London

SEPTEMBER 20–22, 2001

CHAPTER 5

People don't look into their own backyards very much, not even people like Abu Seif, who should have been looking over his shoulder all the time. It was early night and I stood outside the plate-glass door behind his two-story house on the outskirts of London. Muddy plastic toys and soggy cardboard boxes littered the little plot of scruffy grass. He didn't notice them. Didn't notice me. I might as well have been invisible. He never looked up.

Abu Seif had gained a lot of weight since I knew him in Bosnia. He was one of the preachers who came and went, pushing us to fight and die. I never saw him lift a weapon, or even his own bag. But, Lord, how his language moved us. We were fighting against Evil itself, he said. We were spreading the word and the will of the Lord.

And whatever it was we actually believed about the Paradise he promised, or the Almighty Allah he said we served, there was no doubt at all about the Evil that we faced there in the dark cold core of the Balkans. Every village we saw after the Chetniks were driven out was overwhelmed by cruelty. Muslim girls were raped and dismembered, Muslim grandfathers mutilated, Muslim children burned alive where they hid, cowering, too scared to cry and too young to know how to pray. We had seen this for ourselves again and again. We told Abu Seif, and he took the message of righteous fury to every new group of recruits, playing on their anger until they—we—were ready to do whatever it took to stop the slaughter. And so we learned, ourselves, to slaughter. We waded through the blood and learned to love the fire.

Then Abu Seif came to England. To this suburb called Ealing, with its gray rows of half-repaired houses, where I had been tracking him, watching him, looking over his shoulder now for two days and three nights in streets that smelled like curry and cigarettes, mildew and vinyl.

Abu Seif had claimed political asylum in England. He couldn't go back to Algeria, where he was born, he said. So he collected welfare checks. He married two women, both of them teenagers. He fathered four children in three years. He kept on preaching the duty of holy war—Good Lord, he could make it sound glorious!—inspiring the sons of Pakistani grocers and Sudanese cabdrivers, inflaming the restless younger brothers of Palestinian bankers and Yemeni doctors. He told so many tales of bravery, some of them were stories that he'd heard, some of them he made up, and all of them he claimed to have seen with his own eyes. Videotapes of his sermons were everywhere in Europe. There were French kids who'd embraced the cause, some Italians and Spaniards, and even pink-cheeked Englishmen. When Abu Seif thought the recruits were ripe for blood and fire, he helped send them to Peshawar and on to Afghanistan, Chechnya, the Philippines, while he stayed here, safe in Ealing.

Abu Seif sat in front of his computer. He was wearing a short white robe like the friends of Muhammad were supposed to have worn. His legs were spread wide to let his belly push out. His beard was long enough now to rest on his gut. He moved his balls around with his left hand but couldn't seem to get them in the place he wanted them.

On the desk near the computer screen were a microphone and headphones, a jumble of Arabic newspapers, a glass full of tea, a couple of Bic pens, a few envelopes, and a letter opener that looked like a dagger. The steel blade was about four inches and engraved with red and green curlicues and crisscrosses. It had a hilt like a tiny Crusader sword. Now Abu Seif put on a pair of earphones and spoke into a microphone. *"Bismallah al-Rahman al-Rahim."* I watched the words take shape on his lips. "In the name of God, most Gracious, most Merciful." So began his sermon about hate. Every Saturday night he preached jihad online. This night, as I looked on from the gloom of his little backyard, I could see dozens of names in the chat room auditorium on his screen. He talked and talked. More names popped up. Others disappeared. As he mumbled into the microphone, Abu Seif looked like a trained bear in a glass cage, a beast in a circus who was perfectly harmless, until you were inside the cage with him.

I knocked on the sliding door. Abu Seif turned faster than you'd think a man that fat could move. He looked at my hands and saw they were empty. Now, as he switched off his mike, he studied my face. His eyes recognized me, but he didn't know from where. I knocked again, and he slid the door open about six inches.

"Salaam aleikum," I said. "They're watching out front."

"Aleikum salaam. They are watching all places." He had not lost his heavy North African accent. His voice sounded like gravel under water. "Why do you care?"

"I met you in Cazin," I said. "I'm the American."

The memory surfaced behind his eyes. "And now you are in my yard? No. I do not know you," he said.

I braced my hand and forearm in the door and shoved it wide open. Abu Seif stepped away, but kept his balance, ready to come back at me. I held up my hands, open and empty. "You know me, brother, and if you don't help me, I don't know where I'm going to go."

"This is not right," he said. "There is no reason for you to be here."

"Listen. I was in the middle of America when the thing happened. Some people know I was a mujahid, and they came after me. I got out through Canada and came here. But I don't know where to go now."

"How did you get into England?"

"It's easy if you look like me."

"But you came with your own passport."

"Yes."

"So they know you are here."

"They'll figure that out," I said. "That's why you've got to help me. I need a new passport. I need to know where to go."

Abu Seif looked me up and down. "I will search you," he said. I raised my hands again. He patted down my legs and felt under my arms. I couldn't read his expression. "Would you like some tea?" he said. "Have a seat. I will get some." He stepped out of the room and closed the door behind him. I heard him shouting in Arabic, and a woman's voice answering. Then there was silence for a minute or two. I picked up the letter opener from the desk and studied the designs. The blade was surprisingly sharp against the sworled surface of my thumb. The scabbard, which I hadn't noticed before, was half-hidden by a newspaper. "Granada," it said in flowery letters. A souvenir.

I watched the door as I heard Abu Seif's heavy footsteps. I couldn't be sure if he'd be bringing reinforcements, or carrying a weapon. But all he had in his hand was a tray with two glasses of hot tea and a bowl of sugar.

Abu Seif sucked the steaming drink into his mouth. "Why do you think I can help you?" He wiped his mustache and beard with his sleeve.

"I'm hoping," I said.

His expression seemed to consider my hope. He looked me up and down again. Then he glanced at his watch, which looked like a Rolex. The steel band was embedded in the fat of his arm. "I must get back to my audience," he said. "The interval is over. And—there is nothing I can do for you."

"Just a contact," I said, trying to control a kind of anger I hadn't felt in a long time. This fat, phony son of a bitch held the keys to what I needed, and he was going to sit on them.

"You may finish your tea," he said, and put the earphones

on again. "*Bismallah al-Rahman al-Rahim.*" On the screen in front of him, nickname after nickname appeared: Zamzam, slaveofallah, SAD412, ameer_20, friendlyboy, alf_laylah, tiger-eye, amaze_15. Abu Seif took his finger off the Control button on the keyboard, turning off his microphone for a second. "I am not going to help you," he said, and turned back to the screen.

"Brother, I understand," I said. "I am sorry, but I understand. Can you give me a number to call a taxi? I will have it meet me down the road."

"A taxi?" Abu Seif was turned completely away from me and toward the screen. He shook his head like he couldn't believe I would ask for a taxi. I looked at the roll of flesh bulging behind his neck. He pulled up his address program on the screen and typed in the password.

I rammed the point of the letter opener into the back of his neck, driving it home like a tenpenny nail, straight and true above the third vertebrae, then widened the hole with a quick move back and forth. The cartilage popped, and with it the nerve. Abu Seif rolled off the chair, twitching just a little, then he lay still. More tea spilled across the floor than blood.

He was the first man I'd killed in almost nine years, and I was glad it was clean. I sat down at the microphone and watched the text messages roll. "Can't hear you," wrote alf_laylah. "Something wrong with mic," wrote slaveofallah.

"Moment . . ." I typed. "Someone else speak?"

SAD412 came on the earphones, and began to talk about *takfir*—the "anathema" heaped on hypocritical Muslims.

I opened my Yahoo home page, and started uploading Abu Seif's address files into my online briefcase. Then one by one I clicked on the nicknames in the chat room to get their user profiles. Tiger-eye wore the *hijab,* the veil, and was looking for a husband. Slaveofallah was a student in Minnesota. SAD412—"not available." Friendlyboy did not list a name, but there was an address, in Spain, in Granada. In itself that was strange. And there was the coincidence of the letter opener. I clicked the Start button on the Windows program and launched the "Find" function for files containing text "Granada."

I pulled the phones off one ear. I could hear Abu Seif's children running upstairs, and one of his wives in the kitchen. But I was sure they wouldn't bother us. They'd be trained not to see, or be seen by, strange men in the house, and Abu Seif must have told them I was here when he went out to get the tea.

In a box on the screen, a little magnifying-glass icon circled clockwise over a little page icon. Circling. Circling. I heard SAD412 proclaiming all Arab rulers *kafir,* or unbelievers. Circling. Circling. A message appeared on the screen: "There are no items to show in this view."

I typed in "Grenada." The magnifying glass circled. Nothing.

Someone was knocking at the door. I took off the headphone to hear better. Sounded like a small hand knocking. A child's. And she wasn't giving up. "Baba?" I could hear her voice. "Baba?" I didn't see a lock on the door. If it opened, there would be a baby standing there, looking at her dead father, and at me. In a kind of panic I pulled the earphone jack out of the socket. The room was filled with SAD412's voice denouncing the hypocrite rulers of Arabia. The little girl quit knocking. Hearing men talking, she went away.

The files in My Documents were mostly in Arabic. I uploaded everything after August 1 into my Yahoo page so it would be stored online for me to access anytime from anywhere.

Abu Seif's skin was white now beneath his beard. His black eyes were still open and clouded like wax paper. "Welcome to Paradise," I said, and pulled the letter opener out of the back of his neck. I wiped the blood off on his robe, put the blade under the leg of the desk and jerked up so it snapped. It made an okay screwdriver. I lifted the cover off the computer's tower to expose its innards.

"Jump Start Restaurant, best burgers in Kansas, what can we do for you?" Behind Betsy's voice I could hear the clatter of dishes. Lunch would be over now, and she'd be ending her shift soon.

"Hey, Sugar," I said, careful not to use her name and hoping she'd remember not to use mine.

"Why how you doin', Sunshine?"

I laughed. That's my girl, I thought. We were more than lovers, she told me one time, more than husband and wife. "We're accomplices," she said. I never forgot that because it was just so right.

"I'm fine. Just fine," I said. "Customers paying their bills?" The first check should have arrived from Griffin's shop, and that should help put Betsy's mind at ease. She always worried about money, and she had a right to. We lived pretty close to the edge sometimes.

"So far so good," said Betsy.

"Glad to hear that. Sometimes they stiff you, you know. I always feel like, when they pay up, you ought to cash that check and put it away someplace safe. Someplace they can't find it."

"Sounds like good advice," she said. "So what can I do for you?"

"I was hoping I could make a reservation there for a big party around my birthday."

"When would that be?"

"February second," I said. Not my birthday, in fact. "Groundhog Day. By then, we'll know if winter's over."

I heard a dish shatter on the floor. "My goodness," said Betsy, "you do plan in advance. That's a long time from now. Four and a half months."

"Lots to do. Really an awful lot. And it needs doing."

"And nobody but you can do it."

"Nobody."

"Sounds like lonely work."

"Very lonely," I said. "Very, very lonely."

Griffin was out of breath as he fell in beside me and we ran along the edge of a long, shallow lake in the middle of Hyde Park in central London. He didn't say hello at first. He concentrated on keeping pace, and keeping control.

"You're toast," he said at last. "You killed the wrong man."

"That's what you think."

"That's what the Brits think. He was one of theirs."

"Fuck he was."

"He was."

"He was a user," I said. "Using them." I picked up the pace. More breaths, less words is what I wanted. "They know about me?"

"Nobody made connection—but me."

"So no problem."

"It's over."

"Just beginning." Faster now. "Five. Six. More like him."

"No."

"You firing me?"

"Sending you home."

We ran for a few hundred yards without saying anything, through a little tunnel under a road, then up toward a huge fountain and pond. The sun was up now, and we were starting to have company in the park.

"What'd Brits tell you?" I asked.

"Asset murdered. Ealing."

"His hard drive?"

"They got it."

"No, man, you got it," I said, "if you want it."

We were in the middle of a small meadow with a stone monument in the center that looked like a miniature Washington monument. From there we could see everyone for 360 degrees around, and nobody was close. I sprinted toward the monument and stopped beside it like I'd just crossed a finish line. Griffin came up about five strides behind me.

"*You* got the drive?" he said.

I nodded. "You'll get it."

Griffin laughed. "Lord," he said. "Lord. There is justice."

I laughed, too.

"When it comes to this stuff," said Griffin, "the Brits don't share shit. But—"

"But—?"

"But seriously. Time for you to go home."

"Think so?"

"Know so."

I took a long, deep breath. Then another one. "You were smart to find me, Griffin."

"Yeah. Right."

"Smart enough. But you don't know these guys. You don't know what they can do."

"I know 'em as well as anybody in my shop," said Griffin. He put his hands on his knees and tried to get more air. I thought he was going to puke. "I know the faith. Like you. I know the files, which you don't. And"—his face went stone hard —"I saw Ground Zero."

"Yeah, well, they can do that again." I took another deep breath. "And again." One more breath, slow. "And worse."

"They're smart," said Griffin. "Smart as hell. Unpredictable as hell. And that's why . . ." He groaned. "That's why we got to coordinate, got to keep everybody on board—the Brits, the Germans, even the fucking French —work with the other services."

"Uh-hunh."

"This thing with Abu Seif. Shit! Your mission was to penetrate the organization, not take it out all by yourself."

"Let me ask you something. How much time do you think we've got?"

"Don't know."

"Me either. But somebody out there is checking off days on a calendar, maybe even setting his alarm clock. And you're not going to find out who that is and what he knows with some interservice liaison committee."

"You don't follow procedures and I get fucked. I don't like that."

"We stick to procedures and we all get fucked. Big time. And you know it. You keep catching bait fish and pretending you're going up the food chain. We got to move faster than that. I will do what I have to do whether you help me or not."

"You're fucking crazy."

"Sure. Crazy, and worse: I've got common sense. You think these assholes like Abu Seif are complicated? Unpredictable? That's because you got to have everything approved by committee, you got to have your flow chart, you got to have salaries and pensions and bonuses, and you think they do, too."

"Spare me."

"You know what jihad is about for these guys, Griffin?"

"Holy war. Paradise."

"Think 'glory,'" I said. "I don't believe for a second that the smart ones really think when they die they'll wake up with virgins waiting on them hand and foot. And if they do, that's just a bonus. What they *know,* what they count on, is that their names are going to be up in lights—here—right on earth—and right now. Ground Zero's not about God, it's about Hollywood. It's *The Ten Commandments* meets *Independence Day,*" I said. "I've been inside their heads. I know that. And so should you."

"We're a whole lot smarter than you think," said Griffin.

"Yeah? Ask those poor dead bastards in the Trade Center how smart you are."

"Fuck you," said Griffin.

"Yeah? You've been grabbing people all over the map for three years, and you didn't know shit about that attack."

"I ain't got all day to listen to your Power Point presentation," said Griffin. "We know what goes on."

"Tell me something, Griffin. Every intelligence service in the Middle East has spies in those camps: Egyptians, Jordanians, Algerians, Israelis, the Brits, the French, the Russians—maybe even your Agency. Right?" It was a guess, but it was obvious. Griffin just looked at me with that stare-into-space expression that comes with a security clearance. "I bet half of Osama bin Laden's bodyguards are working for 'friendly' services. But you didn't have a clue what was coming ten days ago."

"And you are so fucking smart, you knew. Right?"

"What I know is this. When a recruiter like Abu Seif spots a baby shark instead of a bait fish—someone who's smart, who's got the right look in his eye—that recruit gets tagged for a different program. The sharks get special care, special feeding, become part of a different food chain. Might not go to the camps at all. In fact, probably don't. Who runs *them*? We've got to find the man who handles the sharks, who knows where they swim, and who comes out to swim with them. And you can bet he's not sipping tea with Osama these days. Because the sharks are already in America. They're already in Europe. They're sleepers. They don't do anything until they get the signal. Then: BAM! And while they wait to launch the second wave of terror, and the third, and the fourth, they're leading perfectly ordinary lives in, I don't know, in—"

"In Kansas," said Griffin.

"Could be," I said. "Or in Langley." I stood up straight and arched my back in a long, yawning stretch. "You want that hard drive? Let's find an ATM machine."

CHAPTER 6

"Tell me something about you," I said.

"What do you want to know?" said Griffin.

"Something that's true," I said.

We were on the edge of the park, now, and headed on foot into a collection of town houses and small hotels. I remember there was a statue of a general on horseback.

"I am thirty-six years old," said Griffin.

"Yeah."

"I was born just outside of Jackson, Mississippi."

"Where's your accent?"

"It finds me whenever I go back there."

"All right."

"In my family," said Griffin, "there's a lot of kids, and not a lot of money."

"And a lot of Muslims?"

"Nope. Everybody's African Methodist Episcopal."

"So what happened to you?"

"I was looking for something. Didn't find it. You know the rest. After the Rangers the Secret Service. Now this. Along the way I got myself a degree in Middle East studies at George Washington."

"You got a wife? Kids?"

"Two little boys. They live with their mother."

"You love them."

"Hell yeah."

"At some point, the bad guys are going to go after America's children."

"Bullshit."

"Read their declarations of war, the way they talk about the children martyred in Palestine, the children martyred in Iraq. You know what? Children *are* martyred in Palestine and Iraq. They blame us. And it ain't a big jump from 'an eye for an eye' to 'an innocent for an innocent.'"

"You got anything else to back this up?"

"I hope I'm wrong," I said. "Here's an ATM. We're going to make this a cash transaction, and you can start pulling the money out now, as much as it will give you, as a down payment. I want fifty thousand dollars in my pocket by the end of the day, and then you get Abu Seif's hard drive."

"Bullshit!" said Griffin. "You're practically on the payroll. You don't get bonuses. And we don't pay murderers for stolen property."

"I thought I told you, Griffin—just like you told me—I ain't working for you anymore. You don't want to pay up now? You will. I'll call you mid-afternoon."

I jogged back into the park through a narrow alley with flowers all around, across the wide green lawns and among the trees toward the Oxford Street hostel where I'd spent the last couple of nights. It was time to take a shower and pack.

The escalators took me down into memories of wars before I was born. The deepness of the London subway was like nothing I'd ever seen before, the moving stairs so long that you lost your sense of the surface of the earth. There were posters to read for musical shows and for lingerie, all kinds of things to distract you. But by the time you got to the bottom of the stairs, all of that seemed like another world, and I understood now what I read about the British taking refuge in the Underground during the Blitz. No bomb dropped from the sky could blast through to these man-made caves. But here and now at the end of September 2001, the people around me were scared.

They had the idea that death could erupt in the tunnels around them, that it could filter through the enclosed air that they breathed, that it could blow apart the subway cars they rode in. When we stopped for a couple of minutes between stations, nobody spoke. The only sound I heard was from the earphones of people wearing Walkmen.

The newspapers that were lined up on the racks at Paddington Station didn't have anything that I could see about the death of Abu Seif. They were still running headlines about the number of people who'd died and, mostly, disappeared in the World Trade Center. It was like nobody could believe it. Maybe six thousand dead. Maybe less. Not twenty thousand, like a lot of people thought at the beginning. Not ten thousand. Just eight thousand, or six thousand. Like it might be possible to whittle down the horror by whittling down the numbers. I picked up a copy of *The New York Times* and stood in the station reading it, waiting for the train. At the bottom of the front page was a story about people making a lot of money speculating in airline and insurance stocks just before September 11. But who the hell would do that? Or could? I never met anybody in the muj who was that smart, or, at least, smart that way.

"Pardon me. You're a Yank, are you?" The voice belonged to a man with long white hair and the gray stubble of a beard. He was as tall as I was, but hunched with age. His eyes were a dead brown and yellow around the edges, his skin was sunless bloodless white, like he hadn't left these tunnels for a lifetime. His sport coat and his pants looked like he slept in them. The scarf around his neck was dark with dirt, and he smelled of dust. But he was smiling. "A Yank?"

"Yes," I said.

"Terrible thing," he said, nodding at the headlines. "Terrible. But you'll pull through. God bless America. That's what I say." The old man touched his head like a stage salute. "God bless," he said, and he was gone.

I wanted someplace lonely but public. I wanted it well marked and easy to find if you followed directions stage by stage. I wanted it outside of London. But I'd never been here except for a training mission we did with the Special Air Service when I was in the Rangers, in some rough hills near Hereford. We flew in and flew out and they didn't even stamp our passports. What I knew about England was from reading about its wars and what I could pick up in the Soho Internet café these last couple of days.

The place I found on the Web was on the way to Birmingham near a village called Little Compton. It was a tourist site, according to the Web sites, but there were no tourists anywhere in the world right now. If I could get out there early enough, I thought, I could get a feel for the place. I took a train to Oxford, then climbed in a big London-style taxi, and threw my backpack on the floor.

"The Rollright Stones," I said.

"In the Cotswolds, then, near Chippy?" The driver looked at me in the rearview mirror.

"I guess," I said. "Supposed to be near Little Compton."

"That's right. Cost you about fifty pounds." It was a good thing I was about to get some fresh cash. As we drove through town, I checked out the little mobile phone I'd bought in London for about a hundred dollars cash. It was perfect, I thought. It worked anywhere in England, and you bought scratch cards to pay for the calls before you made them. No bills, no statements, no identity.

The afternoon was warm, one of the last breaths of summer, and the windows of the cab were rolled down wide. We drove through countryside as quaint as Disney movies, but real. The air smelled of straw. Sheep grazed in rolling meadows marked off by stone fences. Stone cottages with big old trees around them looked like they'd been around for five hundred years. Elves could have lived in them.

Betsy and Miriam would love this place, I thought. Miriam would feel like a fairy-tale princess, and Betsy would feel like a lady. I thought about bringing them here someday soon. And then I thought that "soon" might not exist for me, or them, or us. All this, even this, could be destroyed.

"Excuse me, governor?"

"Just a sigh," I said.

I talked Griffin to me, following his progress on my map. He was coming by car up the M40. He was taking the exit at Banbury. He was driving, after a little confusion in Banbury, down the A361 through Bloxham. And I was waiting near a circle of enormous stones that had been in this place for four thousand years.

Griffin's headlights swept along the narrow road that rolled through the countryside beneath me, cones of white cutting through the last of the twilight. There was no sign of other cars around him. I listened for the sound of a chopper, but all I heard, in the distance, were sheep.

"Where the fuck am I going?" Griffin shouted over the phone.

"You're almost there," I said, taking up my position and talking into the wire mike that came with the phone. "When you see the little rest area on your right, pull over."

"Got it."

"You're alone."

"Yes."

"Step over the rope, and come down the path. It's just a few feet."

"What the hell is this?" Griffin shouted in the open air. I could see him now, but there was no way he could see me. "You planning a human sacrifice? Better not be me!" He was a lonely shadow squared off in that circle of stones, like a gladiator not knowing where the attack might come from.

I kept talking softly into the wire earpiece-microphone. I didn't want him to hear me except on the phone. "Put the bag down behind that big rock." Griffin's black face was lit green from the glow of the telephone screen. "Repeat," I said. "Put the bag down behind the biggest rock in the circle, the one over there to your left."

"Done," he said, not sure whether to answer into his phone or into the emptiness of the night.

"See those three big rocks outside the circle?" I whispered.

"Which?"

"Up to your left. You can see them outlined against the sky at about a hundred yards. I left the hard drive there in a white plastic shopping bag."

Griffin put his phone in his pocket and let his eyes adjust to the night, working his way up the hill with practiced moves while I took a few steps from among the tall fir trees that circled the site and recovered the money bag. It was a loose net sack made out of nylon, just like I told him. I could smell the used bills, part paper and part sweat. I retreated back into the dark.

Griffin came down the hill with the hard drive in his hand. When he got to the middle of the circle he stopped and turned around, looking closely at the branches, bushes, and stones now that his eyes were part of the night.

"You still here?" he shouted. He held up the wrapped metal box like a trophy. "Thanks for this," he said. "Stay safe, you son of a bitch. And get the hell out of England."

That night I slept in the shelter of trees near the stones, wrapped in the Mylar blanket I'd packed. I watched the crescent moon rise, and saw a helicopter pass twice over the site. There was no spotlight. The chopper could have been looking for my heat signature, but the Mylar would hide that. Maybe it wasn't looking for me at all. Maybe.

The next morning when the sun came up, I counted the money. Part of it was in pounds, part in dollars, but it added up. There was enough for me to send some to Betsy, and to do what I had to do. I walked into the town of Chipping Norton two miles away. Nobody bothered me. I took a taxi to Birmingham airport.

Granada

SEPTEMBER 24–26, 2001

CHAPTER 7

The wife of the man I wanted to see in Granada was veiled almost like a nun, and much prettier than I was ready for her to be. When I arrived, she was alone behind the counter of a small wholesale shop for Middle Eastern foods and spices in a run-down collection of warehouses on the edge of the city.

From the moment I walked in, early on that stifling afternoon, I had the feeling I'd guessed right. Abu Seif's address book had a lot of potential leads in it, and some of them were people I knew. But they were farther away, in the Balkans and Africa. I couldn't afford any misses at that range, and this address in Spain for "friendlyboy," somebody supposed to be called Bassam al-Shami, kept jumping out at me. Instinct told me to come here, and now the Agency's money let me follow my instinct. If this didn't work out, I'd know quickly, and I could head for Africa, where I thought I might have at least one good connection.

"Le puedo ayudar?" asked the woman behind the counter. She was a little younger than me, and taller than a lot of women, and she had a kind of pretty strength about her face and her hands that was surprising. But that was all I could see of her. Her sleeves were long, the cuffs buttoned tight, and of course she wore that gray scarf—the *hijab*—of a modest and pious woman. It was a kind of uniform, especially for the wives and sisters of the Muslim Brotherhood. It revealed none of the

hair on her head and was pinned beneath her chin, but, still, it framed high cheekbones, a sharp nose, and bright, deep brown eyes that did not turn away when I looked into them. There was no air conditioning in the shop, and her clothes must have been stifling. She shifted slightly on her feet.

"Le puedo ayudar?" she said again.

"Tell me you speak English," I said.

"Sí—yes, a little bit."

"That's great." I was as friendly as could be. "Is Mr. Al-Shami here?"

"He is not here," she said. A thin dew of sweat dampened her upper lip.

"Will he be back today?"

"No," she said. "He is not in Spain."

I stayed friendly, and our eyes stayed on each other's. "I hope he is coming back soon," I said. "I was sent by a friend."

"Bassam has many friends," she said.

"I guess he does."

I looked around the shop, and for a second thought it might be fortified, there were so many burlap bags piled against the walls. But the place smelled liked spices, not sand. Some of the bags were open so buyers could taste what was inside: pistachios, black pepper, a green powder I didn't recognize, a reddish-orange powder I couldn't name, chunks of resin that looked like rock candy but smelled like perfume. I picked up a piece and sniffed it.

"Incienso," she said.

"In sea in so?" I spoke a little Spanish, but had no idea what she was saying.

"In church, you know?" She made a motion with her hand as if she were swinging something. *"Humo*—smoking?" Now she opened her hands in a gesture of helplessness. And she smiled.

I put the resin to my nose again and closed my eyes. It was the smell of the Serb churches, and it sank into the pit of my stomach. "Incense," I said, and tossed the rock back onto its pile.

"Incense!" she said. "Thank you." She pulled a notebook

and pen out of a drawer like a schoolgirl getting ready for her lesson. As she wrote I noticed just how powerful her hands were for a woman.

Along the opposite wall were shelves holding jerry-cans full of liquid. *"Gasolina?"* I asked, and she laughed.

"Noooo," she said. "Honey."

"Honey?"

"*Miel.* Honey? This is the word?" She came from behind the counter and opened one of the cans. Her dark gray dress was long and shapeless and covered her legs to the ground. She took a plastic stick and dipped it into the can, then let the thick brown liquid trickle off the end back into the container. She touched the last drop with her forefinger and held it up for me.

"No thanks," I said.

She smiled and, without making too much of it, she licked the sweetness off her fingertip.

"Is Señor Al-Shami your father?"

"He is my husband," she said.

"And will he be away long?"

"I do not know," she said. "He is away two weeks now. Sometimes he is away two months. He no want that I talk about his trips."

"Sure," I said, looking one more time around the store. Then I pulled the empty scabbard of Abu Seif's letter opener out of my pocket. "Do you know where I can find a letter opener that fits into this?"

"Everybody, I think. But—maybe the brother of my husband. In his shop. In Albaicín." She looked at me, and at a clock on the wall and shrugged. "It is closed now, and I must to pray. I will write for you address. Is near San Nicolas church." She wrote down a street name in schoolgirl handwriting. "Where you stay?" she said.

"I don't know yet."

"You have a car?"

"No."

"Maybe I take you there, to shop? I know a place to stay, also. We meet here at bodega—four o'clock?"

"What is your name?"

"Pilar," she said, and shook my hand, holding it in hers for a long moment.

"Pilar," I said. "A Muslim name?"

"No," she said. "Spanish. But I am Muslim for my husband."

At a phone shop a few hundred meters from the bodega, I bought a Spanish network chip for the mobile phone, then found a seat outside at a café full of construction workers. In the front, near the cash register, was a rack of postcards for sale: scenes from places in Granada I hadn't seen yet, the Alhambra, the Generalife, the Court of the Lions. In Bosnia, I used to listen for hours to preachers who talked about the greatness of the Muslim world, and about Granada. When Europe was in the Dark Ages, the Muslims here were in their glory. But somehow they'd lost it. Maybe because the Christians were crueler, more ruthless, more hungry. Maybe just because their time had run out. They were forced to their knees, scattered into tribes. And that was five hundred years ago, and they were never allowed to stand again like men.

Most of the rest of the postcards were for truckers who didn't give a damn about the glories of Granada. They showed women with tits like pillows bulging out of bikinis, girls with bare asses on the beaches of Andalusia, penis heads with funny faces drawn on them. *"Viva España!"*

The phone was ringing at the Jump Start. The voice that answered wasn't Betsy's.

"Ruth?" I said. "My wife there?"

"We're right in the middle of breakfast, don't you know?" said Ruth, who was Betsy's best friend at the restaurant. "That you, Kurt?"

I hung up. I could call back later, tonight or tomorrow. No rush, I thought.

The steel door at the front of the bodega was locked. Even in the late afternoon the reflected light off the white cinder-block building turned my pupils to pinpoints and drilled into my skull. I knocked again. To my relief, the lock rattled as the key turned from inside. *"Adelante,"* said Pilar. *"Un momento, por favor."*

"Thanks," I said. "This is so nice of you." In the gloom of the shop, I could barely see her shape, much less her face. She closed the door and reached for the light switch, slowly, waiting for—what?

"Freeze!" shouted a man's voice behind me. "Right there!"

I spun around, of course. But the blast of the shotgun sent an adrenaline jolt through me, and now I did freeze. I heard something spilling from one of the sacks against the wall.

"I do not want to have to kill you," said the man, whose accent sounded like put-on British. "But you are going to answer some questions."

"You a cop?" I asked. I was trying to see his face, but couldn't.

"What do you want with Bassam al-Shami?"

"His help," I said.

"I do not believe you. Where did you get the scabbard?"

"From Abu Seif."

"He is dead."

"No! When?"

"You are not going to ask questions," said the man. I still couldn't see his face clearly, but I focused on the shape of the gun, a side-by-side double-barreled twelve-gauge. Two shots. One gone. I was judging the distance between us when an iron bar smashed against my skull and sent me stumbling toward the back of the store. The woman hit me again, and again, stepping into each swing with all her weight. I went down on one knee. The shotgun was still trained on my gut, too far for me to reach, but close enough to cut me in half.

Fear gives you a powerful rush of sensations and I remember now how sweet the spices smelled all of a sudden, how sharp and hot the bile was that rose in my stomach, how salty the taste of blood at the back of my mouth, how cool the tiles of the floor against my cheek.

"Sit up," said the man. "Sit up!"

I wanted to obey, but every time I raised myself on my elbows or forearms, the iron bar cracked against my shoulders or the small of my back.

"Up!" he shouted again, and I saw he was signaling the woman to stop. I rolled over, grateful to be able to obey his orders and, slowly, to sit. I looked at my legs straight in front of me and wondered if they were still part of me.

The man handed the woman the gun. She handled it easily. More easily than him. He had a limp. I hadn't noticed. A limp. He walked as quickly as he could to the back of the store. A bad limp. How about that? Now he was lugging something big and round. The limp was much worse. This guy was a real gimp with a limp. I smiled.

"Put your hands in your lap," he said.

I obeyed.

The tire dropped around my arms, pinning them to my body.

CHAPTER 8

"I know how you feel," said the voice. "The panic begins now." He took the point of the steel rod and shoved the tire. I fell over again, a rag doll, no spine, just bloody lint inside. I tried to twist into some position so my feet, or knees, shoulder, could get some purchase on the tiles. The woman rested the shotgun across the top of two open bags and picked up the iron bar. She swung it hard against my shoulders, my arms, again, again, then the neck, the head, hammering me toward the floor. Without defense, my face smashed down on the tile again, the tire pushing my diaphragm. There was no air. No air. The panic did begin. But my body did nothing. Nothing.

"You are lucky," said the man. "I have questions. When this was done to me, there were no questions. So no answers could make it stop. So you see you are lucky."

"Lucky," I said, or thought I said.

"You are working for the American government."

In my mind I was laughing. I don't know what kind of sound came out.

"Take off his shoes," the man ordered the woman. I felt my trainers leave my feet, my socks slip off. The steel rod smashed against the soles and pain exploded through my entire body.

"Again," said the voice.

Again, the explosion. My bladder lost control, then my sphincter.

"I—I . . ."

"You are . . ." said the voice.

"I am one of you."

"You have come because—? Ah, yes, because America has been hurt and you think, perhaps, Al-Shami has some connection to that? Is that it? I'm having a great deal of trouble understanding you, so speak up."

"I—am—one of—you."

"Do not test my patience," said the voice.

"La Allah," I said, repeating the profession of the faith, *"illa Allah, Muhammad—"* The heart-stopping pain of another blow cut me off.

"Blasphemy," he said. "We will not hear it. When did you see Abu Seif?"

"Ealing mosque."

"When!"

"Month . . . month ago."

The explosion again. And again. The questions were repeated. Again. Many times. And the pain. And then for a time, I can't tell you for how long, there were dreams. I do not remember what they were.

When my eyes started to open, the nightmare was still real. I was on the floor face down in my own blood and shit. The tire had cut off the circulation in my arms and my hands didn't have any feeling at all. The rest of me was in pain. Nothing else you can say about it, just—pain. But now there was light like a sun burning through my eyelids.

"We must rest," said the voice. "We must reflect." I heard him sipping something. "You have been badly hurt today. You are wondering if you will—if you could—ever recover. You are wondering if you will die. You are thinking that you would like to die. You see? I know every step in this process. I am a well-practiced, a very well-practiced, victim." I heard the woman's footsteps come and go. I heard the sound of the man sipping again.

"I was ten years in the prison at Tadmor. Do you know where that is? No. You wouldn't. It is near a great tourist attraction in Syria. Little old English ladies come and go to the ruins of Palmyra and marvel at the pagan temple of Baal, and they pass by Tadmor's prison and look the other way. They send postcards to friends about their fabulous visit, and they have no idea, I think, that the prison is there, or that inside it the tire—what you are experiencing—is a way of life. Whether you live or die, my American friend, you will never be able to say that the tire was your way of life. And you should be thankful for that."

I heard a yawn. The woman was yawning. The voice said something to her in Spanish. They talked for a couple of minutes and then I heard her walk out the door. I did not know if she was gone for the night, or where, or if she would be back. I did not know anything except that, for this moment, the beating had stopped.

"You are broken now," said the voice. "Are you not?"

I couldn't speak.

"I know. Torture has its own physiology," he said, "its own chemistry. They never taught us that in medical school (I am a physician, you see), but in ten years one can study, and one can learn a lot about endurance, or the lack of it. And there is a kind of—what would you say?—a fascination.

"At Tadmor the torture is public. You have the chance to live the pain in your mind, watching others, listening to others, even before you experience it firsthand. And once you know what the screams mean, because you have been there, there is a reaction that sets in when you hear a certain noise—say, the crack of a metatarsal."

His words came through to me very clearly, but I couldn't seem to control any of the sounds that came out of my own body.

"You know," said the voice, "I didn't hear that particular sound tonight." He was silent for a time and somewhere in the empty cave of my brain the thought came that the beating was about to begin again. The voice got up, turned out the light that was in my eyes, and walked into the other room. My face was flat and still on the slick tiles. I couldn't see what he was doing, but I heard water running.

Suddenly the bodega's overhead lights went on. "Lie still," said the voice. "And close your eyes." A stream of cool water washed over my head and neck.

"Thank you." I croaked the words. The water ran in a small flood toward a drain in the floor. It was pink with my blood.

"You are most welcome," said the voice. "Water, you see, is one of the greatest of pleasures. That is why it is so present in Paradise, so absent in Hell. Would you like more?"

"Yes," I said.

The voice walked away into the other room and again I heard the water running. I tried to twist to see his face, but could not. Every muscle in my neck and shoulder was knotted with the pain, and he was behind me.

"Listen to me," he said in a doctor's tone. "You are filthy and I am going to remove your trousers, but only to clean you."

Twice he splashed the cool water over my rear and my genitals, and I watched the filth flow into the drain.

I was beginning to think now a little more clearly about what he was doing. In the dark, during the beating, he was the bad cop. In the light, with the blessed water, he was the good cop. First he would be feared, then he would be loved. I saw this mind-fuck for what it was, and I was grateful anyway for the water.

"Pilar will be back soon," said the voice, "and we will have to start again, unless . . ." He let the idea settle in on me. ". . . unless you can tell me a little more about yourself and what you are doing."

"I—I don't know."

"That's not a good beginning."

"I was afraid . . ."

"Go on."

"I was afraid after New York."

"Why was that?"

"I was a mujahedin."

"Really? That surprises me."

"I was. My father—Bosnian. I was in Cazin, in Zenica."

"There are many spies among the mujahedin."

"I do not know."

"Maybe you are a mujahedin. Maybe you are a spy. Maybe both. This is not such a bad thing. The elements are mixed in any of us."

He wanted me to have hope so he could take it away from me. This would not end soon, and when it was over, I would be dead. I didn't know if that mattered to me now. I had fucked up so bad. So bad. Where had I gotten the idea I could save America? Or even my own family? Betsy. Miriam. Thinking about them should have given me strength, but it took the last breath of hope out of me. My muscles, tight with pain and fear, surrendered. I couldn't resist anymore.

The tire, wet from the water, slipped a tiny bit on my arms. I tried to move my fingers under my body, but they had lost all sensation. My legs felt my hands against them, but the hands did not feel the legs. I had to make my fingers work again, I thought. Concentrate on that. As much as I could, I tightened my stomach muscles to give the blood in my arms more room to flow. The tire slipped again, but clouds of pain filled my head.

"We all make compromises with power," said the voice. "Have you ever bargained with God?"

"No," I said.

"I see you are still able to lie," he said. "No more questions until Pilar gets back."

He walked away, and was gone for some time. When he returned, he was sipping tea. I could smell the mint in it.

I started to speak. "I went to Abu Seif for help."

"No more lies for now," said the voice. "Abu Seif is dead. Murdered. And for all I know, you are his killer. You're not his killer, are you?"

"No."

"You are his killer, aren't you?"

"Yes."

"Ah," said the voice. "There you go. That is really *the* problem with torture: If someone is telling the truth, how do you know?"

"Please," I said. "Please listen."

He sipped his drink and said nothing.

I started to sob. "Please . . . Please . . ." I kept repeating the word until it lost all meaning in my mouth.

"People will say anything to stop the pain," said the voice. "Anything at all. If there is time, one can check the information, one can look at the files. But when you have no information, when you have no files, how do you judge? In that case, pain becomes the only measure of truth. Pain and the interrogator's instinct."

"Please . . . listen."

"But, you see, there's a trap there, too. There comes a time when the interrogator will not believe anything without the pain—anything at all. Do you think I can believe you now?"

My fingers began to tingle, and to ache, as if they'd been numb with cold. I lay there as still as I could and focused all my energy on my hands, on my forearms, willing them to work.

Outside was the sound of a car pulling up. The door to the bodega opened and the woman came in, dressed now in blue jeans and cross-trainers, with a kind of smock over the top of her body, a black *hijab* over her hair and neck. She put her purse down on the counter as if she were getting ready to start a normal work shift.

She and the voice talked for a couple of minutes in Spanish. The overhead lights went off. The halogen light was back in my face, like a sun burning in the blackness of space. But nothing else happened. They kept talking. The front door opened. Someone left in the car. I could hear the engine start, could hear the sound of it fade as it went away. Someone went into the back room to boil water. The ritual of pain would begin again soon, but they would make me wait, and wonder, about when.

CHAPTER 9

If you know you're dead, you know you can do anything. The doctor's voice wanted a little candle of hope burning inside of me. As long as it did, I'd be careful. But I knew I was a dead man. My faith in that fact was stronger than anything he could tell me. And I only had one idea about Heaven: I wanted to hold that shotgun in my hands and pull the trigger. Maybe there wasn't another shell in it. Maybe that's why they left it lying there on top of the fucking pistachios somewhere in the dark. Maybe it wasn't there at all. Maybe they moved it when I was passed out. Maybe I couldn't remember just where the hell it was. Who the fuck knew? Who cared? If I failed, I was already as fucked as I could be. Freedom's just another word for nothing left to lose. And the doctor's voice had made me as free as I was ever going to be.

A moan came from the back room. The moan of a woman. I shivered. Whatever she was doing, I hoped she kept at it.

My face and shoulder slid across the floor as I pushed with my right leg toward the gun I thought would be somewhere to my left. Too slow. I rolled over so the tire was in the small of my back. Flashes of light, pure pain, shot behind my eyeballs. But I was moving. In a wild flailing back-kick, I was moving faster. Faster! My head hit a burlap bag and suddenly I was breathing some kind of spice like powdery fire. Gagging. Coughing. But on my knees. Felt the front of another bag with my face.

Another choking powder. Then the rocks of incense. My face felt the cool of blued steel.

The main lights of the room went on. She was coming from the back. Let her. Let her get close, real close. Falling as I stood, I twisted on top of the bag. The tire around my gut sank into the loose contents of the sacks. I hadn't expected that—but it was everything. Now I had some leverage. The gun was underneath me, pointing somewhere into the room. I angled over it, burying the tire deeper into the soft bags so I could get a better grip. There, the trigger. The gun jumped to life; the heat of the barrel touched my leg; the noise rang in my ears. I wrenched myself upright and turned, ready to be beaten to death, but, now, to stand and see it coming.

She was on the ground. The blast, like the bite of some enormous shark, had taken a huge piece of her side and stripped most of the flesh from her right arm. Blood and pieces were sprayed across the white bags of couscous on the far wall. Her long white legs were bare beneath the shredded smock. Her back arched impossibly, inhumanly. She quivered and jerked for a couple of seconds, the circuits in her body out of control, and then she was dead as she could be. Her veil, still pinned beneath her throat, soaked up the blood seeping from her mouth and nose.

I limped to the counter and used it slowly to pry the tire off me, my hands and arms shaking, my whole body shaking now beyond my power to control. In the back room near the neatly folded jeans she'd left on a chair, I found her purse and spilled out the contents. Her identity card, Maria Pilar Seco de Shami, showed a brunette, and gave her home address. Stumbling, I gathered up my own pants from the floor and took them into the back to wash them as best as I could, and as fast as I could, in the sink. I wore them wet into the heat of the Granada night.

The police who came to the hospital didn't believe me when I told them I was just a backpacker who'd been mugged. But this was a tourist town. If the victim didn't want to push it, the cops weren't going to press the question. They didn't ask me anything about Pilar. I don't think they found her until days later, when the stink of the corpse overpowered the smell of the spices.

I went to her apartment the afternoon after she died. I had the keys from her purse. From across the street, I watched the place for about two hours before I made my move. It was in a block that was square and modern but already run-down. There were not many people around in the early afternoon, a few women, fewer men. None had a limp, none could show me the doctor's face that, I realized now, I'd only imagined.

The inside of the apartment was almost sterile. The computer was in a little bedroom just off the front hall. The hard drive was gone. There were no floppies, no CDs anywhere. All cleared out.

I started rooting through the closets, the cabinets, under the beds. But this was a strange kind of home. There were no wedding pictures, no albums. There had never been any children here, I thought.

On the wall in the living room was an embroidered plaque with the Arabic script for "Allah." I looked behind it. Nothing.

Nothing.

A television with a box of cheap videos next to it, mostly kung-fu movies I'd never heard of.

I checked the answering machine. No messages. I looked in the trash cans for some scrap of paper, some receipt, anything to give me a clue. But they were clean and empty.

The shred of paper from my pocket, the one Pilar gave me, seemed to puzzle the taxi driver. "Albaicín?" he said. I nodded. He looked closely at me, like he was trying to read the bruises on my face. We drove up a hill into tiny, winding streets. At the entrance to an alley he couldn't enter, he stopped and declared, "Aljibe del Gato. Is not long. You find number four."

There was no number four.

I looked around the corners to see if there was a tourist

shop, or any kind of shop right there that might sell souvenir letter openers. I checked the street signs again. Calle Aljibe del Gato. At one end was Calle María de la Miel. At the other was Calle Pilar Seco. Less than nothing.

"Jump Start Restaurant, best burgers in Kansas, what can we do for you?"

"Hey, Sugar."

"Hey, Stranger."

"How's everybody?"

"'Everybody,' is fine. My little girl's not so good."

"What do you mean?"

"I mean she misses her daddy."

"He misses her. He misses her so much you can't believe it. And her mommy, too."

There was a long silence.

"You get a package?"

"I picked up a package yesterday."

"Good. Good. But, you know, some folks might stop paying their bills."

"What's that supposed to mean? What are you talking about?"

"I mean—I mean, that was a good package, wasn't it?" It was twenty-five thousand dollars.

"Very good, but I don't understand what's going on. What are you talking about? Quit playing this damn game."

"Yeah."

"I don't care about the damn money. I want you back here."

"Yeah."

"Don't you think the President and the army and the whole U.S. government can do this without you?"

"No. I—I can't have this conversation right now. I have to go, Sugar."

"Coward," she said. "You fucking coward."

All I wanted to do was sleep, and for an hour or two I did, but the painkillers were wearing off and the aches in my legs, my shoulders, and along my ribs were excruciating. I popped 800 milligrams of ibuprofen. "Ranger candy," we used to call it. Short of morphine, it was the best you could do. Next door there was another American, so drunk that he knocked from one side of the hall to the other every time he went to the bathroom to get sick, which was a lot. Once he leaned in my door and I thought he was going to heave right there. I turned on the light and got ready for a fight. All he had on were his jockey shorts. He stared at me with glassy blue pupils that jumped out of red nests of veins. I don't think he really even saw me. Then he managed to choke back the puke and stagger away.

The room in the hostel was like a cell. The air was still and hot. There was nothing to stop my mind from spinning, and when I was completely awake in the dark, thinking of Betsy, I felt my heart turn to dust.

I could not give up, I thought—and I thought I could not go on. Could anything be more important than going back to Kansas? If I don't go home, I might lose everyone I am trying to protect. But how can I protect them from my past? And when the second wave of terror comes, what then? I hoped Griffin and the Agency and even the fucking Feds were doing a better job than I was. I hoped to hell they were. Maybe it was time to pray, I thought, and then hated myself for thinking it.

After Bosnia, and after the terror that I almost unleashed, I realized men were better off not asking God for help, because the answers they thought they heard were too horrible. I stared at the ceiling. Yes. About that much I was right. It was better to look for God than to find Him. I had searched, and while I was searching I was as good a man as I could be. It was when I thought I'd found Him that I was the worst.

What you need right now, Kurt, is not prayers, it's reasoning. There are explanations for what you've seen. Al-Shami may be many things—doctor, terrorist, torturer—but he is also a businessman. Import-Export. He trades in spices and foods. Where does he get them? I couldn't begin to think. But I could begin to work.

The drunk was heaving his guts out down the hall. I looked in the open door of his room. His passport had fallen on the floor beside the bed.

The little hole-in-the-wall cybercafé near the center of Granada was still open and I could hear the sounds of gunfire, explosions, and the groans of death even out on the street. A bunch of teenage boys were on half the terminals playing Quake III or Counter-Strike, interactive shoot-outs in dark passages among mystical enemies and imaginary terrorists. The noise distracted me, rattled me. A couple of other kids were playing interactive American football and every so often I found myself staring blankly at their screens. I felt like a player running downfield waiting for a long pass: I was way out in front of everybody else, but I didn't know the pattern, didn't have any blockers, didn't even know what the quarterback looked like.

Concentrate. Read. It's just over two weeks since the attacks on New York and Washington and there is a tremendous amount of information available from public sources: newspaper articles, court documents, endless opinions by instant analysts. At home, Americans are still mourning, still sifting through what they thought they knew about the men in the suicide planes. And it isn't just the death and destruction that makes them grieve, and it isn't just revenge that they want. There is a question at the center of their sadness and anger that only Americans would ask: "How did it happen that those nineteen men lived and worked and ate and drank and laughed among us, right here in the Land of the Free and the Home of the Brave, and they didn't learn to love us?"

Overseas, President Bush is focusing everyone's attention on Afghanistan: Osama, Al-Qaeda, the Taliban, and all those "evil doers" in Kabul and Kandahar. Meanwhile the Europeans are rounding up the usual suspects—people they've been watching for years. But there is a big problem, and you can see it just from reading the papers. The teams that hijacked flights AA077, AA011, UA175, and UA093 didn't operate out of Afghanistan. They operated out of Europe. And America. And they never were the usual suspects. Now their operation is over. Their lives are over. Their trail is a dead end.

A lot of the information that was coming out as news was really years old and a lot came from an Algerian caught at the Canadian border in late 1999 with a bomb he was going to use to blow up L.A. International Airport. He turned state's evidence and testified in court about Osama's operations. He said the terrorist training camps in Afghanistan were organized by nationality. He said he'd seen Swedes and Germans there. He said he'd seen dogs killed with cyanide gas, and had been told you could use gas like that near the air intakes of big buildings to kill hundreds of people. He also talked about the gatekeeper, a man who received the holy war's volunteers when they came, and told them where to go when they went out. Abu Zubayr. The recruits were sent to him in Pakistan, where he looked them over with his one good eye.

Abu Zubayr was the man who finally separated the minnows from the sharks. But in 1999 Abu Zubayr dropped out of sight. Nobody seemed to know what happened to him. Maybe he was in Afghanistan. Maybe he was in some Pakistani dungeon. Or maybe he disappeared because he was the one man who knew every fish in the sea, and he had a new assignment: to prepare the second wave.

What interested me most was Abu Zubayr's cover. He was a honey merchant. In Abu Seif's address book there were addresses for several different import and export companies. To the extent that I could cross-check what they traded, they all seemed to have one product in common whether they were in New York, Granada, Aden, Peshawar, or Nairobi, whether they were called Shami Goods and Services or Asl Sweets. They all sold honey.

I left the cybercafé at about three in the morning. The guns, groans, and splashes of gore were still echoing down the street. Above me I could see the Alhambra. Maybe it was the greatest achievement of Islam. I don't know. I didn't see it up close. But from where I was it looked like my idea of Alamut, the city where the Old Man of the Mountain lived in the Crusades, the place where he built a paradise and convinced his followers he held the key to it before sending them to spread terror all over the world and down through history.

The apartment blocks where Pilar and Bassam al-Shami had lived were brutally lonely late at night. One or two lights were on, but the main street and the alleys that led off it were dead silent. The only footsteps in the stairwell were mine. The turning of the key in the door echoed down the hall.

I was not sure what I was looking for on this second trip. Nothing had changed in the apartment since I left it. The curtains were still drawn. The little oriental carpet in the front hall was still crooked. The mess in the computer room was the same.

The box by the TV had a dozen or so videos in it, some in the cases, some not. I started popping them in the machine and fast forwarding. They weren't even from Hong Kong. Most looked like they were made in the Philippines. The only Bruce Lee was *Enter the Dragon.* But when I opened the case, the tape had no label.

A home movie: The first scene was a street scene where most of the people in the street were black. Men were dressed in short-sleeved shirts and, some of them, in ties. The camera seemed to be shooting aimlessly, like it was left on by accident. A couple of shop signs had the word "Nairobi" in them, so I guessed that's where we were. A blonde woman in a safari hat and shirt and khaki slacks was standing in a busy square. Behind her were a couple of skyscrapers and a low building. Africans walked in front of her and behind her and took no notice at all. Now she was standing across the street in front of a craft shop, with a bunch of carved giraffes on each side of her, waving. Now she was in another city street, waving again. I could see the same skyscraper again. Black glass front, white stone sides. A parking lot with a guard at the entrance. Another low building. Lots of cars. Lots of traffic noise. Lots of Africans in short-sleeved shirts with ties. A street vendor passes with a cart full of brilliantly colored fruit. The blonde woman in the safari hat is waving again. Same skyscraper and same low building in the background. She turns and looks at it and looks back at the camera and waves.

I rewound that section of the videotape. The woman waves, and turns, and behind her, flying above the low building, is the American flag. I rewound the whole tape and started it again. Every scene except the one with the giraffes shows the same low building. Now I see the guards around it more clearly. There is another scene of the parking lot, another shot of the guardhouse in front of it. In all of them, the blonde in the safari hat is laughing and waving. You can't hear what she's saying over the noise of the buses and cars, but she thinks the person behind the camera, who is saying nothing, is just the funniest person on earth. There was no time and date on the video. But I knew it must have been taken before August 1998. The building in the background was the American Embassy in Nairobi. On August 7, 1998, it was blown up by a hit team from Al-Qaeda.

The image turned to gray snow and I got up to look for a pen and some paper to make some notes. In the room with the computer I finally found the stub of a pencil and a yellowing envelope.

"Más lento. Muy, muy lentamente." The voice was coming from the living room. The doctor's voice. *"El cinturón."* I could feel the hackles rise on the back of my bruised neck. The voice was on the tape. *"Primero, el cinturón."*

CHAPTER 10

The video was still rolling. The blonde was in what looked like a big hotel room. The white curtains were drawn, but there was still a lot of light. She still wore her safari hat, and she was looking down at her waist, unbuttoning her safari shirt. Underneath she had a short, thin T-shirt that showed her navel and was tight against her heavy breasts. Something was written on it. Her stomach was flat, and she flexed the muscles a little for the camera. She unfastened the canvas belt, the *cinturón*.

The woman was standing at the end of a bed and in the foreground I could see a man's naked legs. The right one was scarred and withered. "Give me the belt." His hand reached out and she looked into the lens as she dangled it in front of him. Only then did I recognize her as Pilar.

She took off the safari shirt and dropped her pants to the floor, standing before the camera with her hands on her hips, wearing nothing but a thong, the hat, and the T-shirt. The logo across the front read "friendlyboy." Now the hat came off. She shook her head. Her dyed blonde hair, thick and heavy as a mane, cascaded over her shoulders.

This was the woman who had shaken my hand so warmly, swung a steel bar so painfully, and died so quickly. The tape kept rolling.

She pulled off the T-shirt and the thong, and stood completely nude in front of the camera. There was not much tease, because there was no sense of modesty. She had the same kind of matter-of-fact confidence stark naked as she seemed to have when she was covered from head to foot. The muscles in her arms and stomach were all softly outlined. There was no hair on her body at all.

In a mirror behind her, I glimpsed the man who was filming. He had his shirt open, and no shorts and he was clearly aroused. But the camera blocked his face. Apart from his graying hair and trim salt-and-pepper beard, I couldn't tell much about his features.

"Put the camera on the desk," he said. She took it from him, still running. Now I could see the whole bed, but the light from the picture windows behind it turned the man into a silhouette.

Pilar straddled him, rubbing herself against his groin even as she slid the belt around his waist and his hands and strapped down his arms. She rose up on her knees and he twisted himself beneath her until he was on his stomach. She kissed and bit his shoulders, the small of his back, working her way down his body. As she got nearer his ass, she put her hand between his legs and reached under him. Now her tongue was between his cheeks, lingering there. She was kissing his legs, running her tongue along the scars. She climbed down off the bed and began to run her tongue up and down his feet, his instep, his toes—and the tape ended.

"Wow," I said to the empty apartment. "You are one sick son of a bitch. What the hell do you look like?"

I went over the parts of the tape again, where I thought I might be able to get a better look at his face. I played with the color and contrast. But the best image I had of him, when he was prostrate on the bed looking at the lens of the camera, was so badly shadowed and so full of ecstasy or horror or both that it was hard to know if I would ever be able to recognize it again.

The next morning I addressed the tape to Marcus Griffin, Government Office Building No. 2A, Langley, Virginia, with an unsigned note: "You're going to love this. Be sure you run the tape to the end. The woman is Pilar al-Shami, and she is dead. I think the man is Dr. Bassam al-Shami. He did ten years in Syria's Tadmor Prison. Probably part of the Islamic resistance. Now he sells honey. I am sure he knows where the sharks are swimming."

I sent the cassette regular mail. That would give me some time.

East Africa

OCTOBER–NOVEMBER 2001

CHAPTER II

Flies with red eyes the color of matchheads crawled across the map of Kenya on the wall of the Summit Vision Development Agency. The chart was covered with tiny brown spots, and near Lake Victoria in the west you couldn't really tell where the villages ended and the flyspecks began, but the danger zones in the east were clearly marked: entire provinces along the Somali border were shaded in black.

"Looks like you need a security escort in half the country," I said. The secretary, who spoke with an Indian accent, said, "Mr. Faridoon will be receiving you shortly. Perhaps you would like to have a seat?"

"Thank you," I said, and kept looking at the map. Even in peacetime nomads roamed the provinces near Somalia. But peace was a long time ago, and the wars had erased, redrawn, and erased again what there was of a border. Hundreds of thousands of Somali refugees were holed up near the town of Dadaab. There was drought and flood, hunger and famine—thousands of square miles of no-man's-land where any man could hide if he had the money, the guns, and the right God to protect him. In the middle of the blackened badlands were three little pins: the development agency's projects.

"Mr. Faridoon will see you," said the secretary.

The man behind the large metal desk looked to be about forty, maybe a little older. He was clean-shaven, in a white shirt with long sleeves and a tie. His skin was olive, almost gray. He greeted me with a smile that was friendly but wary, like he was trying to place my face.

"I had a beard in the old days, in Bosnia," I said. "And the old days were nine years ago."

He looked at my eyes, then at my hands, and back into my eyes. " 'The Demolition Man!' " he said.

"Is that what they called me?"

"That and 'The American.' "

"Yeah."

"You *are* the one who blew up the Chetnik prison camp?

"Yeah."

"Incredible. That was about the bravest thing I remember from those days. You saved a great many lives."

"Yeah, well," I said, "that's ancient history."

Mr. Faridoon looked at me and smiled. "History counts," he said.

"So does the future," I said.

"Yes," he said. "Yes!" He shoved the papers on his desk aside like he was clearing a path between us. He gestured for me to sit down. "And what brings you here?"

"I always kind of wanted to see Africa," I said. "My marriage—well, I had some personal problems and some time off. So I came."

"That's it?"

"Came here on a wing and a prayer, I guess you'd say, and then I remembered you."

"Really?"

"Yes," I said. He knew I was lying. He just wanted to know why. "Yes," I said again, "and while I'm here I thought maybe I could make myself useful."

"I see," said Mr. Faridoon. "You mean you want a job."

"I mean, if you've got something for a few weeks or months, I'd be happy to help out, even as a volunteer."

Mr. Faridoon laughed. "Do you even know what we do?"

I did not. And I did not know whose side they were on,

either. When I saw this Faridoon and the Summit Vision Charitable Trust in Abu Seif's address book I wasn't absolutely sure that this was the man I remembered from Bosnia. There were so many charities in the Balkans, and so many people from so many places connected to them. Some were Saudi, some Iranian, and some were, I thought, a little more mysterious. This was an Ismaili charity, and in those days I had no idea who the Ismailis might be. I knew nothing about the ancient cult of the assassins, or the modern charities of the Aga Khans. All I knew was that they had a project in Bosnia to help distribute safe heating stoves, which might have given them good cover to bring in heavy metal objects: guns, RPGs, even mortars. And in those days, that's what I hoped they were doing. I remembered liking Faridoon. My gut and what I'd read about the Ismailis told me he could be friendly with the British services, or the Indians. Or playing on his own. Or a true doer of good deeds. Or none of the above. I laughed. "Not really, no, I don't know what you do."

"I supposed not," he said. "We build beehives, mostly. We're helping people who have nothing to develop a grassroots economy into something. We don't have much call for a demolition man."

"I've spent a lot of the last eight years as a carpenter."

"Useful," said Faridoon.

"And, of course, the other area where I might help is with security."

"Security." Faridoon sat back in his chair and shook his head, still smiling, thinking. "What precisely did you do after you left Bosnia? Did you just give up on the jihad?"

"After what I saw in Bosnia—after what I saw that night at the prison camp—yeah, I quit. I realized that kind of war was never going to solve anything. I went home. I settled down."

"You're from the Midwest, I believe? I can tell by the accent, although I can't quite place it."

"Kansas," I said, a little impressed.

"Precisely." He sat back. "Precisely." His smile was not the easiest to read. "We learned many things in Bosnia, didn't we, Kurt?"

"Not enough to stop what happened on the eleventh."

"If you could have stopped it, would you have stopped it?" He leaned forward. "Don't answer too quickly."

"Yes."

"I mean *then,*" he said. "Would you have stopped it if you could have back then? In Bosnia?" He listened to my silence, then went on. "Were you at the Ansar house in December 1992?"

"Yes."

"That tall, gentle Arab who visited. So tall. So gentle. So rich, they said."

"I saw him. Yes, from a distance, at night."

"And you knew his name."

"Osama."

"And if you had known what he would do, then, would you have killed him then?"

"I was a different man—then."

"Yes." Faridoon sat back. "Yes. I think you were." He nodded in answer to himself, and smiled. "What are you doing tomorrow morning?" said Faridoon. "I don't think I can use an employee, but maybe"—he seemed to search for the word—"a consultant."

"Jump Start Restaurant, best burgers in Kansas, how can we help you?" Ruth, the other waitress, again.

I hung up and lay back in the king-size bed at the Nairobi Holiday Inn. God, I was tired. God, I was sore. God. The minibar beckoned, but there wasn't enough energy in me to get up. I closed my eyes and tried to remember what a cold beer tasted like. It hadn't been such a long time since I had one, but that was in Kansas. It was before that clear Tuesday morning in September when everything changed. How long ago was that? Three weeks? Just a little less than three weeks. And I had the beer on . . . the Sunday before the Tuesday. We went with Miriam on a picnic up by the lake. There were trails up there that weren't too crowded, even on a Sunday, and years ago Betsy and I found a little stand of trees right by the water that felt like it was all ours, and usually was. We started taking Miriam up there when she was less than a year old, and now she showed us the way. That Sunday we ate Betsy's deviled eggs and fried chicken and potato salad, and I washed it all down with a Coors Light from the cooler, so cold it tasted like spring water. Ah, God.

"Jump Start Restaurant, best burgers in Kansas, how can we help you?" Ruth, again. I hung up, again.

I picked up a copy of *Kenya Life Monthly* from the bedside table and leafed through photographs of celebrities who came to the country to take safaris or donate money. Former President George H. W. Bush was among them, alongside the Aga Khan, at the opening of a cultural center in Mombasa. Caught in the camera flash, the old Bush looked almost like I remembered him from the Kuwait war, dignified but a little confused. The Aga Khan stood beside him, full of confidence, with a smile as comfortable as old money. The Ismaili faithful used to offer their leader his weight in gold. That was one of the things you always read about them; there were so many stories and myths. But the Ismailis were something else today. Quiet. Present. Taking care of themselves, defending their vision of their faith. They didn't have scales, they had portfolios.

The Old Man of the Mountain was long behind them. His fortress of Alamut was overrun by the Mongols, and his followers became just another minor, persecuted bunch of believers in Persia—until the British thought they might be useful, and moved them to India during the Raj. The British always liked to work with minorities who relied on them for protection. In India the Ismailis didn't have any friend but the Crown, and they served it well, and it served them, for more than a hundred years. Ismailis spread all over the Empire, from the jungles of Uganda to the most remote mountains of northwest Pakistan. Since the Empire ended, they stood on their own, and served their own interests, whatever those might be. The Aga Khans became playboys, and philanthropists, and hung out with ex-Presidents. But why was Faridoon's number in Abu Seif's computer?

I turned off the light and fumbled for the remote control, clicked on the TV, and zapped through the channels to CNN. The present President Bush was on the screen. "The battle is joined," he said.

CHAPTER 12

As the war in Afghanistan got under way, the television reports were all about cruise missiles and stealth fighters. From Kabul came a few of those computer-video images of "bombs lighting up the night sky," running over and over again. They looked like they were cut apart and pasted back together. There was no way you could tell what was happening.

I dialed Kansas.

"Jump Start Restaurant—"

"Ruth, let me talk to my wife."

"That you, Kurt?"

"Ruth, right now. Please."

"You hear the war started?"

"I heard. Please?"

"You anywhere near it, if you know what I mean? . . . Oh, Betsy. Betsy, it's Kurt. He says—"

Betsy must have grabbed the phone out of Ruth's hand. "Kurt, where are you?"

"I'm far, far away from Afghanistan."

"Ah," she said. "Ah, thank God. And you're okay?"

"I'm totally okay, except I miss you, Darling. Are you and Miriam doing all right?"

She hesitated for just a second. "Yes. Fine," she said. "Miriam misses you. I miss you."

"You're sure you're okay?" I wanted to reassure her. I wanted to reassure me. "If there's anything wrong, I'll come back, no matter what."

"No!" Her voice broke. "No. No, don't say that, Kurt."

"I—"

"Kurt, listen to me. I don't know where you are and I don't know what you're doing, but it's got to be done, right?"

She sounded scared and strong and angry and loving all at once, and for a second I didn't know what to say. Then the words came out. "It has to be done."

"And nobody else can do it. Tell me that. Tell me nobody else can do what you're doing."

"It's true."

She started to speak but her voice choked. I couldn't say anything either. After a second the electric life went out of the line. "Betsy?"

"I'm here, Kurt."

"Betsy, what's wrong? What is it you're not telling me?"

"Kurt, listen. Miriam and me, we're here and we're alone. Do you understand that?"

"But you got our friends, and you got—"

"*Listen* to me. If you aren't here, we are alone," she said. "And I'm gonna tell you something. I'm scared. Scared about you, and the world, and this war, and about the next paycheck, and I'm so, so scared I'm going to lose you. Can I just say that? I look at the TV and I'm terrified. You hear me?"

"I am not in Afghanistan."

"*Listen to me!* What you're doing—whatever the hell it is, wherever the hell it is—it's got to be done. Right? *Right?* Don't tell me you can just come home because you're worried about us."

"But I just wanted—"

"What you're doing has got to be done. That's what I tell myself every morning and every night. That's the only excuse. The *only* excuse."

The line sounded dead again, and I was afraid she was gone. Then, "Kurt?"

"Yeah."

"Just come back to us," she said. "When it's all over, come back to us."

CHAPTER 13

We flew into the rising sun and every feature of the earth below was outlined in morning shadows. Near Nairobi, farms cluttered the land. There were patches of tall corn, and rows of sisal with leaves like clustered bayonets.

"I expected"—I had to shout above the noise of the Cessna's engine—"I expected wild animals."

"Not many here," shouted Faridoon. "Farmers drive them away if they can."

"And around the camps?"

"The shifta killed them all a long time ago. When you've got so many guns around, you don't have many animals."

"Shifta?"

"Somali raiders—they're warriors, bandits, poachers. Take your pick."

I nodded and sat back. It didn't seem worth shouting. "Mind if I doze off?"

"Be my guest," Faridoon shouted back.

Maybe I'd been asleep ten minutes. Suddenly the plane turned hard to the left, real hard, and one of the instruments began to scream a warning. The turn continued, and the screaming got more urgent, but Faridoon was smiling. He took one hand off the wheel and pointed. "Elephants," he said. We were making a tight spiral above them—tighter than the Cessna wanted to go.

At first I didn't see the animals because I didn't understand what I saw. The earth beneath us was a rich iron red and so were the enormous things that moved across it. We were only a few hundred feet above them now. I had never seen anything living that was so huge. They had nothing to do with the elephants in circuses and zoos. It was like the difference between a scout car and main battle tank.

The plane was screaming again. "What's that sound?" I shouted.

"Stall indicator. No problem."

"Right."

"Really," he said, "relax." He leveled out. We headed again toward the rising sun and a land that grew flatter, emptier, with every mile that passed. The plane was climbing slowly until, at about three thousand feet, we felt like we were standing still and the land beneath us was as red as the deserts of another planet. The Cessna's engine wasn't working so hard now, and it was just a little bit easier to talk.

"What's your biggest security problem?" I asked.

"Rape," said Faridoon. "Rape is the worst."

"So you know who's doing it?"

"Sometimes."

"Can you take them out?"

Faridoon's expression let me know I'd probably failed his test already. "We don't want to start a war. The cycle of vengeance never ends in these parts, and we do not want to be part of it. We cannot be part of it. But we have to figure something out."

"And you were hoping I've got some ideas."

"I'm hoping," he said. "Some of our best people at Summit are women. And they won't—they cannot—even begin to think about working out here. Except . . ." Faridoon grinned. "Except Cathleen," he said, and shook his head.

"What makes her so special?"

"You'll see." And once again, Faridoon smiled.

Now clouds held back the sun, and heavy raindrops started to rattle on the front of the airplane like bursts of machine-gun fire. We flew low and slow over land that was dead from drought, mutilated by floods, until a sprawl of people appeared below us like ashes scattered across the earth. We circled once over rows of battered tents, small huts patched together from twigs and garbage, and a few low stucco buildings. As we approached the water-slick landing strip, I could see a large figure in a long white shirt and blue jeans—a woman with a scarf over her head—talking to three men in rumpled uniforms beside a Toyota pickup. Faridoon gentled the Cessna down onto the mud runway and we half rolled, half skated to a stop, then taxied over to the reception party. The second the engine quit turning, the woman pulled open Faridoon's door.

"You've got to talk to these bastards," she said.

"Good morning, Cathleen," he said.

"Top of the morning. Are you going to talk to them or not?"

"That's what I'm here for," he said, climbing out of the plane. "Cathleen, meet Kurt. I'm hoping he can help us with some of these problems."

"Pleased to meet you," she said, starting to head back toward the soldiers.

Faridoon put his hand on her shoulder. "Wait," was all he said. Her face turned red and there was a terrible mix of emotions there—anger and anxiety and relief and frustration, all magnified by her size. Cathleen was a force of nature, with huge breasts and heavy arms and a kind of passion in her movements that made me think she was going to explode, but she didn't. She waited. Faridoon went on alone to talk to the soldiers.

"What's wrong?" I asked.

"The little girls," she said. "You'd think they'd spare the little girls." She shook her head. No, finally she wasn't going to wait. She headed for the soldiers and I followed. "Can't they bleedin' do something?" she shouted at Faridoon and at them.

Faridoon turned and headed her off. "We'll discuss this when we get back to the compound," he told Cathleen, and even though she seemed to be mad as hell, she listened to him the way someone does who knows the voice of reason when she hears it. "Now let's unload the plane," he said.

In front of the Summit house, .50-caliber cartridge boxes were piled like enormous Lego blocks. "Sure looks like you're ready for war," I said. "You've got enough ammunition here for an army."

"No, no," said Faridoon. "The boxes are empty. But they're very common, especially on the other side of the border, and we've found that they make good hives."

"Wish we did have some ammunition," said Cathleen.

"Let's start with some tea," said Faridoon as we walked into the main room of the house, which was part living room, part kitchen. "And that big survey map, is it still here in the cabinet?" He spread the chart on top of a 1950s kitchen table with aluminum legs and a Formica top. We sat on lawn chairs with most of the webbing frayed or gone. Cathleen put the pot and the cups on the table and let us pour our own.

"This is the border with Somalia," said Faridoon. A straight line ran north and south, highlighted in pink. "This is where we are." Just to the left of it, and about eight kilometers inland. "Now," he said to Cathleen, "tell us what's been happening."

"More of the same," said Cathleen. "A whole lot more of the same. Oh, Faridoon, the little girl they brought in last night. Oh, God, you must come see her with me. Ten years old, Faridoon. And every night there are more. And we know we only hear about a few of them."

"It's the shifta doing this?" I asked. "These Somali bandits?"

"No," said Cathleen. "I've been out here a long time and I know shifta better than I know some of my cousins in Dublin. The shifta take advantage. They get what they can get. But this is more like an organized campaign, like there's a method to the madness."

"How's that?" I asked.

"It's a protection racket these sick fucks are about. And in Allah's name no less. The men here see that they can't defend their wives or daughters. They see the soldiers and police don't do the job. But over here"—she pointed to a town called Wolla Jora on the far side of the border—"there's a lot of Itihaad people. Just when the rapes are increasing, some of their preachers show up in the camps. Quiet like. And they say they're going to do the job the police don't. They say they're going to give men back their dignity, they're going to protect their womenfolk. You know, 'Islam is the solution.'"

"And nobody does anything."

"No. A few years ago the Ethiopians went into the northern areas—here." She moved her hand over a corner of the map. "They were going after Itihaad for their own reasons. But, you know, it's like trying to clean with a dirty mop. You just spread the dirt around. Then last year we started hearing about new arrivals across the way, in this area." She drew a circle with her finger. "Not sure who they were, but the Itihaad people were very impressed with their new guests. You could see that right away. Their guns got better. Their trucks got better. And, you know what, the rapes increased."

"Al-Qaeda?"

"Some of its best and brightest," said Cathleen.

"A long way from home," I said.

"For them the rapes are bonus pay, don't you know."

CHAPTER 14

The clinic was four grimy stucco walls beneath a tin roof dense with cobwebs. There were eight metal beds. The paint on them was worn away by the clenched hands of patients in pain and the iron legs were rusted by pools of sweat. Some of the sick were on the floor, crowded inside because of the rains. The girl was curled up on a stained mattress, wrapped in a coarse wool blanket. She had a high forehead, delicate features, and large, warm black eyes that seemed to see us, but not to follow us. The air near her was stale with sickness. She smiled when Cathleen spoke, but did not lift her head. Cathleen ran the back of her hand over the girl's cheek and said something else to her in a language I did not understand.

Outside the clinic a tall man with midnight-black skin stood beneath the eaves clutching a stick. He looked into the distance like a sentry and his jaw was set, whether in pain or anger was hard to tell. Faridoon approached him and spoke a few words, but the man said nothing. He just nodded his head slowly, almost rhythmically, the way some athletes do when they're about to sprint out of the blocks. But there was nowhere for this man to go, nothing for him to do.

"That was the girl's father," said Faridoon as we drove back toward the compound.

"That little girl is his only child," said Cathleen. "Her mother's dead. But after something like this, some men in these parts might walk away from the shame, you know. Not him. I think he really is a good man."

"What did he do before he came here?" said Faridoon. "He doesn't look like a farmer."

"Shifta," said Cathleen. "Ivory poacher back in the old days."

"Ah," said Faridoon.

"Ah, Mother of God!" said Cathleen. "It just breaks your heart. You won't find tougher people than these in the whole world. Too tough for their own good. And so proud, and so completely fucking hopeless." She turned on me. "Do you have any idea what that girl has been through?"

"I saw women who were raped in Bosnia," I said. "I have an idea."

Cathleen shook her head. "In Somalia, girls are mutilated already when they are six or seven years old. Did you know that? All of their genitals are cut away with a knife or a razor blade and they are sewed almost shut."

"Why the hell would they do that?"

"*Women* do it to them—the mothers to the daughters—because that's what the men expect. So when a little girl like that is raped, the sheer physical damage to her, and the pain, is almost beyond belief. She is lucky, very lucky, she did not die. And she still might. And we don't even have tests here to see if she's been infected with HIV, which she might well be. And I ask myself what kind of men would do that to her. And I can't get over the idea that this is part of some sick goddamned game by the people across the way."

"You don't know that," said Faridoon.

"I see what's happening," said Cathleen.

"Do you hear any names?" I said.

"Abu Zubayr is the name I heard," she said.

Early in the afternoon, as soon as there was a break in the weather, I drove Faridoon back to the airport. "See what we can do here," he said as we pulled the blocks out from under the tires of the Cessna. "Develop an action plan. But don't cross the border under any circumstances."

"If you say so."

"I do say so." He climbed into the pilot's seat but left the door open to talk. He looked over the controls. "You're going to be tempted to talk to Abu Zubayr, but that could be a trap—and almost certainly will be."

"How do you know that?"

"I know him. And so do you."

"I do?"

"I'm sure you met him in Bosnia. Very quiet. That was before he lost the sight in his eye. In those days he was called Salah."

"The Salah who used to sleep in the Ansar house? The one who sat next to Osama when he came."

"That's the one."

"Have you talked to him?"

"We met in Wolla Jora town when he first came. He said he's in the honey business now."

"Salah."

"Leave him alone, at least for now. Are we clear about that? Perfectly clear?"

I nodded, and couldn't think why I felt relieved, then realized that was the connection to Summit. Or might be.

Faridoon swung the door of the Cessna closed and cranked the engine. A couple of minutes later, he was skimming the bottom of the clouds.

Cathleen brought a Coleman lantern to the table. The blue-white glare shone like a cold sun on the contour lines of the map. She leaned over the chart, planting her hands on both sides, seeming to want to take the chart and the land it represented into her arms and smother it all in her breasts.

"Wolla Jora is the town, but the place you want to know

more about," she said, "is this farm about two miles outside, which is where the distinguished visitors from abroad hold court and make their plans. Or so I'm told by some of the Orormo who wander back and forth through here." She traced lines with her finger through small valleys and riverbeds. "You see how easy it is for them to cross the border. Nobody's watching." She shook her head and took a deep breath, studying every curving line on the map like a sorceress reading chicken guts before, finally, she heaved another sigh. It was hard to keep my eyes on the map with her huge breasts right in front of me. She looked up into my face. "Would you be wanting a little of mother's milk?" she said.

She must have seen I looked a little confused.

"Whisky," she said. "Would a glass of whisky do you?"

"Yes. Yes, it would," I said.

Cathleen and I sat in the dark in a pair of the low lawn chairs, our drinks cradled in our hands, talking to each other's outlines.

"Have you known Faridoon a long time?" I asked.

"About six years," said Cathleen. "Since he first brought me out here from Ireland."

"How'd he find you?"

"The world of beekeepers is not so huge, you know."

"His good luck."

"Hah. And mine I suppose."

"Are you Ismaili?"

"No thanks. We Catholics have enough strange beliefs." I could hear her take a swallow of whisky. "Well, maybe if the Aga Khan was to propose to me I'd give it some thought, you know. But I haven't had him come courting in quite some time. I take it you're not a convert yourself."

"No."

"Know much about the Ismailis, do you?"

"A little bit I've read."

"Don't know much myself. Sure you've heard why they were called 'assassins'—*hashishin,* because they were after smoking dope to help them on their way to Paradise. Seem to have given that up, though. More's the pity."

"Hah! Yeah."

"You know they scared the bejesus out of Richard the Lionheart and his crew, and scaring the English is no bad thing. I'd send them to Heaven for that. Did you ever hear how they'd jump off towers when the Old Man of the Mountain told them to? They'd do anything he commanded. Jump off towers. Disguise themselves as women. Spend years working in some rival's court, just waiting for the order to kill."

"I read about that, yeah." I took a long sip of the whisky. "Sounded like fairy tales, but . . ."

"But what?"

"Now it sounds like Bin Laden."

"I reckoned you'd say that. But the Old Man, you know, he was after something different. He was playing with the idea of Paradise, not just for the hereafter, but for the here on earth. You know what he used to say?"

I shook my head in the dark.

"'*Nothing* is true.'" Cathleen slurred a little. "*Everything* is permitted.'"

I tried to see her face, but I couldn't make out any of the features.

"And Faridoon is part of all that?"

"Oh no, darlin'. Nobody was ever part of that. It was all made up, don't you know? The Ismailis don't bother anybody. They've got schools, they've got foundations, 'the Aga Khan this,' 'the Aga Khan that,' and there are charities like this one."

"So Faridoon's not an assassin?"

"No more than you are," she said.

"He said he talked to Abu Zubayr in Wolla Jora."

"He told you that, did he?"

"Is it true?"

"Yes."

"What did Abu Zubayr tell him?"

"Oh, I think it was a right difficult conversation. Abu Zubayr called him a heretic. But, then, you'd expect that, wouldn't you? And Abu Zubayr called him a British spy. Can you imagine that? Faridoon?"

"I guess it's hard to imagine."

"And he told Faridoon he would kill him if he ever saw him again."

"And he meant it?"

"Oh, I think so."

The dark settled in on us. The whisky in my glass was almost gone.

"So tell me," I said.

"Tell you what?" she said.

"Is anything true? Is everything permitted?"

Cathleen laughed.

CHAPTER 15

On the edge of the camp was a small mosque built out of mud and a few stones with a big mud cone for a minaret and a piece of scrap metal cut into the shape of a crescent moon on top of that. It seemed to me to be, in its way, very beautiful. The imam was an old man whose hair was white against the tight black skin over his skull. His body was bent, but his voice was still strong when he sang out the call of the muezzin before dawn, wailing in Arabic to tell us that prayer is better than sleep. Then, a few minutes later, Cathleen's short-wave radio would click on, and we'd hear classical music telling us the BBC news was about to start.

According to the reports we heard, the war in Afghanistan was going pretty slowly for the Americans, at least at first. But it was going well, they said. The American bombers were doing their work day and night hitting "Al-Qaeda training camps" that Washington called "the terrorist infrastructure."

It was hard for me to listen. I kept hearing about our surveillance satellites and planes, our U2s and B52s, our electronic intercepts and our Predator drones, which flew over the enemy's hideouts like huge dragonflies. Washington was real proud of those. But I knew the news didn't have anything to do with the war on the ground. All that Washington saw were buildings that exploded in gun-camera flashes, or tiny people-shapes wearing turbans who were carrying guns and grouping and regrouping. And all they heard were the voices that wanted to be listened to. You couldn't count on that to tell you, really, what was going on. This war had to be fought up close and personal.

Cathleen and I got into a routine pretty quickly. At night, when the place got quiet, she'd tell me everything she heard from the nomads and the refugees who came by that day. They always had bits and pieces of information, but what nobody ever told her, she said, was "I don't know." So a lot of what she heard were lies made up to please her. We were trying to put together a picture of the farm outside Wolla Jora: who was there, what they were up to, and also how they were defended. But some folks told us there were hundreds of strangers at the farm, and some said there weren't any.

"I've got one man that I'll be talking to who goes back and forth quite a bit," Cathleen told me one night. "A regular commuter he is to Wolla Jora, and he's got the brains to figure out what we need. Of course, it's been weeks since I saw him, but he should be coming around these parts again soon."

"I'd like to meet him," I said.

"Oh, he's my little secret," she said.

That night we stayed up late, talking in the dark. I told her about Betsy and Miriam, and she just listened. Other nights we'd have a little of mother's milk, and go to bed early. And every few days, real late, I would ask Cathleen's permission to use the satellite phone and call Betsy at work.

I worried about her and about the loneliness that was eating away at her—at us. But I was also getting more and more worried about that package I'd left in the freezer at the Jump Start. Too much time was passing. Every day the odds got worse that someone would find it. And if they did, there was no telling what could happen. Maybe the virus wasn't dangerous anymore. But I didn't believe that. I figured it was probably just as dangerous, just as deadly as it always had been: the Sword of the Angel of Death.

When Betsy answered, we didn't talk for long, and mostly we said the same things, like we were reading from a script:

"Are you okay?"

"We're fine."

"I'm making progress here."

"That's good."

"I love you. I miss you so much."

"We love you, too, and we miss you."

And that was all. It wasn't what I wanted or needed to hear. But it told me they were alive and well, and that none of the disasters that might have happened had happened. The calls kept me hoping that when I got home again, somehow we'd be able to pick up right where we left off. As long as Betsy and Miriam were living and safe, I thought, there would always be time for that.

Each night as I was falling asleep on a cot in that mud house in the middle of the wet African desert, I'd go dream-walking through my own place in Westfield. I'd go past the big sofa in the TV room that we bought in a discount mall outside of Wichita. It was big enough so all three of us could stretch out and share the popcorn. I'd look into Miriam's room, at the bunk bed I made for her out of two-by-fours and four-by-fours. It wasn't really a girl thing, but I thought she'd think it was fun to climb on, and she did. Now Barbie and her friends lived on the top bunk. A lot of times in my mind I saw Betsy sitting up reading in our bed. She kept the sheet pulled under her chin, but she was naked underneath it. She never did believe in sleeping with clothes on if she could help it. I saw Miriam in the kitchen. She had a milk mustache and her hair was hanging down around her face. She was studying her Fruit Loops as carefully as a code breaker, moving the pink ones to one side with her spoon, and the yellow ones to another.

I thought if I could make my home live in my head while I was still awake, it would stay with me into my dreams, and sometimes I think it did.

My day job was carpentry. The .50-caliber ammo boxes had the right basic shape and size for a beehive, but we had to make frames that hung inside them for the honeycombs. Before I came, Cathleen taught a Somali carpenter to do some of the work, but then he disappeared, nobody was sure where, so she taught me.

"You have to be very precise, you know," said Cathleen, "because bees are very precise. So you'll be wanting to make the tops of the frames thirty-five millimeters wide so they hang just so, with about seven and a half millimeters of bee space between them. Are you writing this down? Any more than that, and the bees look for some place else to build their combs, or, they just get sloppy. And we wouldn't be wanting sloppy bees, would we? Any less, and they get too cramped. The little darlings are creatures of habit, you know. Like most of us."

"I've been looking around for tools," I said.

"Tools, eh? You think tools are a problem, do you? Well let me ask you this: Seen many bees around here?"

"Just the ones in back of the office."

"And flowers?"

"No, now that you mention it. None."

"Right," said Cathleen. "There's some. But we're not building these hives for here. A lot of the people come from parts of Somalia where the earth really is green. Hard to believe, I know. But there are plenty of bees there. And there aren't plenty of precise tools. What we'll be doing is giving them hives, then teaching them the skills to take home to build their own, so that someday they *will* go home and use what they have, instead of waiting for the things that they don't have." She pulled a rifle cartridge out of her pocket.

"Recognize this?"

"Kalashnikov."

"Good for you, boyo. And the Kalashnikov cartridge casing is precisely thirty-five millimeters long at the top of that little shoulder where the cartridge tapers in," she said. "And the bullet is 7.62 millimeters wide. Perfect measurements for bee space, don't you see?" She was pleased with herself. "We improvise with what we have," she said.

And so we did. I worked under a piece of canvas spread over a couple of poles that kept off the sun and sometimes kept off the rain. Nothing could keep off the flies. Solid ammo boxes were fine for hives, but others were cracked or beat-up. I took them apart for the wood and the nails. Cathleen wanted me to train an assistant for after I left, but she couldn't seem to find the right prospect. It was slow work alone, but it was good work, and it cleared my head while I was doing it.

I knew I'd made mistakes in London and Spain, moved too fast, and still managed to keep going where I needed to be. But I was in the wilderness now, and no mistakes were allowed. I could wait a few more days until I really knew the lay of the land and the disposition of forces on the other side. Just a few more days. Then, we'd see.

About a week after I arrived, Cathleen came back from one of her visits to the KPF headquarters to see the local commander. She looked strange—excited, upset—I couldn't tell which.

"What did you find out?" I said.

"No rapes in the last couple of days," she said. "But we knew that."

"Good news."

"But don't be thinking it's not dangerous out there. Seems they turned up two dead men about eight kilometers from the camp. Don't know who they were. The captain said they're shifta."

"Near the border."

"That's right."

"Dead how?"

"Dead in pieces," she said.

That Friday, just an hour or so after the midday call to prayer, I saw a man walking toward the workshop with a child in his arms. He was carrying her like he'd just lifted her out of bed, and at about fifty yards I recognized the little girl from the clinic and her father. He stood tall and the little girl hugged his neck to steady herself, but she was as light across his arms as a piece of cloth. He did not look left or right, but walked straight to the door of the foundation office, and then inside. I put down my hammer and followed.

"What have we here?" said Cathleen, running the back of her hand across the girl's face the way she had in the hospital. "We're looking much happier and healthier," she said. The man spoke to Cathleen in his language, and she listened closely, then talked for a long time herself. The girl nuzzled her head into her father's shoulder. Finally, the man nodded and Cathleen turned to me.

"I think you've got a new assistant," she said.

CHAPTER 16

Faridoon came back the morning the mosque began to melt. The rains were driving down hard, and the mud walls just started to crack. The old imam kept trying to push stones and dirt back into place. But the crumbling wouldn't stop.

The rains cut all the roads to the west, and at the big camps north of us around Dadaab there were shortages of food already. It was almost impossible to fly in this weather, but somehow Faridoon waltzed his Cessna under the clouds and managed, once again, to land in the mud. "The boy's got a great touch," Cathleen said as she watched him coming in, and there was no denying that. We hauled a couple of duffel bags out of the back of the plane, threw them into the Land Rover, and got drenched to the skin doing it. But we were glad to see him.

"Are you both all right?" he asked.

"We're good," I told him.

"That's what Cathleen said on the phone. Glad to see it. I don't like the sound of all these killings in the bush."

"Six dead now," I said.

Cathleen was about to switch on the ignition, then stopped. "Is that why you decided to come out so sudden like?"

"That and some problems I wanted to talk to Kurt about."

"So talk," said Cathleen, before I could say anything.

Faridoon finished pulling supplies out of the back of the plane. Like he was waiting for his moment. Then he said,

"There's a lot of ugliness with the Americans right now, especially down on the coast."

"Like what?" I said.

"Your compatriots have been all over Mombasa, Malindi, Lamu."

"Which compatriots?"

"FBI. CIA. Whoever they are, the KPF are following their orders. There are too many arrests. It's indiscriminate. It got so bad in Mombasa people rioted."

I shook my head. "That's just like the Feds. Making friends wherever they go."

"They came by our office in Nairobi. They asked me a lot of questions about our work," said Faridoon. "Not just here. Everywhere. In Yemen, in Pakistan, Afghanistan, Bosnia. They asked me a lot about Bosnia."

I didn't like the sound of that. They must have made the same connections I did: the Summit entry in Abu Seif's address book, and the Kenya tape I sent from Granada, which must have landed on Griffin's desk. "What sort of questions?"

"Questions about money, questions about people. I told them to go to hell. I also told them we'll be calling our friends in Washington."

I thought about that magazine picture of the old President Bush and the Aga Khan. "So what are you worried about?" I said.

Cathleen answered. "Let's just say these are unpredictable times."

Faridoon focused in on me. "I'd very much like to know what you've been telling your compatriots."

"I don't talk to those guys. And they sure as hell haven't been around here."

"I think you should come back to Nairobi with me this afternoon, then be on your way."

"No!" said Cathleen. She looked like he'd slapped her in the face.

"I think it's necessary," said Faridoon. "We can find out

what we need to know about Abu Zubayr without your help. No hard feelings. My mistake. We don't need any Americans here."

"Let's go back to the house," said Cathleen and started the engine.

Nureddin didn't seem to notice us. Rain hammered down on the canvas roof of the shed and on the tin roof of the house so loudly you could barely hear, and he concentrated on the frame he was putting together. Inside the house, his little girl was at the stove making tea for him. Now that we were there, she put some more water on for us, too.

Her name was Waris and she'd gotten a lot stronger and healthier since she left the clinic. Whenever you smiled even the littlest bit in her direction, her face lit up so bright that everybody's mood seemed to change. She smiled now at Faridoon, and he just couldn't not smile back. But he had business on his mind, and the smile didn't last.

Cathleen looked at me. "Kurt, my boy," she said, "I'd like to talk to Faridoon for a couple of minutes on my own if you wouldn't mind."

A minute after I walked out the door, I heard Cathleen shouting. The noise of the rain made it hard to know just what she was saying, but the tone would have carried over Victoria Falls. Waris came out to join Nureddin and me. She was upset about the arguing, I guess, and she was just about to cry, but her father put his arm around her, and she put her head against his chest, and he just held her like that until she calmed down.

I looked away at the rain splattering in puddles and watched the puddles turning into ponds, and I watched the mosque. It was in terrible shape now. About a dozen men from the camp were trying to help the muezzin shore it up, but they were losing the battle. Nureddin watched the mosque, too. The north wall, the one that pointed toward Mecca, was starting to lean. He and I looked at each other. We had to do something. But there were no boards big enough to brace the walls. All we could do was join the muezzin and the men from the camp using our bodies to press against the building, hoping somehow that the clouds would part or the liquefying ground beneath the walls would steady, that if we could hold them long enough, some miracle of faith or luck would allow them to stand. The rain poured over us. I pushed my hands against the side of the mosque and felt the grit under my palms oozing away like the wet sand at the beach that slides under your feet with an outgoing wave. Nureddin was beside me, throwing his shoulder into it. There were about twenty of us now, pushing, holding, bracing, but it wasn't working. We were covered in mud and Nureddin and the other men wearing white robes looked like they'd been dragged from graves still wrapped in their shrouds.

I heard Waris's voice. She was shivering in the rain, shouting and pointing—pointing up—at the minaret. It was starting to lean. The sheet-metal crescent tumbled off the roof and into a deep puddle. The whole cone began to slope, melting, cracking, toppling off the collapsing roof. There was nothing left for us to brace and we stepped back. Little streams of water ran along the seams of the old muezzin's face as he watched his handmade house of God turn into a pile of mud and rock.

Faridoon stood in the door of the Summit building waiting for me to be done with the struggle against nature. "Two weeks," he shouted.

"Thanks," I said, still out in the open, stripping off my shirt and letting the rain shower me clean.

"Thank Cathleen," said Faridoon. "She seems to have a lot of faith in you."

"She's the best," I shouted over the rain.

Faridoon tossed me a towel. While I dried off under the tarp, he looked at some of our handiwork: the hives, the frames. He didn't say anything, like he was waiting for the air to clear. Then he said, "I like you, Kurt. But those men in my office . . ." He shook his head. "There was a black American named Griffith, I think. He kept insinuating—well, that's just it. I don't know what he was insinuating." Faridoon shook his head slowly back and forth. "I felt I was a fool to have an American mujahid working for me."

"Ex-muj," I shouted. "But, yeah, I see what you mean."

"Better for you to stay out here for now."

"Probably."

"Do what you've got to do. In a couple of weeks I'll fly you back to Nairobi and we'll part ways."

"I get it," I said.

"I want a full report—the rapes, these murders in the bush. I want to know if we have to close this place down."

"You'll get it," I shouted.

"Good," he shouted back, and the subject was over, but there was nowhere to go. Faridoon and I just stood under the tarp looking out at the ruined mosque while I tried to towel off the grit.

"Valiant effort," he said, nodding toward the fallen minaret.

"We had to try."

"God didn't want it to stand."

A chill went through me. "Maybe they just didn't build it so good."

"Sure," said Faridoon, his voice getting hoarse from the half-screamed conversation. "But that's not the way they'll see it. They're going to see this as God's will. And they're going to be even more in awe of Him than when the mosque was standing."

"If you say so."

"Oh, I most certainly do. What else is God but awe?"

The downpour was coming in huge bursts, thundering on the tarpaulin above us, sending a mist through it into the air around us, beating down the ruins in front of us. Faridoon stepped just inside the door of the house and I followed.

"You mean the fear of God," I said.

He shook his head. "Awe is what you feel for something so magnificent, or so terrible, or so frightening or glorious that even to think about it overpowers you." Faridoon smiled his easy smile. "Like the God in the rain who overpowered this mosque and defeated every man who tried to hold it together. You inspire awe by building or by destroying, you know. Destruction is easier, of course." Faridoon nodded toward the ruined mosque. "Even a building like that, when it was put up, people wanted to show the awe they felt—to shape that feeling with their hands, to get a hold of it somehow. To communicate it."

"Yes," I said.

"Think about the great god-awesome structures of this world. The pyramids in Egypt, those huge Gothic cathedrals in Europe, the enormous Buddhas at Bamiyan that the Taliban blew to bits. They were all designed to inspire that kind of awe." He coughed and wiped some of the rain-mist off his face with the back of his hand. "They were built at the limits of the society's possibilities—and beyond. They took more than a man's lifetime. No one who saw them at the end saw them at the beginning. This mosque was not so grand, but it was"—he looked in the direction of the desolate camp—"it was at the limit of this society's accomplishments."

"Yes," I said. "Wow."

"Yes. 'Wow.' Awe is worth pondering, you know. Isn't that what Bin Laden was after? I mean, think about it. He saw a world where it was not just Allah, it was *America* that created 'awe.'" Faridoon practically screamed the word America. "*America* had everything for everybody—money for nothing and chicks for free." He laughed. "It was like a dream of evil and a nightmare for good. And what were the greatest symbols of that awe? No cathedral in America is as grand as the skyscrapers of New York. No symbol of American force is more obvious than the Pentagon. And they were so vulnerable! Hit them and the awe of America evaporates. It goes back to where it belongs—to God." He took the gritty towel out of my hand and wiped his face. "You can see how Bin Laden would think that."

"Yeah. I can see," I said.

Faridoon grinned sadly. "If I were American," he said, "I'd give a lot of thought to the nature of awe. Because in the end, you know, that's all that protects you."

CHAPTER 17

Kabul was falling, and I fell asleep with my ear against the speaker of the short-wave radio. Three hours later I woke up in exactly the same position, still listening. It was dawn in Kabul and the streets were empty. The Taliban had disappeared from the Afghan capital and my eyes were wide open in the African dark. The rain had stopped. I turned off the radio and, for the first time in days, I heard real silence settle over the compound. In another hour I'd be able to hear the muezzin calling the faithful to pray near the ruins of the mosque.

A man was moving out there. The shape of him passed just at the edge of what you could see in that dark. He was running at an easy pace, but ghost-like, moving almost without sound. Then he was gone. In my last glimpse of him I saw he was carrying a rifle. I eased myself off the cot and crouched closer to the screen door. Like a hunter in a stand, I waited, and waited some more. I couldn't follow in the darkness. Slowly a predawn glow outlined the scene in front of me: the workshop, the Land Rover parked next to it. But no one appeared until the old muezzin arrived to sing out *"Allahu Akbar."*

I checked Cathleen's room. Through the door I could hear her breathing easily. No need to wake her. With no radio alarm, she would sleep for a while now. The sky was silver, clear and bright in the last minutes before sunrise. The ground was still soft. I followed the barefoot tracks of the man toward the refugee tents, then toward the long slit latrine where hundreds of footprints surrounded the ammonia-stinking sludge of shit and lye. If he was headed back into the camp or through it, I'd lost him. I walked a wide arc around the outer edge. There were still dozens of tracks. Some were women and children. Many were men. I walked one more arc, still wider. Still too many tracks. But there was only one set that belonged to a man running, where the front of the foot pressed much deeper into the earth and the space between the prints was much farther apart. The rising edge of sun in the east blasted straight at me. The tracks were headed for the border.

His legs must have been about as long as mine, I thought, starting to pace his footprints and falling into an easy stride. He moved quickly and surely over the red earth. I moved much more carefully. He did not find the straightest lines but the firmest ones in the still-wet landscape. He didn't slow down, he didn't search. He'd been over this unmarked path a lot, knew it well, knew right where he wanted to go.

A bright green stubble of grass was starting to grow across the land. Life was erupting in the first dry warmth of the day. There were even some tiny flowers. The bees would be happy, I thought. But for the first few miles outside the camp there was no hint of a tree or a bush. They'd all been ripped up and burned long ago. Only after I'd been running for about forty minutes, five miles at this pace, did I start to see little clusters of shrubs here and there, and also clusters of women in black shawls, who were gathering twigs. They must have started before light. They had to walk a long way to find anything at all to burn in their cooking fires. But the situation was desperate, and because there hadn't been a rape for more than a week, they were a little less frightened.

The footprints carried over a rise, then into a shallow stream. And there the footprints disappeared. On the far side, none of the new grass or flowers were broken by the weight of a man running across them. I walked up and down the edge of the stream. But there was no track to be seen. I turned in a slow circle beneath the wide-open sky, looking for any sign of the man with the gun, but all I saw in the distance was a cluster of about a dozen women, like a little flock of crows. One of them broke away from the group and started to run. She was strange and beautiful to watch, moving as light as air across the land, her cloak fluttering behind her long legs. She was running toward the camp. Too fast. Too damn fast. The women were looking at something out of the ordinary. The girl was running to take news.

As I approached, a cloud of flies rose up as thick as black smoke from the middle of the circle of women, then settled back. One of the shawls kicked something in front of her. The cloud rose again. The smell of raw guts, sweet and stomach-turning, caught in my throat. As I got nearer, the women started backing away from me, and from the swarm of flies on the ground.

"God Almighty," I said.

The crawling, buzzing blanket of insects covered a sort of structure—a sort of horrible shrine, really—made from parts of a man. The ground all around it was black, stained by the blood. The legs and arms were hacked and torn apart at every joint, then leaned up against the gutted torso like logs on a bonfire. And on the top of all this, stuck on a long piece of gnarled wood, was the head. The eyes were wide open in the black face, showing flashes of white beneath the crawling flies. The mouth was wide open, too. Out from between the teeth hung the man's dismembered sex like a Satan's tongue.

I backed away, and the women started to close in again. They had some unfinished business with this oozing, seething pile in front of them and they were looking at each other to see who would make the first move. Finally, the tallest of the women, holding her cloak around her with her left hand, reached into the cloud of flies with her right hand to grab the stick beneath the severed head. She shook it hard to pry it loose from the torso. The man's cock dropped out of his silently screaming mouth and the wide-eyed face tumbled onto the ground. A weird trilling shrieked from the women's tongues, like cicadas on a summer night, but more shrill, and angry. The tall woman added the wood to the little bundle she had at her feet. Then all of them turned and walked back toward the camp. When they were gone, I used my foot to nudge the butchered man's head away from the main swarm of flies. The cheeks were puffed out. I figured the testicles were in there. And there were other things I didn't notice before. The man had a thin beard and his hair wasn't long like most of the shifta wore theirs. It was cut short like a mujahedin. "God Almighty," I said again out loud, trying to break through the empty noise of the flies.

Beyond the circle where the women had stood I found tracks of men, and I thought I could read the story they told. Before the body was cut apart, it was dragged by a large man, whose footprints pushed deep into the earth. The trail backward was easy to follow. In a few places the feet of the dragged man made impressions at strange angles. "Still kicking," I said, wishing there was somebody to hear. A shiver ran through me, and I thought how much I'd like to have a weapon out here. How much I needed one.

Walking back up the trail of the dragged man I came to a shallow dip in the ground. It would be easy to lie up in a place like this without being seen, unless somebody was hunting you, and knew your ways, and knew the kind of place you'd go. I crouched at the edge of that hiding place. There were tracks all over and I didn't want to disturb anything. Two—no, three men had been here. One was the man dragged away and butchered. One was the butcher. And the third, he took off running. You could see he was wearing some kind of trainers and the tracks were easy to spot.

In Africa you always see buzzards in the sky. They circle over the bodies of dead game or cattle, and you don't notice them. But now I paid attention. A flight of vultures spiraled in front of the low sun about half a mile away. I studied the line of the tracks. The toes of the running man's shoes dug deep into the soft ground. For a few yards, the bare feet of the butcher followed the tracks, then stopped. The butcher kneeled down. You could see the impression of his leg. Nearby was a brass cartridge—a casing for a 7.62-millimeter bullet. A NATO round. I followed the running man's last steps to the center of the vultures' spiral.

I waved my arms and shouted. The huge birds backed off a little, loping around, shifting from one foot to another, flapping their enormous wings, but they didn't fly away. Through the veil of insects, I saw the man's eyes were gone already. Beaks and claws had ripped his guts open, but most of his body was intact. His head was still on his shoulders, bearded, the hair cut short. And now I saw what looked like a third bloody eye socket. The bullet had hit him from behind and the exit wound was right in the middle of his forehead. The butcher was a hell of a shot, I thought. He'd gone down on his knee and taken aim from five hundred yards away. He'd let off one round. And then he went back to his business with the man he took apart. What I could not find were any tracks showing where the butcher went when he finished. All of this must have taken place at about dawn—maybe an hour and a half before I got to the scene. He might still be around, but I couldn't begin to tell you where. The police would be coming soon, I figured, and I wanted to be gone by then. But in the meantime, I hoped there'd be movement, maybe birds flying up from the scrub, maybe the shadow of the man himself, something, anything that would give him away. What I would do if I saw him I wasn't sure, but I watched the flat horizon like a sailor looking for a sign. There was none.

When I got to the Summit house, Nureddin was standing at his bench as usual. I pointed at the house. "Cathleen?" He pointed toward the airstrip. When Cathleen wasn't there, sign language was the only way Nureddin and I communicated.

He was putting together frames for the hives. I started tearing apart a box for more wood and nails. Waris brought us coffee. This could have been any morning in the last couple of weeks. There was nothing different at all about the way Nureddin looked. He stood tall like a soldier at attention, but was never tense. His face was serious, his eyes sharp, but you could never say what the feelings were behind them.

I wondered where he kept the gun. It was probably an FN FAL. They used NATO rounds and a lot of African armies had them in the seventies and eighties. The barrel was long, so it was good at a distance, but it wasn't so easy to hide. You could wrap it and bury it, but you really wouldn't want to put your fine rifle in this wet ground.

Nureddin came from the camp to our compound before light to get that gun. Unless he knew that I followed him, it would be right back where he kept it, probably right in front of me. Not the bench where he worked. That was too open. And not inside the house. That was too close to Cathleen and me.

I finished pulling apart one box and went to get another from our empty ammo-box wall, and that's when I knew. Because we always took the boxes from the top or the middle, down at the bottom they were pushed together tight. If you knocked holes in the adjoining sides you could hide an FAL in there, ammo, whatever you wanted.

Waris came out of the house with some more coffee for her father and for me. He nodded thanks. And she put down the tray and hugged him around the waist, the way she sometimes did, just happy he was there.

CHAPTER 18

Cathleen was gone a long time at the airstrip. Now that the sky was clear, a lot of planes were coming in with supplies that had been held up for days, even weeks. So it wasn't exactly unusual that Cathleen hadn't come back yet. But nothing was sure out here. Nothing and nobody was safe. Not here. Not anywhere. Not anymore. And I felt like I didn't really know anything for sure about anybody.

Time to make a move, I thought. With Cathleen's help I had put together a pretty good picture of what the farm near Wolla Jora looked like. There were four low buildings including the main house and a small mosque. Usually there were about thirty men there, more or less. Most were from the Abir clan. They served as a guard force. They all had Kalashnikovs or M16s and they had four "technicals," pickup trucks fitted with .50-calibers. But the actual precise number of men at the farm changed from day to day, and you couldn't really know. The Al-Qaeda contingent itself was small: three Arabs who had been in Afghanistan until a few months ago. They were Abu Zubayr's close-in protection. But Abu Zubayr didn't always stay at the farm. He had another house he went to sometimes that was closer to the coast. And sometimes he just disappeared.

It was time to call in reinforcements. Griffin was on my tail? Well, let Griffin figure out the best way to take out Abu Zubayr. The USG would probably fuck it up. But I was at the limit of my possibilities. I didn't have any decent weapons, any explosives, or any backup to carry out my own operation. I was sick of this world, where nothing was true and everything was permitted. I was tired. I wanted, more than I'd ever wanted anything else in the world, to go home.

As if nothing had happened that morning, Nureddin stood in front of me sawing joints in the miter box.

Yeah, time to go.

The Land Rover rumbled into the compound, and Cathleen was grinning when she got out. "Come inside, out of the sun," she said. "I've just been meeting with my secret source. By tomorrow we'll have the whole picture."

"Tell me more."

"Deep Throat is flying over to Wolla Jora right now. I told you, he goes back and forth all the time. He buys honey over there."

"What does he know about Abu Zubayr?"

"Just about everything, I suppose. He was making jokes, you know. Said Abu Zubayr must be the best-protected honey merchant in the world."

"What did you ask him?"

"All the things I've been dying to ask him for the last couple of months, don't you know. Bassam's much more reliable than anyone else I talk to."

"What, exactly, did you ask him?"

"I asked him, who is with Abu Zubayr? How long is Abu Zubayr planning to stay around? You know the questions as well as I do."

"Did he have any answers?"

"He's going to get them."

"That's great. Who is this guy? He's Somali? Kenyan?"

"No, no. He's Arab. Lebanese or Syrian, I think. Very cultured."

She hesitated for a second. "Oh no, you don't. I've said too much already."

"Cathleen, you have to tell me more about this guy."

"I don't think so, Kurt. We have kind of a special relationship, and I wouldn't be wanting to betray that."

"Is he a doctor?"

"Why would he be after buying and selling honey if he was a sawbones?"

"Does he have a limp?"

"You know Bassam?"

I shook my head. "Never heard that name." If this was Bassam al-Shami then we were right on track. And if he was helping Cathleen, he was sucking us all into some kind of trap. I could feel time running out the way you do when you wake up before the alarm.

The 703 area code was going to show up on the bill for the sat phone, and whoever looked at it might guess it was Langley, but that didn't seem very important just now. There were two rings, then a click, then the silence of a call lost in space looking to reconnect somewhere, then another ringing tone, and finally the recorded voice of a woman with a British accent: "The mobile phone you dialed is currently occupied or has been turned off. Please try again later."

The mid-afternoon sun burned the water out of the ground and nobody wanted to move in that wet heat. Nureddin was taking a siesta in the shade of the workshop. Waris was dozing inside with Cathleen, who had plugged an electric fan into the diesel generator. The thrum of it roared in my head.

In Kansas the leaves would be turning and the autumn cool would have settled over the land. I suddenly realized I'd missed Halloween and didn't even know what costume Miriam wore. What was wrong with Betsy and me that we couldn't find a better way to talk, to say more, even if there wasn't much time, even if somebody was listening in?

Betsy. I figured Betsy was just getting ready to go to work; might even be in the shower. I needed to hear her voice. The phone rang but there was no answer. I should have fixed the ringer. Why hadn't I just sprung for a new phone? I waited five minutes. No answer. Another five. None. I dialed the house again, and again. Probably she was dropping Miriam off at her Aunt Lea's or something. I could get her at the Jump Start in another fifteen minutes.

I lay down on the cot and tried to take a siesta myself, just a quick blackout to take the edge off my tiredness, but unconsciousness wouldn't come.

I called Langley again. The signal wandered through space and led nowhere. Griffin was in my face when I didn't want to see him, and never there when I needed him. I started to dial again, then stopped. "Fuck him."

I called the Jump Start.

Ruth recognized my voice and she asked me right away, "Is Betsy with you?"

"What are you talking about?"

"She's been gone for two days. Nobody knows where."

"Two days?"

"She shoulda left some kind of note or something."

"Where's Miriam?"

"She's gone, too."

"They're over at Lea's, aren't they?"

"Nope. Lea came here looking for them. I thought—Kurt, you mean you don't know where they are?"

"No."

"Should we call the police?"

"Yes." Think. "Yes. Has anybody been to the house?"

"Lea went over. She said everything's okay there."

"The car?"

"That's there, too. It's okay."

"Ruth."

"Yeah, Kurt?"

"I'm really, really worried."

"I am, too, Kurt. And I been thinking, ever since that break-in, I been kind of worried about Betsy. But you know how she is."

"What break-in, Ruth?"

"She didn't tell you? That's what I mean about Betsy, keeps so much to herself."

"Ruth, tell me exactly what happened."

"It was weird, really, you know? We all said it was weird. But then we just sort of forgot about it, I guess."

"Weird—" I counted a couple of breaths. "Weird how?"

"Cleaned out your refrigerator and freezer and, like, that was all. Must have been some bums or kids or something. 'Kids with the munchies,' Betsy said. Mighty hungry, I guess."

"When did it happen?"

"I don't recall exactly. End of September, beginning October maybe? Right in the middle of the day. Betsy was here. But nobody saw nothing. Guess everybody was off working. Somebody broke your back door and just cleaned out your refrigerator. Now ain't that weird?"

"Did they take the TV or the stereo?"

"No, like I said, nothing."

"Anything in the garage? My tools, maybe?"

"No, don't think so. No. But they did break in there, opened up that old freezer of yours. But Betsy said it was prob'ly empty already. Oh, Kurt, I'm so worried."

"Did you see anything or anybody strange around the Jump Start?"

"Nothing more than usual. I mean, no, not around the Jump Start. Um—"

"I'll call you back in a few minutes. Find out everything you can, okay? It's going to take me a couple of days to get home, but I'm coming. Got that?"

"Yes, Kurt."

There wasn't much I could do until we could get Faridoon to fly back out and pick me up, and I couldn't seem to get through to him on any phone or radio.

I sat on my cot with my back against the cool wall and looked out through the screen of the porch at the emptiness of the sky. Nothing moved out there, least of all the air. I wanted to steady my mind, stop it from racing while I tried to put together the pieces of what Ruth told me. But there wasn't enough to work with yet. Betsy and Miriam had gone someplace and they didn't tell anybody. That was all I knew. Weeks before, somebody broke into my house, and it looked like they were after the Sword of the Angel.

A small speck on the southern horizon started to take on the shape of a plane. It was going very low and very slow, and without my really thinking about it, some part of my brain worked to classify the thing. Not a Cessna or Beechcraft. It was too small, too thin. It had a V-tail—but the tail was upside down. I leaned forward, like that would help, and tried to get a better look. It was flying toward us, but it wasn't flying toward the airstrip. I stepped outside.

During the Gulf War I saw cruise missiles, and I thought this might be one of them. But why would a cruise be coming after us? And this thing was different. It looked like a huge dragonfly. A Predator.

The Agency was taking a look around with one of its unmanned surveillance craft. From what I'd heard on the radio, when these things were armed with Hellfire missiles they were the CIA's new favorite toy. The Agency boys and girls thought they were great for terminations. You could sit back with your joystick and video screens wherever you were and home in on whoever you wanted to hit: death by remote control. Distant, soundless, clean, safe. But there was so much you just couldn't figure out from the air, like who really was who and what really was what.

I wondered if this Predator scanning the desert saw the fly-covered shrine left by Nureddin. What would they think about that when it showed up on their screens back at Langley?

"Anomaly," they'd say.

The white dragonfly passed right over the Summit house at about a thousand feet. So now they were taking a look at us. Or at me.

"Ruth, have you heard anything?"

"I talked to Bud Nichols down at the sheriff's office. Oh, Kurt, I am so worried. Where are you?"

"What'd Nichols say?"

"He said he's looking. He's looking and he's calling. But technically she's not missing yet. Not until tomorrow. Can you believe that?"

"That's not good enough."

"That's what I told him, Kurt. Especially after that thing last week, when that guy showed up at the house."

"What guy? Ruth, quit surprising me with this stuff, for God's sake."

"Don't Betsy tell you *anything*? She said he said he was an old friend of yours. But Betsy didn't like the look of him. 'Too slick,' she said."

"Did she tell you his name?"

"No. She said he just stood in the doorway—she didn't let him in—and he asked a bunch of questions."

"What questions?"

"She didn't say, really. She just said they were about you, and she didn't like them. And I thought it was, you know, not really that important. But now all kinds of things seem important—"

"Did she tell you what he looked like? How old he was? Anything like that?"

"'Too slick.' Yep. That's what she said, which I thought was kind of funny. She didn't make a big deal out of it. You know Betsy. Oh, Kurt, I am so upset I can't think straight."

"Was he black? White? Mexican? Arab? Eskimo?"

"I guess he was just white. 'Too slick' is all she said, and—wait—and she said—she made a kind of joke out of it—you know Betsy. He told her he had a message for you from a friend of yours named—and that was the funny part—anyway it was funny when she talked about it."

"What?"

"He said your friend was named—what was it?—'Zoo

Bear.' Betsy said, 'What zoo bear? Kurt's a teddy bear, but we don't know any zoo bears.' Weird, huh? We laughed about that. Do you know anybody named Zoo Bear, Kurt?"

"Nobody," I said. "Did he say what the message was?"

"That's what I asked Betsy, but she said he didn't tell her. He just said, 'It's personal.'"

Nureddin opened his eyes when he heard the double click of the FAL's bolt. Apart from that, he didn't move. I kept my eyes on his eyes.

The FAL was a gun I knew real well, and every piece of it felt familiar. I'd already taken the magazine off, and now I worked the cocking handle back and forth. I hit the release catch near the pistol grip. The barrel broke forward. I pulled out the bolt. Nureddin never looked at what I was doing. He just looked at me.

The metal under my fingers was clean and well oiled. I twisted the gas plug and lifted it out, then removed the piston and the hand guards. All the pieces were on the workbench now, but I didn't look down. I just raised my hands beside my face to show they were empty, and then without looking at the rifle put it back together piece by piece. When I finished, I snapped on the magazine and chambered a round, then flicked up the safety.

Nureddin never took his eyes off mine, but now he stood up and took one step toward me, face-to-face across the bench. His hands were at his side. He didn't make another move.

I put the rifle down on the bench and took one step back. He picked it up. Still looking at my face, he clicked off the magazine and pulled back the cocking handle. A bullet flew out the side and landed on the ground. Now Nureddin stripped the gun just the way I did it, never looking down, always looking at me. When he was finished putting it back together, he chambered a round, flicked up the safety, put the rifle on the bench again, and stepped back.

I nodded toward the wall of ammo boxes. He nodded. He knew I'd found everything in there: another FAL, three Kalashnikovs, an M16, three M67 fragmentation grenades, and one M18 smoke grenade. From the look of them the grenades dated back to the US mission in Somalia in the early 1990s. There were also a couple of long knives, almost like machetes, a little quiver full of arrows with handmade points, and an African bow. The M16 was useless. No ammo. There were just a few rounds in the clips of the Kalashnikovs. But the second FAL's magazine was full, and there were about a hundred loose rounds besides. It was quite a good little arsenal, I figured. Anyway, it was enough to change the limit of my possibilities.

I picked the FAL off the bench and held it up between us. "Wolla Jora," I said, and for the first time since I met him, I saw Nureddin smile.

CHAPTER 19

I follow the rhythms of the solitary shifta running through the lightless desert, my feet striking the ground but the rest of my body and my head somewhere else, without sight, without any sense of what is around us, lost in space in the middle of the moonless night. The pain in my muscles doesn't reach me after a while, but in that empty-headed, hard-breathing trance the fear keeps catching up. If Abu Zubayr's people have Betsy and Miriam, then Abu Zubayr is the only chance I'll have to save them. He is going to have to tell me where they are. He is going to have to tell his people to release them. And he is going to have to do all of that in the next few hours. I know after September 11—we all know after September 11—these guys don't take prisoners, and hostages don't survive. A running cadence from my Ranger days keeps slipping into my open-eyed dream. "C-130 rolling down the strip, Airborne daddy gonna take a little trip. Mission unspoken, destination unknown, don't even know if we're ever going home." Destination unknown. Going home. Destination unknown.

But now there's a light. The destination is known. It's there up ahead. The first light is in one of the farm buildings about six hundred yards away from us. Nureddin, in one smooth movement, takes up a prone position. So do I. Another light goes on and casts a dim glow over the ground outside, just enough so we can pick up the movement of a man walking from one building to another. The sound of a generator rolls across the empty terrain between us.

Nureddin takes a sharp breath, inhaling the scent of decay on the air, and he points to a space about halfway between us and the first building, but I'm not sure what I see. Something big is silhouetted dead-still against the glow coming from the compound. An animal corpse, maybe a camel. And it's not the only one. There are at least three other bare-boned skeletons of some sort out there. Nureddin makes a gesture with his hands, opening them like an explosion. He points to each of the big stinking carcasses, and each time makes the same explosive gesture. There are mines. Goddamn mines. I can clear our way through the field, probing inch by inch with the knife on my belt, if I haven't lost my touch. But by the time I finish, the sun will be rising.

There has to be another way. What can we see here? One four-door Toyota pickup "technical" with a mount for a .50-caliber in the back—but no gun there. There's supposed to be three other technicals. Where the hell are they? And where are the sentries? Where is everybody? And why is this man who is stumbling half asleep from one building to the other so relaxed? He's acting the way any soldier does when the thing he's supposed to guard is gone. Abu Zubayr must have left with the other technicals and probably half his crew or more. Shit. What's it going to take to squeeze something useful out of these characters? What are they going to know? They ain't gonna know shit.

"Abu Zubayr?" I ask. Nureddin nods. "Here? Now?" I point down. He nods again, then holds up his hand to silence me, and stands. He puts his bow over one shoulder and the FAL over the other, then motions me to follow as he starts loping like a marathoner on a victory lap, running straight for the rotting carcasses. If he knows what he's doing and I follow close enough and carefully enough, maybe we'll get through. If he doesn't know what he's doing, we're both going to get killed—or maybe maimed and then killed. But if I hang back, I'm going to be left crawling inch by inch until the sun lights me up. I follow his pace and his footsteps as fast and as best as I can and I think I hear something coming out of his throat. Low. Rhythmic. Not a running cadence or a song. A prayer. Ah, shit, Nureddin, don't you go trusting God to get us through this.

Nureddin takes a zigzag course, running from the corpse of the camel to the skeleton of a goat next to a couple of blown-apart buzzards, then on toward the skeleton of another goat, and straight toward the small building that I figure is the mosque. Nureddin seems to know his way around this place pretty damn well, which gives me some confidence. And also gives me the creeps.

We circle behind the mosque at a distance of about twenty yards and crouch behind a long row of ammo boxes. Each one is mounted on stone supports, and even in the dark I recognize our hives. Most of the bees are still asleep, but a faint buzzing mixes with the distant sound of the generator. We wait.

"Allahu Akbar—" A tape-recorded call to prayer explodes through a loudspeaker on top of the building in front of us. The hives vibrate with the sound and buzz with life. A couple of bees, then a couple more, light on my face. Neither Nureddin nor I move as we watch the men of the compound slowly making their way to their prayers. I count twenty-four of them wandering drowsily into the little building. I can't tell which is Abu Zubayr, or if any of them are, but one is limping like Bassam al-Shami, the torture doctor, the secret source. It would be good to see him here.

Nureddin points to the day pack, where I carry the grenades, then at the mosque. I nod. He's thinking what I am thinking.

The imam begins the recitation. A single Kalashnikov-toting sentry stands, sleepy and bored, outside the door of the mosque. He picks his nose and tries to get a good look at what he dug out. Nothing else in the compound moves. Nureddin pulls two arrows from his quiver and strings one in his bow. It catches the sentry in the shoulder—not a killing shot. Nureddin has the other arrow drawn and aimed, but holds back. The sentry collapses on the ground, twitching like a man with a seizure, but makes no sound.

The two of us creep forward to the open doorway. Bees rise off our bodies and faces and fly back to the hives. The sentry is lying almost still, but not quite. His eyes are wide open, and up close you can see he's shivering with some kind of uncontrollable spasm. Nureddin puts his hand on the man's heart and nods. The sentry is still alive. Still conscious. Completely paralyzed.

There is a hierarchy of prayer. We know the most important men in the mosque will be in the front row of the faithful, so as all kneel together and touch their heads to the ground with their backsides to us, I pull the pins from two of the grenades, then release the handle on one. Counting "four," "three," "two," I toss it into one of the back corners of the building near the door, then I toss the second, and step back. The first explosion sends a cloud of dust out the door. There is a hush, a taking of breath by the injured and the stunned inside, then the second grenade goes off.

I look over my shoulder. Nobody is coming from anywhere else in the compound. Everybody is here. Nureddin lets off a three-shot burst, then another, then another. There is no place for anyone to hide. Five or six men at the back of the building have taken the brunt of the shrapnel. But everyone inside is stunned, and just about everybody who wasn't in the front row is injured. I throw another grenade into the back. A dud. And another that explodes in the air. It tears off half of one man's face and knocks a second man against the wall, his chest gushing blood like a sieve. Now I have my gun to my shoulder, watching for any survivor who is somehow together enough to grab his rifle. One in a turban manages to throw the bolt on his Kalashnikov before I catch him in the gut with a quick burst from the FAL. Now nobody moves. There are about a dozen still standing. Slowly they put their hands up in the air and back toward the wall, their faces a mix of confusion and fury. Half of them have their eyes closed, praying.

I was afraid that Nureddin would kill them all. But he is cool—so super cool it makes the hair on the back of my neck stand up.

I look at the man who limped. I don't recognize his face. But, then, I never really did see Al-Shami. "*Hola,*" I say. No reaction. "*Qué tal?*" No reaction. "You don't remember Granada?" Nothing. Maybe he is Al-Shami, maybe not. He looks too young, and he doesn't look smart enough. "I'll get back to you."

Betsy.

Miriam.

One of these bastards knows where they are. One of these motherfuckers is going to make sure Miriam gets home to play with her Barbies tonight.

If I ask for Abu Zubayr, simple as that, nobody is going to know him, and the more I ask, the more they're going to harden their lies. I rip a piece of cloth off of one of the dead men's thobes and use it to wipe the black grease off my face. I want to make sure I am recognized, even if I fail to recognize him. As I work my way down our row of prisoners, a couple of them look away. Some stare right back. But others, in what looks like the trance of prayer, will not open their eyes at all. This isn't working. I step back.

"Abu Zubayr? Who knows Abu Zubayr?" None of the holy warriors answers. I let off a round into the groin of a dark-skinned Arab I know can't be Salah and he crumbles screaming onto the blood-damp floor. All but one of those saying their prayers opens his eyes. A couple try to make a move. Nureddin drops one of them with a clean shot to the head. We step back a couple of paces.

"Abu Zubayr?" I am looking at the man with his eyes still closed. His features are coming into focus in my memory. One of the younger Somalis looks at him, too.

"That'll do fine. Open your eyes, Salah." His skin is pitted and scarred from acne, so the long, rough beard seems to grow from craters in his face. His lips are thin, his nose broad and broken. Only one of his eyes, the left one, has any life in it. The other is as gray and dead as a spent bullet.

From behind me Nureddin speaks the name "Abu Zubayr." I wouldn't want to hear him say my name like that. Nureddin puts a fresh clip into his FAL.

The screaming man I'd shot in the groin goes quiet. There is a thin metal click: the handle of a grenade springing off. It spins toward me on the floor like a child's top.

Nureddin and I bolt back through the door and step to each side. Nothing. No explosion. But the survivors inside grab up their guns and started blasting. "Shit."

Just that fast the situation is out of control. More bursts of gunfire. And a kind of panic hits me, not that we will be killed ourselves, but that, now we've found him, we'll have to kill the man we came for. "Abu Zubayr," I shout at Nureddin and wag my finger. He cuts loose another burst through the doorway of the mosque, then backs off.

No one moves. Nureddin and I are outnumbered eight to two. At some point the muj will try to break out. But we can't know when. They have the initiative. We can't leave. I can't question them. We are prisoners of our prisoners.

The only grenade I have left is the smoke grenade. I hold it in my hand, trying to think the best use to make of it. Then Nureddin reaches for it. He studies it, handling it like he knows exactly how it works. Then he fires off a couple of blind bursts toward the building and runs around the back. I keep popping off rounds, trying to keep them down inside without using up too much ammunition, backing away at an angle and lying prone about thirty yards away to get a clear field of fire with a little bit of cover.

The thick plume of yellow smoke rises from behind the mosque. "What the fuck are you doing, Nureddin?" A couple of minutes later, he reappears carrying an ammo-box beehive.

The smoke-drunk insects are crawling over his face and arms. He throws the hive underhanded into the mosque, like he was heaving a boulder. I lay down some covering fire. Nureddin disappears again around the back and returns with another hive. He throws that in, too. You can hear it smash and splinter on the dirt floor. There is a scuffling sound. Then nothing. Then someone screams. The bees are waking up.

Now Nureddin takes up a prone position angled opposite mine. We have the door in a crossfire. We wait. The first man through is the one with the limp, his face and arms covered with stinging bees. Nureddin drops him. Now the rest follow, screaming and firing blind as Nureddin and I squeeze off one short burst after another. When Abu Zubayr appears, Nureddin sees him first and lowers his aim to the legs. The bullet shatters one of Abu Zubayr's knees and he starts to crawl. The man behind him takes a round through the lungs and falls on him. The bees, now in the open air, swarm upward and away. Abu Zubayr is trapped by his wound and the weight of the man on top of him, and now Nureddin has the barrel of the FAL pointed straight into his good eye.

"Ibn sharmuta," says Abu Zubayr. Son of a whore.

"My name is Kurt Kurtovic."

"I remember," he says.

"You're going to remember more."

Nureddin looks at the wounded and dying men around us. He takes the long knife out of his belt and, one by one, slits their throats. Abu Zubayr watches with the face of a man who's seen it all before. Then Nureddin kneels down beside the paralyzed sentry he's shot with his poisoned arrow. He feels the man's beating heart and nods, like a doctor checking a patient.

CHAPTER 20

The night was over. The sun was rising. The air was still. The screaming men were silent now, all of them. Abu Zubayr, clutching his shattered knee, made no sound at all as Nureddin kicked him in the head, knocking him over on his face, and tied his hands behind his back with a piece of wire.

An engine coughed to life somewhere out of sight. The generator, I thought at first, but who would do that? A plane. We saw it rising quickly about half a mile away. Small. Single engine. A Cessna. It banked sharp, real sharp, like it was going to fall out of the sky, and it headed south. Abu Zubayr didn't even look up at the sound.

"Who the fuck is that?" I said.

He said nothing.

"Who the fuck is that, Salah?"

Nothing.

"Is that Al-Shami?"

Nothing.

"Nureddin," I said. I pointed at my eye, then at Abu Zubayr, and saw that Nureddin understood he was to watch him. "I'm going to take a look around," I said and pointed at the other buildings. Nureddin nodded.

It wasn't until then, just then, that I really saw what we'd done, how many men we'd killed. And I felt it for a second, felt the whole weight of death like a wave rushing up at me, tightening my throat, shortening my breath. Then I turned away. It was time to think about the living. About all the living. About Miriam. About Betsy. And about all of our American dead.

The extension cords from the half-destroyed generator led into the house and, sure enough, one wire connected to a sat phone, the other to a laptop. The screen lit up, the window-paned flag of Microsoft waved—and the security box appeared. I X'ed it out. Slowly, the programs kept loading. The files in "My Documents" were encrypted. But maybe these guys were lazy. There were some quick bits and pieces I could pick up in other folders. Temporary Internet Files and History showed whoever was on this laptop was doing a lot of Web surfing. I scrolled through the entries, ordered them by date, ordered them by name. There were a whole lot of pages from religious sites. But there were even more from cummslurpingslutts.com. "What would Osama say about that?" I wondered to the four walls.

There were travel agency sites, banking sites. But most of them showed nothing offline when I clicked them. There was a site for Lloyd's shipping registry. But again, the page came up blank.

What else looked interesting? MapQuest: those little computerized plans of states and cities that show you just how to get to any address in America. There were a lot of those in the temporary files. One of them was for Westfield, Kansas, 6970 Pecos Way. I folded the laptop shut and put it under my arm.

The Somali sun scorched everything beneath it, but none of those left alive outside had moved. Nureddin crouched in front of Abu Zubayr as if he could see the flames of Hell burning the Arab's sting-scarred skin, and he enjoyed what he saw.

"Where are they?" I asked Abu Zubayr. But he didn't say a word. "Where are my wife and child?" Abu Zubayr smiled, and his dry lips cracked red. I kicked him in his bloody knee. He let out a choked scream, but no words followed. "Who's got them?" I shouted. I laid into his ribs, kicking the wind out of him, then let him gasp back his breath. Still he didn't talk.

Nureddin touched my shoulder and I swung around. He had his long knife out of its scabbard. He motioned me to be still, then stood over Abu Zubayr for a minute, just looking at him.

"Don't," I said. Nureddin looked at the Qaeda operative, and at me. Then he turned to the paralyzed sentry, and pulled him straight into Abu Zubayr's line of sight. Nureddin used his foot to turn the man's head until the open eyes, now dry, red, and burned, were looking straight at Abu Zubayr's face. Nureddin laced the fingers of his left hand into the sentry's right, pulling the arm upright and taut, then swung the heavy knife in a powerful forehand that cut the sentry's arm completely off at the elbow. Blood spurted from the arteries like red ink from a squirt gun as the stub fell to the ground again. Nureddin released his grip on the hand and put the severed forearm neatly to one side, then took a strip of cloth and tied a tourniquet around the gushing biceps. He was going to keep the sentry alive a while longer. The man's burned eyes were moving in his head, rolling in narrow, agonized circles.

What Abu Zubayr was thinking just then I couldn't tell you, but I sat down in the shade of the battered mosque, forcing back the dry heave that was rising in my throat. It was going to take me a minute to ask any questions. I opened the laptop. My fingers trembled a little as they touched the keyboard. I focused on the screen. On the address in Westfield. When I heard the sound of Nureddin's blade chopping through a joint, I didn't look up, but a small geyser of blood splashed across my hands and the computer. I wiped it off as best I could, but the screen, the keys, my fingers were smeared with it.

"Salah," I said, "I don't know what he's got planned for you. And I'm not sure if I can stop him. But I can try if you give me a little help."

"You are weak," he whispered.

"Yeah," I said. "I guess I am." A bee lit on the screen. I blew gently and it flew away. "And you know—you know what,

Salah? I am tired of killing. I am so fucking tired of killing that I am going to do whatever it takes to stop it. And whatever it takes to protect my own. Whatever. Now let's start with the password to this encryption system."

"America is weak," he whispered.

"Whatever," I said.

"America is—" He stopped short. I glanced up. Nureddin had just castrated the sentry. "You will not let him do anything to me," said Abu Zubayr. "There is too much you want to know."

"What I want to know is in here," I said. "But there's not a whole lot of time. The battery is at—fifty-seven percent. It says that's over an hour. I don't know. My laptop always cuts off real quick when it drops under fifty percent. And when this one goes, I'm out of here. I'll be taking this back to—somewhere we can work on it. Nureddin will stay here with you." Over the next few minutes, the old shifta continued to build his little human shrine beneath Abu Zubayr's good eye. The fountains of blood became a trickle, and by the time Nureddin hacked through the man's neck, there was no blood flowing at all.

"Strange poison," I said. "Lets you live, but doesn't let you move. I wonder what that poor bastard was thinking while Nureddin took him apart?"

No answer.

"Salah, I'm going to ask you just one more question, then I'm out of here. Where is my family?"

"I don't know."

"You know they lived at 6970 Pecos Way."

"I don't know."

"Who does?"

He shook his head.

"Bullshit," I said.

"I don't know."

The laptop's warning beeper started chiming like a digital alarm clock.

"I'm gone," I said.

"*They're* gone, Kurtovic."

"No."

"But you can always find another little whore."

I turned off the computer, put it gently on the ground, and pulled the knife out of my belt.

Nureddin saw the technicals a long way off, coming at us through the late afternoon, racing, bouncing, veering over muddy ruts, men in the back holding onto the .50-calibers like rodeo riders hanging onto their saddles. They didn't aim, they just shot. One round popped into the wall of the little mosque and pocked it a couple of inches deep just above my head. But I didn't have it in me to move. I thought—I thought—I could not think anymore, but there was the idea somewhere in my head that if we could just wait for night, we would be okay, we could get back out through the minefield. Something. Get away from this place and what happened here. Just an hour or so away. The sun was low. Another .50-caliber hit the wall of the mosque and went clean through it. They had to build these places of worship better, I decided. What would God think?

Nureddin was moving all over the compound. He was looking for—something. Nureddin would take care of us. He always took care of us. Nureddin, my friend. I wondered what Betsy would think of him. What would Betsy think? Where was Betsy? Funny name to be saying out here. Betsy. This wasn't really a Betsy kind of place. We were so far from Betsy and Miriam Land. So far. No, this sure doesn't look like Kansas, Toto.

An RPG is what Nureddin found. Good for you, Nureddin. You are one smart son of a bitch. Wish I could move. Wish I could help you. But I am just so tired, you know. You can see that, can't you? Forgive me, old buddy. It's been such a long day of work. Should have left when I said I would. Did I learn so much in the last eight hours? It was such a slow thing. Such an uncooperative bastard. But he was polite after a while. That was good. Good to be polite.

Where are you, Nureddin? The air went hollow for a second and the explosion left my ears ringing. Those rocket-propelled grenades always make so damn much noise. Big noise. One of the technicals is on its side. Good move, Nur. Wish I could help. Those other two bastards are going to be right on top of us in a couple of minutes. Guess—yep, guess I better try to do something. Let's see, prone position. That's good. That's good. Hands shaking? No. Weird they're not shaking now. They were shaking like Parkinson's just a few minutes ago. But the aim's steady now. The bullet goes right through the windshield of the first technical. Should have got the driver. Truck should crash. They always do in movies. But it just rolls to a stop. One of the men in the back gets out, pushes the dead driver aside, and takes the wheel himself.

What's that dragonfly shadow moving over the ground and up the walls of the buildings? Something is coming out of the sun. Hello, Predator. Taking a little look-see? Hello, Langley.

One of the technicals has stopped and the .50-caliber man is pumping a stream of bullets at the great metal gnat in the sky. That technical stops firing. It's in fiery pieces. Hellfiery pieces. But the other technical is just fine. Too bad. Going to have to fight, I guess. Maybe get shot. Maybe die. So many maybes.

The back of the head of the Somali manning the last .50 blows away like the Zapruder film. Nice shot, Nureddin. The technical turns and pulls behind a low dune. Another shooter gets up in the bed. A better shooter. The bullets are coming so close I can feel the heat under my skin.

It's darker. The night curtain has dropped real quick. Or I'm real slow. The shooting has stopped. Good. Can't see so good to shoot.

Somebody is on my back, on my head. Arms pulled behind me. Strap around my wrists. Plastic cuffs. Where'd they get those? *We* use those. Standard government issue. Pulled to my feet, patted down. Thrown against the wall inside the mosque.

"Jesus," someone shouts. "Get in here, Archangel. Take a look at this."

Fluttery noise outside. Silenced gun cutting loose three-round bursts. I hear the loud report of the FAL. Then somebody coming in through the door. And somebody else. Can feel their movement better than I can see them.

"Out!" one of them shouts at the other. "Get out now! Cover from outside."

"But—"

"Now!"

"Yessir."

The op commander is close to my face. I smell the dryness of his mouth. Flashlight on. Cold light. Bright. Blinding. Sweeping room. Light focusing. Stopping on the naked, bloody thing lying almost next to me on the floor. "God Almighty." Not my voice.

"Abu Zubayr," I say. "Still alive. Can still talk." I look at my chest in the white glow of the Maglite. At my legs. Everything caked with dust and blood. "I—I—can't do more."

"It's me."

"You?"

The man shines the light on his own face. "It's me: Griffin."

"Griffin. Good Griffin. Griffin, my friend. Ahhhh." I bang my head on the wall. Still isn't working. "Miriam," I say. "Miriam and Betsy. Gone."

"No," says Griffin. "No. We've got them. They're okay. But I don't know what the hell we're going to do with you."

X Ray

DECEMBER 2001–MARCH 2002

CHAPTER 21

The sandpaper feel of my eyes moving under the skin of the lids and the chill of the sweat seeping down my back told me I was alive. There was something pressing against my cheekbones like the rubber rims of goggles, but there was no light, only the smell of fuel and disinfectant in the air, and the engine vibrations I felt in my bones. An airplane. I was sitting on the steel floor of some kind of transport, tethered to it with canvas straps. My hands were cuffed, my ankles were shackled, and there was a chain around my waist. Earphones connected to nothing were clamped on my head like a padded vise. When I spoke I heard my voice inside the back of my skull. Nobody answered. When I listened, the sound closing in on me was the sound of the sea, like the sound you hear in a shell on the beach, the sound of blood rushing in my ears.

Panic hovered near. I tried to speak again and realized the voice was not making words but groans the way someone sick or wounded sounds. Was I sick? Was I wounded? My mind floated in blackness like one of those eight-ball toys where little sayings about the future surface through black ink. Acid surged in my throat and for a second I fought it. Then it came again in a second wave and I opened my mouth wide to let go whatever poison was in my gut. The burn rushed through my mouth and the back of my nose. I shook my head and screamed to clear my lungs. Suddenly water splashed over my head and drenched whatever clothes were on me. In seconds I could feel the cloth cold and clammy against my skin. I was conscious. How long had it been since I was conscious? I sat back. I listened to the sound of the sea in my ears, and waited for messages to float out of the ink.

I remembered the day of the knives. I remembered asking Abu Zubayr questions. I did not remember, completely, what they were. We talked about—about—weddings. About ships. About weddings. I remembered Griffin whispering in my face, and me repeating as much as I could about ships and weddings, names and places. And Betsy and Miriam—yes, both of them—safe, he said. That's what Griffin said. Safe. But where were they? And where was I?

I remembered a helicopter out of Somalia (I thought it was a helicopter), but the rest of the memory was lost in clouds of dust and the mist of dreams. There was a pill "to help you," someone said. Help me what? And why did I take it? There were other pills. I took those, too, in different places, at different times, but I had no sense of place or time. The day of the knives could be yesterday or last week or last month.

And now I was a prisoner. And from the way I was shackled, I'd say I was a dangerous one.

The pressure changed inside my ears. The plane was going down, slowly settling toward a landing. The wheels smashed onto something solid and g-forces flung me to my left, then back to my right, like the "Octopus" ride at a county fair. Then we stopped dead. There was no sound but the blood-sea in my ears and the vibration in my bones from the plane's engines. Then another vibration, deeper and farther away, took its place, deep and low, rumbling from inside enormous machines. Hands grabbed each arm and jerked me up onto my feet, but my legs weren't working so good. "Where we going?" I heard my voice in my head again. No voice replied. The hands pulled me, lifted me, and my feet slid and shuffled forward, stop, forward, turn, stop, stand, turn, stop. The hands never left me. We walked down an incline and I felt a breath of hot wet air and the burn, for just a second, of what I thought must be the sun. Fuel smells filled my nose. Then the chill again. And the shuffling, the shuffling.

The hands pushed me up against a wall, but the wall was soft. My forehead was pressed against it. I started to stand back but a hand pushed my head hard into the wall. I stayed there. Someone pulled the earphones off my head.

"You understand English?"

"Yeah," I said. "I'm—American." I wanted to sound friendly, but my tongue was thick and my voice drunk.

The hand pushed my head against the wall again. "If you understand, then do what I say. We're going to take off the chains now, but I don't want you turning. I don't want you moving. Do you understand?"

"Yeah, buddy. Where—where're you boys from? I've got to talk—somebody."

"Do you understand? Yes or no." He'd memorized a script.

"Yes," I said.

"Stay in that position until you hear the door close," said the voice, and finally a hand I didn't see took off the goggles. The door closed. The room was completely dark.

You don't think when you don't have senses. The mind doesn't work like that. It navigates by dead reckoning, and it needs reference points: images, sounds, smells, tastes, textures. Take them away and the thoughts that come and go have nothing to hang on to. After a while, they stop being thoughts at all, just rushes of fear and excitement. We learned something about this during the survival-evasion-resistance-escape courses when I was a Ranger. The goal of the interrogator is to turn you into a child again, make you dependent and obedient, and make you want to please Daddy. But, hell, that was just book-learning. And the book said nothing about a padded cell with no light, no cot, no nothing.

I wanted the faces of Miriam and Betsy in front of me. I

wanted to see them through the dark. But when they came to me, the feel of missing them and the fear of losing them was so terrible that it tore away at whatever organization was left inside my head. It was Griffin's face that kept me together, at least at first. "Won't be long," he said in one of the last moments I remembered in real time. "Won't be long." And those were the words I hung on to so hard and so tight that they were like a hymn in my head for a while. And long after I didn't know how long "long" was, his words were there.

But what had *I* said to *Griffin?* Did I warn him? Did I tell him what Abu Zubayr told me? Did I know myself? There was something about ships. When the horror of what was happening to him was too much for Abu Zubayr to stand, he talked about ships. Or did I dream that? There were so many dreams. Constant dreams. And in one of them Abu Zubayr and I were floating down a long, narrow river that ran in and out of buildings like a flood. We sank and surfaced, and Abu Zubayr became Griffin and I kept shouting at him "The ships! The ships!" but he just rolled over in the water like he was rolling over in a bed and pulling the covers, the water, with him. Whatever I knew about the ships from the day of the knives, I hoped I told Griffin, because it was real important. But here in the dark I couldn't separate memory from dream.

I waited for the interrogation. I wanted the interrogators. Wanted them so bad that I had to try to stop myself, because wanting is what this is all about. They make you want. They give you a little. You want more. They make you pay with whatever you got, which is whatever you know, and maybe what you don't know.

One thing I knew they wanted, but I knew they didn't know they wanted it: back in Westfield in the Jump Start freezer, back there with the forgotten gray-green pork chops, all sealed up in a red thermos canister that looked like a fire extinguisher wedged behind a bag of ice, the magic elixir that could become the Sword of the Angel of the Lord. Mine eyes had seen that glory. And if the interrogators knew, they'd take it from me.

And if they knew, they'd take me and keep me and this would be my life forever here in the hole in the dark with my brain eating itself the way starving flesh eats its own fat. Must tell them. Cannot tell them. We'll put that knowledge away, won't we? We'll migrate it out of the mind like a maggot burrowing through meat, and push it into a place they won't find it.

And sleep came.

But the interrogators never did.

My world exploded with white light. The first thing I saw was my own hand covering my eyes, trying to shield them, but the light burned through the fingers blood red. "Get up. Face the wall," said a man's voice. The light was flaming through my lids now. "Shower time," said the voice. "Strip."

I fumbled open the Velcro fastenings of the jumpsuit, stepped out and kicked it away from me. Every stinking bodily fluid I had was in there somewhere. I kept blinking, trying to handle the rush of light. I looked down at myself and I had this weird feeling that the body parts didn't belong to me, like they weren't hooked up somehow. I looked at my hands in the white light. The nails were black and the creases between the fingers were stained dark brown with Abu Zubayr's blood. I looked up at the two guards. Both were wearing body armor, with helmets and visors that kept me from seeing their faces. All padded out like that, they looked like a cross between Darth Vader and the Pillsbury Doughboy. Neither carried any weapons that I could see.

"Against the wall." I did as I was told, and one of the guards locked shackles around my ankles and a belly chain with separated cuffs around my waist. Then the two of them grabbed my arms and half-carried me stumbling naked into a steel-walled hallway. I guessed before that we were in a carrier, and now I knew we were. But where we were on the sea, and where we were going, I had no idea.

The first stop for me was the toilet. The chains stayed on

and the guards stood there and watched while I pissed and shit. Then we went to the shower room, which was empty except for us. I stood in chains under the steaming water. It scalded my face and shoulders and poured over my chest. But because of the cuffs and the belly chain I couldn't do anything to clean myself, couldn't even rub my hands together to get rid of the blood.

"When do we talk?" I asked.

"Not now," said one of the guards, and I realized he was the only one who ever spoke.

"We shouldn't waste time," I said.

"Not now." He still had that script, the one that told him to "impart no information." There was not going to be any pleading with these guys, or persuading them.

"What's the date?" I asked.

"Not now!"

Time is one of the first things they take away from you. They keep the lights out or the lights on so you lose any sense of day or night, and you're just tired all the time. After a while, even if you don't answer any of their questions, they can create a kind of special world for you where every new bit of information you have comes from them. *Everything.* Is the war on terror over? It is if they want you to think it is. Have the ships sailed? What ships?

But the fact was, nobody talked to me about anything. The only way I guessed how much time was passing was by the length of my beard and hair, but that wasn't really reliable. Every so often, in silence, they shaved my head and face. Just like, every now and then, they brought me food or led me to the toilet. But how often? There was no way to be sure. In the padded cell the light was on sometimes, and off sometimes. But only they knew when. They took on a power the Qur'an gives to God: "He merges Night into Day, and He merges Day into Night, and He has full knowledge of the secrets of all hearts." But they didn't really give a damn what was in *my* heart. What I wanted. They didn't even ask.

Belonging. For too much of my life, that was all I wanted. I tried to belong to the army and to the Rangers. I tried to belong to the world of the first woman I loved. I tried to belong to the ranks of Allah's Holy Warriors. I learned their skills, I learned their ways, I learned their minds. But I never fit in with them. The only place I ever found where I could be who I was, and where that feeling of belonging wrapped around me with all its warmth and comfort, was at home with Betsy and with Miriam. And now they were farther away than I could imagine. Where was my sweet milk-mustache baby? Where was my smart loving tough caring more-guts-than-a-burglar little tadpole of a crying laughing fighting kissing sleeping-with-her-head-on-my-chest-and-her-breath-stirring-across-me wife? Ah, Lord. I could go crazy wanting them and wanting home, and it was slipping away from me fast. I had to fight to pull the faces of Miriam and Betsy out of the shadows, but the shadows were too many, and then the faces of the people I loved were lost and all that lingered was the idea of them.

No one talked to me in the hold of that ship. They gave me nothing to read, nothing to distract me from their light and their dark. Nothing, from their point of view, not even the game of interrogation, to keep me from going insane. And after a while I thought all I had left was my anger and my discipline and my faith in the power of hate, a faith I had almost forgotten.

Hate is hard and bright; it has a clear edge like a spotlight, and when all else fails, you can use it to get your bearings, I thought. That was what guided Nureddin and me through the night. That was what would get me through this.

I began to remember and recite chants I learned as a Ranger and verses from the Qur'an and even from the Bible, all from a long time ago in my life, and all of them built on rhythms of hate. "I do well to be angry, even unto death." Isn't that what Jonah said? And call it prayer or call it what you want, five times between waking and sleeping, I would try to clear my mind of everything but a dream of fire. The important thing was to remain my own man in my own mind, not theirs, not ever, not anywhere, no matter what they did. "They" who slaughtered in the name of God. "They" who slaughtered in the name of democracy. "They" who put me here for reasons of state or security or just because they couldn't think of anything else to do with me. They all wanted to keep me away from my home, my life, my peace. But I would have my own. I would look at them and they would be consumed by fire. That was the vision that kept me going for a while longer in the dark, a pure flame, blue and hot; a curtain of flame, and just beyond it, peace. When ants began to crawl under my skin in the blackness, the flame steadied me. When I heard my voice wailing inside my head, the flame guided me, until a kind of calm settled into my soul. Hate would keep me going, hate would give me the power to lie or to tell the truth, to fight or to fall back, to do whatever needed doing. That's what I tried to believe. Hate would free me, and then there would be time enough for love. "Won't be long," I said out loud. "Won't be long." Until hate failed me, too.

I was dead.

Drifting.

Nowhere.

I was lost—when the house began to build itself.

I saw a rolling meadow above a pond, and I saw the foundation start to outline itself in the blowing grass. There were no shovels or backhoes, yet there it was, tracing its way into the ground where a deep, cool cellar appeared, with solid walls of cut rock. What kind of house could I build in a place like that, on a foundation like that? I saw the shape of it: two stories with a porch that wrapped around three sides of the building, and half-moon dormer windows in the roof. It was covered in white clapboard. The windows were tall and those that looked out on the porch reached almost to the floor. There was a fireplace in the living room, and a big kitchen where you could eat around a wooden table. But there were no people here. The house was not finished. I had to work to make it real. I had to hammer in every nail on every joist. I had to lay every floorboard and every shingle. That would be the only way to finish the house. And then we would see—then we would see who would come to live in it.

CHAPTER 22

"You've been with us seven weeks." The man behind the steel desk glanced over the file in front of him, then looked up at me with all the interest of an Orkin man looking at another termite. His face was square and his head shaved into an old-style crew cut, the frames of his glasses were thick and black. His BDUs bore no insignia, but there was a thick white line on his right ring-finger. Probably he wore a Naval Academy ring. But he wouldn't want me to know that.

"Yeah," I said. "Yeah, sure."

"Yes." He flipped back a page in the file. "Seven weeks and one day."

"Lost track," I said.

"Yes."

"And—"

"Yes?"

"Why am I here?"

"Above my pay grade," he said.

"Yeah."

"The medical report says you are in good condition."

I nodded.

"Do you have any physical complaints?" he asked.

I shook my head. "Why am I here?"

"I told you, that's above my pay grade."

"Why haven't I—been"—the words came slow for lack of practice—"been—questioned?"

The guy just looked at me with that expression that guys with security clearances love to cultivate. Not a frown and not a smile, but not quite blank either, as if the question had never been asked at all. He smelled like soap, I thought, like those little bars you get in a cheap motel.

"I am an—American citizen," I said.

"Yes, well, we hear that a lot."

"You know."

"Do I?"

"You know my name—Kurt Kurtovic, and that I am—U.S. Army Ranger. Panama. Gulf War. In your file."

That look again.

I asked, "What about ships?"

"I don't know what you're talking about."

"What about goddamn *ships*?"

"I can tell you we have detained you for your own protection."

"I see," I said. "I—can I see somebody?" I was trying to force myself to speak in full sentences.

"No."

"Griffin?"

"Who?"

"Somebody."

"You're not making sense. You want to see a lawyer?"

"Yes."

"Impossible. You are not under arrest."

There didn't really seem to be anything else to say. "What—what now?"

"You're leaving in a few minutes."

"Back to—States?"

"Let's not play twenty questions."

I sat back and looked at my handcuffs and shackles, my maximum security smock with the Velcro on the sides so they could leave the belly chain on all the time, and my paper slippers. "Will I—will I have time to pack?"

The guy didn't smile. "You're very controlled," he said.

"Yes," I said. "I have—a—job—to—do."

"What's that?"

"My country—expects me—to move farther—uh, farther—faster and fight harder," I said, repeating the words of the Ranger Creed that was my faith before I found God, that had come back to me in the hole.

"Whatever," he said, closing the folder.

I looked at him and for just a second his square face was consumed with fire. "Whatever," I said.

To the orange jumpsuit and the blacked-out goggles, the earphones, and the chains, they now added mittens and a little cap. They'd taken away sight and sound. Now touch. But the more my senses were taken, the more I absorbed whatever sensation was left. Shuffling shackled, shuffling mindless, suddenly a wave of feelings hit me. The earphones didn't block everything, they just muffled it, and a wall of sounds came at me so loud that I could feel them with my whole body. I felt the deep shock of jet engines. I felt the heat of the sun burning through the cloth that covered my body; the wet, heavy air filling my lungs. And the smells—the smells of fuel and of burned rubber, of sweat and of the sea—rushed at me from every direction. All those weeks in the ionized air of the cell, I smelled next to nothing. Now I was catching scents like a bird dog in a cornfield. And one of them was—was—so fresh and so pretty. And so out of place. I stopped my shuffle for a second and surprised the two guards who held my arms. What was the smell? I turned my head trying to catch it again. There. Just for a second when I turned my head to the right—I couldn't tell you what was in it, but I could tell you what it was: the perfume Betsy used to use. The little bottle had two little doves on the top. Her grandmother gave it to her and she wore it when we got married, and sometimes she wore it when we made love. And there was no way I could smell it without thinking of her. The guard's hand pushed my head back and the hand had the smell on it. Now something else was being put on my face. A paper mask like a painter's mask. But I could still smell the perfume. And Betsy's face came to me out of the shadows and filled my mind and I started laughing, and I couldn't stop. This guard—must be a woman sailor—this guard was wearing Betsy's perfume. How crazy was that? I kept laughing and laughing as they chained me inside the chopper.

On the long flight to land, and then on board another plane, which flew so long that I slept and woke and slept and woke four times, I remembered the smell and laughed until the rubber of the goggle rims and then the paper of the mask were damp with sweat and tears.

The airplane rolled to a stop and we were led down the ramp onto solid land and into the heat of the sun. I was shuffled onto some kind of bus, then off. There were other prisoners around me now. Getting on and off these vehicles, we stumbled into each other like blind mice in an old cartoon. Somebody moved my cuffs from front to back of the belly chain and forced me to get down on my knees on gravel. I settled back and waited. If they'd wanted to kill me, I was in just the right position for a bullet to the back of the head. But I knew the U.S. military well enough to know they hadn't brought me all this way to kill me. At least not like that. Even so, I flinched when somebody touched my shaved scalp.

They were just taking off the earphones. "Name," said a deep Southern accent.

"Kurt Kurtovic."

"Nationality."

I said nothing. I didn't know where I was or who was listening.

"Up! Get up!"

I tried, but the only way to get up if you're shackled and chained is to rock back and balance a second to steady yourself, then stand. The gravel slipped under my feet and I went down on my side. The blacked-out goggles shifted on my face and I saw the orange suits of two other prisoners nearby on their knees, and the legs of guards in BDUs. And that was the first glimpse I got of the cage that was going to be my home.

"A little help?" said the Southern voice.

Hands grabbed me and lifted me up, shuffling me forward. Through that sliver of an opening between my face and the shifted goggles I saw chain-link fencing and steel posts, a cage with doors like a kennel. I couldn't think what this would be. The door opened. No dogs inside. I was inside. The chains came off and I could move. The goggles came off and I could see. The guards closed the door.

There were a lot of cages: at least ten right here in two rows of five, back to back, and another set beyond that and another beyond that. There were no walls. Everything was wire, so that when you looked around, you could get a pretty good view of what was happening just about everywhere. Just like in a kennel.

But, my God, the air. It was late afternoon and there was a breeze blowing. A sea breeze. I peeled the orange overalls off my arms and shoulders to let the air move across my bare skin. I stepped back to the back of my cage and sat down on the cool cement with my fingers laced into the chain-link fence above my head. It felt so good to stretch. It felt so good to have breath from the open sky. Life was rushing suddenly back into me in ways I didn't dare think it could. My mind began to shed its web of dreams like it was coming out of a cocoon.

An officer stalked down the walkway in front of the cages, a Marine colonel who looked like he spent a lot of time on the weight bench. He surveyed the cells, reviewing the enemy troops. Some of the men behind the wire looked at him, others paid no attention at all. No one shouted. No one shook the wire. It was like all the prisoners were just waking up from a long sleep but didn't know yet if they could move, or if words could come from their throats. The only sounds were of the seagulls overhead, the far-off rumble of an airplane engine, and the crunch of gravel beneath the colonel's boots. I stayed back at the back of my run.

"You are now at the United States Naval Station at Guantánamo, Cuba," said the Marine colonel. "You've been brought here because of your affiliation with terrorist organizations that attacked the American people. The United States is now at war, and you will be held here until the end of that war. You will be treated humanely, but you will be interrogated and you are expected to cooperate. In a few minutes, you will be supplied with basic necessities. Captain Jackson will inform you of the camp routine." The colonel turned and left. Captain Jackson saluted and watched him go. And we watched Captain Jackson, whose face was sharp and narrow and mean, like some Georgia cracker you'd meet at an all-night truck stop, and who looked too old for his rank.

Gitmo, I thought to myself. This is Gitmo! This is fucking Cuba! I tried to look through the walls of interlaced wire to see how many others were here. Was Nureddin somewhere nearby in another cage? Was Abu Zubayr here, whatever was left of him? Did any of his men survive? What about Al-Shami? He seemed to be everywhere else. *Everywhere.* Why not here? But in the cages around me everyone was a stranger. To my right was a tall, black-skinned man with a sharp Arab nose. He reminded me of a Sudanese I used to know in the Bosnia camps, but this wasn't the same guy. His left eye was closed and the skin around it scarred. So many one-eyes in the muj, their sight lost to shrapnel and their own homemade bombs. The right eye was moving, staring, without stopping to focus on anything.

"Listen up!" shouted Captain Jackson. The one-eyed Sudanese turned his back on him and started pacing off the space in his cage: the length was two and a half of his strides, the width was less than two.

To my left was a guy who could have been from Pakistan or India. He had very dark skin and black eyes, and he squatted in the corner of his cage like a frog ready to jump, but he was deadly still. I looked at his eyes. His mind was far, far away.

"Listen up!" the cracker captain repeated, pulling a little spiral notebook out of his pocket. "Each of you will receive the following items," he said, and started to read. "'Clothing: two prison overalls orange color. That includes what you have on. One pair of rubber sandals; what we call flip-flops. For sleeping: one foam mat, standard issue. We get the same thing in the field, so I don't want to hear nothing about that. One blanket. Yeah. Personal hygiene: soap, a bottle of shampoo, and a tube of toothpaste. You are not going to get toothbrushes. Just use your fingers."

The Sudanese was still measuring his cell, the Squatter was still ready to jump to some far-off place.

"You will have two buckets," said Captain Jackson. "One is for water, which we will fill several times a day. The other is for waste. You do your necessaries in it, and it will be emptied twice a day. Now, this is important: I understand some of you use water to clean your posteriors. Well, you do what you like. But do not *repeat* do not use that water from that bucket for drinking purposes. You will also be given a canteen. Use that for your drinking purposes if you want. And there will be bottled water with meals. And"—he consulted his notebook—"there should be enough water for washing up before your prayers, or whatever it is you need to do. And speaking of prayers, we have a Navy chaplain who is a Muslim and who will be—" Captain Jackson turned to a sergeant and looked at him. The sergeant shook his head. "—who will be speaking to you later today or tomorrow." He looked around to see if there was any reaction, but there wasn't. He nodded like that meant something. "You will get a wash cloth and two towels. If you want to, you can use one of those towels as your prayer rug." He nodded at his notebook. "And we will also be distributing Ko-rans and I'm pleased to say there are Bibles, too, for anyone who wants to discover the Gospel according to Jesus Christ." He flipped the notebook closed and put it back in his pocket. "Any questions? Fine then. Some food will be distributed in about twenty minutes." Just as he started to walk away, Jackson noticed me. He walked over close to my cage door and stared into my eyes, which were just about the same freezer-blue as his. "Where the hell are you from?"

There was nothing I was going to say. Not to him, not then, and not in front of anybody in any of these cages. I just stared straight into him. Then he turned away, followed by the sergeant and a couple of privates.

The food came in a clear plastic bag full of smaller plastic bags: barbecued potato chips, a pack of peanuts, a couple of cereal bars; there was a box of sugar-frosted cornflakes and there was a little pack of raisins. It was like I had America in my hands—my old America from when I was a kid lying on the sofa munching in front of the tube. There were Tony the Tiger and Mr. Peanut, and that was the Sun Maid, who smiled at me from the plastic, her hair covered by a red bonnet and dark locks falling over her shoulders, her arms reaching out over a big basket of grapes. She looked different than I remembered her. Her skin was lighter. Why was that? Who was this Sun Maid who'd never seen the sun?

"Bosnian?" The voice came from behind me, a loud whisper almost next to my head. "You Bosnian?" In the cage that backed onto mine was an Arab with a boyish face who looked like one of those foreign students at Kansas State who wear backward baseball caps instead of headdresses and spend more time at Hooters than the mosque. "Are you Bosnian, brother?" the Arab asked again. "Or Albanian? Where are you from?" His English was very easy to understand, with almost no accent, like he'd grown up in California—but not quite. I remembered that kind of accent from the Gulf War. "I am from Kuwait," he said. "Where are you from? When did they get you?"

I half smiled at the Kuwaiti, but said nothing. Let the prisoners spread the word I was Bosnian Muslim. Hell, I used to think I was. Let them believe what they wanted.

Dusk seeped around us and a loud electric crack split the air. Current hummed above our heads and the cold rays of floodlights filled every cage. Now loudspeakers crackled. *"Allahuu-uuu-akbaaaarr."* God Is Great. They were playing a cassette of the call to prayer. That's pretty damned politically correct, I thought. This never happened in the carrier. And one by one we stood up in our cages.

I did not look like anyone around me, but at this moment I knew how to be part of the *umma,* the great Muslim mass of the faithful. Whatever I believed, I knew the routine. With water from the bucket I washed my feet and my hands and my face, and I turned my back on the sun. I bent my head in prayer, and prepared to kneel in submission to God—facing due East.

"Qibla?" someone shouted. The direction to Mecca. I looked up. The one-eyed Sudanese who had paced off the inside of his cage like a linesman looked in the direction of the lost sun, and toward the creeping shadow of night beyond the halo of the floodlights. He turned in a circle searching, like a dervish turning, looking for a sign that would tell him where Mecca might be.

Captain Jackson's superiors didn't think this one through, I guess. In Saudi Arabia and Afghanistan, in Pakistan and Indonesia, Mecca lies to the West. But not in this place, a world away in the middle of nowhere. The faithful didn't know which way to turn. *"Qibla!"* the Sudanese shouted again and again, louder each time. *"Qibla!"* shouted another voice in the next set of cages. Others took up the chant. *"QIBLA!"* Where was the holiest, the most adored of cities? Where was the Ka'aba? Guards shouted, telling the prisoners to calm down. But no one listened. Some of the men in the cages were pushing and pulling the storm-fence walls, pushing-pulling together to make the whole structure rattle. Others stood half-naked, their towels in their hands, looking for a place and a way to pray. The Sudanese threw a flying kick at the door of his cell. The man to my left did the same. Now the whole *umma* of Guantánamo was shouting, cheering, chanting. And now the call to prayer was drowned by the howl of an alarm.

A squad of Marines, helmeted and padded like the guards on the ship, rushed into the gravel alley in front of our cells. Still the chanting continued. They faced the doors of our cells.

They were looking for the leader. But there was no leader. Behind them, outside the fence line, Marines with M16s and M79 grenade launchers deployed as a second line of defense in case the guards lost control. One of the padded Darth Vaders stepped forward toward my cage door. "What's this kibble shit?" he said.

I smiled, said nothing, turned to the East and spread out my prayer towel.

"You!" the guard shouted.

I shook my head and closed my eyes, making a quiet show of speaking to God, then heard a heavy vehicle rolling over the dirt road outside the fence. I said the first lines of the Fatiha, which is the Lord's Prayer of Islam. "In the name of God, the Merciful, the Compassionate . . ."

They were bringing up a water cannon. "Desist!" shouted a voice over the loudspeaker—a woman's voice. The men in the other cages looked at each other and up at the nearest guard tower, where a heavy woman noncom in BDUs and cap with a blonde ponytail was trying to shout them down. The black Arab climbed up the inside of his cage and pounded with his fist against the inside of the corrugated roof. Other prisoners did the same until a kind of thunder rolled through the camp.

The nozzle of the cannon drooled for a couple of seconds then exploded, knocking us off the walls of our cages, off our feet, forcing us back like twigs hosed off a sidewalk. Most of the men hung back at the far side of their cells after that first blast. But I stood up—stood in the center of my cage, turned East, and thinking "fuck you all" started again the routine of prayer. My eyes were closed now, but I could hear the water turning toward me like my own perfect storm. It hammered my head and ribs. I tried to brace myself on the slippery concrete floor, I steadied, I stood. The water moved on. I stood up and walked back to the middle of the cage and began again to pray. The water came back and this time it didn't let up, battering me, drowning me, shoving me across the floor of the cell. A phalanx of four guards assembled outside the cage door. The

Kuwaiti looked on wide-eyed from the far side of his cage, then signaled something to the Sudanese and to other prisoners I couldn't see. From a human throat nearby came the wail, again, of the call to prayer. Suddenly the water stopped. I saw in the next cell and the next and the next, all the prisoners turned toward the East, taking the direction I had set. Then the Darth Vaders were on me, pinning me to the wet cement. For just a second I saw myself lying in a puddle on the driveway in Westfield on a hot summer day when I was three or four, just smelling the water and the cement and feeling good about it, like I was home.

I was cuffed, shackled, carried away.

CHAPTER 23

"Did you sleep well?" A doctor in hospital green was leaning over me, a dark shape outlined against the white canvas roof of a hospital tent.

I shook my head and pulled against the restraints on the gurney.

"I thought they'd given you something," he said.

"They did."

"I see."

The doctor came into focus. He was about thirty-five or forty, a big man with the beginnings of a potbelly, and as he talked he filled up the airspace over my head. His scrubs were wrinkled and looked like he'd slept in them. He had a day's growth of stubble and his eyes were red but alert. From what I could see lying there on the gurney, nothing about this doctor was stupid rules and regulations and drink-from-the-clean-bucket. He looked completely out of place in this military base. If he was good at his job of doctoring, then that was probably all he was good at, and that was enough.

"Doc—"

"Yeah?"

"I'm an American."

"Yeah," he said. "Sounds like it."

"I've got to get out of here. I've got a wife and a little girl."

"Can't help you with that. How are you feeling?"

"Like I'm under water and can't get back to the surface."

He looked at the chart hanging off the gurney. "Yes. I can imagine. Looks like they went a little heavy on the dosage." The doctor looked me up and down. I was naked except for a towel somebody had dropped over my crotch.

"How did you get these bruises on your right side?"

"Water cannon."

He touched them and I felt his fingers make contact. There was a delay. Then I felt the pain.

"So you were making a little trouble for Captain Jackson?" he said.

"I was minding my own business."

"That's why you're here. You're just an American family man minding his own business."

"Doc?"

"Yeah."

"Why are you here?"

"Navy Reserves."

"You're doing your duty for America."

"Yeah."

"So was I."

"Then why are you here?"

"Because—because the government is confused."

"Confused?" He smiled. "Confused is an interesting word."

"Doc?"

"Yeah."

"Is America okay?"

He thought for a minute. "Yes," he said.

"Was there another attack after—"

A screen of suspicion crossed his eyes. "Don't ask me for that kind of information," he said.

"If you know somebody—"

"I can't help you with anything but your health." He listened to my chest with his stethoscope.

"Marcus Griffin, CIA," I said.

"Who?"

"Just get a message to Marcus Griffin, CIA, that I'm here."

"Is he here?"

"Langley will know where he is."

"I can't help."

"I know," I said. "I know. But if you could."

"Will you lie still or do I give you something else to calm you down?"

"I'll lie still."

"You do that, and I'll see what I can do," he said in a soft voice that was reassuring, but not completely convincing. Then he headed for another gurney, an unconscious strapped-down detainee on the far side of the tent. He just wanted to shut me up, I thought. His act was just bedside manner. Gurney-side manner.

"Doc?"

He looked back over his shoulder, but didn't stop.

"My name's Kurtovic," I said. "Kurt Kurtovic."

By mid-afternoon I was back in the cage. As the guards took off my chains I heard a couple of other prisoners shouting: "Qib-la! Qib-la!" But this wasn't prayer time. I didn't understand. "Qib-la!" they yelled.

"That's your name," said the Kuwaiti in the next cage. The black one-eyed Arab on the other side heard him and grinned. "Qib-la!" he shouted.

"See?" said the Kuwaiti. "You showed us the way to Mecca. And look"—he pointed at the guard tower, the one where the woman guard with the ponytail stood shouting at us the day before—"they put your name up on the guard post." A big white cloth banner hung from the tower due east of us. On it written in green was the single word *"qibla."*

I sat down in the opposite corner of the cage and looked north and west toward Kansas. "Won't be long," I whispered to myself. "Won't be long." I put my head against my knees and went back to the house in the meadow by the pond: my big, empty house that still needed so much work. None of the walls were painted yet. The kitchen wasn't in. There were so many decisions to be made that I couldn't seem to make, or at least couldn't make by myself.

The sky had darkened, the prayers had passed. It was after midnight as I watched the Guantánamo mosquitoes swarming around the floodlights. I let myself be hypnotized by clouds of suicide bugs plunging toward the gold heat, veering away, then coming closer again and again and again until they died.

"Qibla?" The Kuwaiti again. "Qibla, you awake?"

"Yeah," I said.

"He speaks," said the Kuwaiti.

"Yeah."

"You think they will keep us here a long time?"

"Oh, yeah."

"Qibla, you are Bosnian?"

"Yeah."

"You are a brother?"

"Are you?"

"I don't remember you from Kandahar."

"No."

"Or Gardez. Or Tora Bora."

"Yeah."

"Where did they get you?"

Wasn't his business. No need to say.

"When did they get you?" he asked.

"And you?"

"End of Ramadan."

"Ah. So you know."

"Know what?"

"The wedding." I said.

"Many weddings," he said.

A knot drew tight in my stomach. "Many," I said.

"Oh yes. Bigger than New York. Bigger than Washington."

"Yes! But when, brother?"

"Soon."

"Hamdulillah," I said. Praise the Lord.

"Soon, brother."

"Shhhhhhh," I said.

"I hear you," he said and fell silent.

Soon, he said. So the second attack hadn't happened. *Hamdulillah* for *that.* The information from Abu Zubayr might have helped stop it. And my prize? This flood-lit storm-fence cell, invisible to the people I loved as they were invisible to me. The light went out. The mosquitoes scattered away from the lost heat, but in the dark I thought I saw the swarm of suicides go on.

CHAPTER 24

There were a couple of Guantánamo mornings when I woke dreaming of my father, and of Charles Atlas.

At our house in Kansas my father never talked about Islam, which had been his religion in a whole world and a whole life I knew nothing about when I was a kid. If my father worshiped anybody, it seemed to me then, it must be Charles Atlas. "He was the one who brought me to America," my father used to say, although strictly speaking that wasn't true at all. And when I was a little boy he used to hold Charles Atlas up to me as a great example of what any man could do for himself. He always used the same word: "'Resurrection' is what it is," he'd say. "This Charles Atlas was a ninety-seven-pound weakling, you see? And he made himself the most perfect body in the world." When my father was just a kid in Yugoslavia he ordered one of those Atlas pamphlets through the mail and somehow it made it all the way there. It was the first book he ever read in English, he would tell me, and when he showed it to me, as he did many times, it always reminded me how old he was, how much he came from—not just another place, but another time.

I was the baby of the family, much younger than my sisters, and only eleven when my father died of a stroke at the age of sixty-eight. So when I looked at the brown-ink pages he showed me when I was nine or ten it seemed they could have come from another century. But I don't think he saw that in my eyes. At least, I hope he didn't.

"The Atlas method is 'dynamic tension,'" my father would say as he pushed his big hands together and the muscles bulged up on his chest and shoulders. "No weights. Just using your body working against itself and what's around you. They give it fancy names now. But it's always the same. One muscle works against another muscle. Brillll-iant." His accent came out in words with double l's. "Brillll-iant. And you know where he learned this?"

"In the zoo, Papa."

"In the zoo. That is correct. He watched the panthers in their cages. He wondered how they stayed so strong, with such muscles, in those little cages. And he saw them leaning against the walls, pushing, you know. This is dynamic tension." Charles Atlas was the god of my father, I thought, and the idea made me smile, because his spirit was with me now in my cage. It was a real long time since I'd thought about dynamic tension, or Atlas, and a long time, too, since I'd let myself think about my father. But the human zoo at Gitmo, it was just ready-made for dynamic tension.

The chaplain showed up, finally, after about three days: a short man with a gut like he'd swallowed a beach ball, he wore BDUs that weren't quite creased. His skin was dark gray, like a well-done steak; his beard was streaked with white; his hair was buzzed short under a white crocheted skullcap. The chaplain stopped at every gate to every cage that morning, introducing himself as Ahmed al-Bakhsh, and talking to whoever wanted to talk. The one-eyed Sudanese always let him pass by, and when he came to me I just stared at the ripples in the corrugated roof. But the Squatter almost always talked to the chaplain, and in a language they both understood. I wondered how this man of God got his job. I wondered who vetted him.

"He is a spy," the Kuwaiti whispered to me through the wire one morning.

I nodded silently. Yeah. But who for?

As the days passed we got to know the guards better, and their routines—especially the hefty blonde woman with the ponytail. She stood on the watchtower with her binoculars and looked at everything below on a 6 A.M. to 11 A.M. shift. We pissed, we shit, we slept, she watched. Most of us didn't wear the jumpsuits anymore. Towels were enough. And when the ponytail was the one in the tower she got a special show from the one-eyed Sudanese.

He had about as big a dick as I'd ever seen. Hanging down, it looked like a riot club. When the ponytail was on duty, the Sudanese watched the lenses of her binoculars, waiting for them to swing in his direction—and they had to, because she had to keep an eye on everyone. Then the towel would drop. He'd put his hands on the wire above his head and just stare at her; didn't even touch himself, just pumped his hips a little to make the thing swing back and forth. It grew hard and grew fast, swelling like a fire hose. The binoculars turned away, but he knew they'd be back. Had to be. Like a mortar at sixty degrees his dick aimed straight at the guard tower and he focused his one eye on the ponytail. When he knew the binoculars were coming back, then, finally, he wrapped his hand around the shaft of his cock. The touch did it. A thick spurt shot against the wire of his cell. There was no reaction in the tower. The glasses kept panning over the cages, and over the animals inside.

After about two weeks the guards started bringing a big-wheeled gurney to the cages. The shackle shuffle was taking too much time. The stumbling prisoners were too clumsy. So the guards stretched a detainee flat out on the cart like a body in a morgue and wheeled him away to the sheds for questioning. Eighteen days after I arrived at Guantánamo, the gurney came for me.

In the air-conditioned cold of the windowless interrogation room they seated me opposite a steel schoolteacher's desk with my back to the door. Two guards fastened my restraints and left. But for a long time no one else came. A chill settled into my shoulders and spine. Then the door opened behind me. Wet heat flooded the room with a thin mist. "It shouldn't have taken this long," said a voice I knew, and a rush of fear and hope and despair and anger swept through me like a sickness. Griffin sat down on the edge of the desk facing me. "It shouldn't have taken this long," he repeated.

I shook my head. "Where are my wife and child?"

"They're in good shape. They miss you, but Betsy's holding everything together."

No words came easy. "You see them?"

"Last time was last week."

"You're not lying."

"No lie."

"Do they know I'm here?"

"Nobody knows you're here. What they know is you're on a mission."

"Where are they?"

Griffin moved his eyes over the room, looking at the corners of the ceiling and at the floor. "When you get out, we'll take you to them."

"When?"

"I can't tell you."

"Then who can tell me when I get out?"

"Maybe the President."

The white noise of the air conditioner filled the room.

"We've done good so far, Kurt. Real good. We stopped the ships you told us about."

I nodded. *"Hamdulillah,"* I said.

"Yeah," said Griffin. "By the grace of God and you," said Griffin.

"Cut the shit."

"It's true. I don't want to have to tell you that you saved America. But, hell yes, you could say that. At least for now."

"So give me a medal."

"Someday."

"And let me get the fuck out of here."

"Soon."

"Yeah."

"Let me tell you what happened with the ships."

"Is that going to get me out of here sooner?"

He looked again at the corners of the box where we talked. "Maybe."

"So tell me."

"The information you gave us from Abu Zubayr identified six possible targets and three ships."

"Yeah."

"And each ship a bomb."

"Yes."

"We got all three ships."

I nodded.

"We caught one freighter in the English Channel just after Christmas. It was held for three days while it was 'searched.' It took us that long to figure out what to do with what we found the first hour we were on board."

I nodded. "Nitrates. Like Nairobi. Like Yemen."

"And worse."

"How worse?"

"Cesium and other medical isotopes."

"A dirty bomb."

"Dirty enough. The conventional blast would have been huge. Maybe fifty times bigger than Oklahoma City. Then panic caused by the radiation would have been much worse. Geiger counters off the charts, and people out of their homes fleeing the slow, silent death; the fear of contamination lasting—who knows?—maybe a generation."

"The target was London?"

"The target was an American nuclear sub near the mouth of the Thames River, which would have been just perfect for Qaeda: you take out a military objective, you attack a symbol of American power, you terrorize civilians, and you drive a deep wedge between the United States and its closest ally, Britain."

"But you stopped that one."

"We did. Watched it from Djibouti on, then closed in as it reached the Channel."

"And the other two?"

"The second was a freighter off the coast of Japan. The Japanese Navy blew it out of the water over a mile-deep trench. Said it was North Korean. Said the whole crew died. And you know what? The whole thing's been forgotten already."

"Same kind of target?"

"Same. U.S. warships near Okinawa."

"And number three?"

"Ships just disappear at sea all the time. They leave one port, they never arrive at another." Griffin smiled. "This one we took out ourselves, and a lot more quietly than the Brits or the Japanese. Qaeda's probably still looking for it."

"And the crews?"

"We got all of them."

"That's good news. I mean, that is good news." I looked at the restraints that trussed me to the chair. "Now do I get the fuck out of here or not?"

"Soon."

"Griffin, look at me."

"Yeah."

"You saved my life."

"I guess I did."

"And you tell me you saved Miriam and Betsy."

"We kept them safe."

"But that's not enough to keep me from killing you if you're lying. I've spent the last two months in Hell. And in Hell you learn to hate real good."

"I hear you."

"Am I going to get out of here?"

"Yes. And if anybody listens to me, you're going to get out sooner, not later."

"I don't like that 'if.' "

"I don't either. But you and me, Kurt, we're in this together."

"I'm in chains and you're not."

"That's your cover."

I just looked at him.

"We need you, Kurt— No, let me be real straight: I need you, and I need you right here right now in this place. Because this war ain't ending." He stopped himself and stared at the corners of the room, then down at the surface of the desk.

"And I'm in here for the duration?" I asked.

"Not if I can help it—and not if you help me—help all of us."

"Fuck you. I paid my dues and then some."

"Help Betsy. Help Miriam."

"That a threat? Touch them and you're going to die," I said.

"No, man," said Griffin. "You're going to help all of us live."

I shook my head.

"Kurt, there are more ships. Maybe a lot more. Maybe nine, ten, twelve more. Some of the crew we caught told us enough to know that. Those ships weren't ready before. They might be now. And the only way to stop ships is with information. If one of them cruises full bore into Boston harbor or Naples or Gibraltar or Miami—if they ever get that far, then there's going to be hell to pay."

"There's nothing I can do about it."

"We think we have one man who knows more."

"Abu Zubayr?"

"No. There's nothing left of him but the rind." Griffin swallowed like there was something bitter in the back of his throat. "It's another man, one we thought was just crew on the boat off Japan when we picked him up."

"And now?"

"And now some of the others say he's a planner. But he's not responding to interrogation."

"Go on."

"I think some of the detainees here respect you. I think maybe they talk to you. Brag to you."

"And?"

"And they might let 'Qibla' know a little about what's going on."

"That's why I spent seven weeks in the hole, no questions asked? Is that it? You wanted to make me one of them again?"

"You were in the hole to keep you safe."

"From who?"

He motioned lazily with his hand and seemed to indicate the walls around us.

"Nobody believed me when I said I was American," I said.

Griffin nodded.

"Nobody had my file," I said.

"Maybe that was lucky for you," said Griffin. "Maybe that was lucky for all of us. An American would have to be in jail in the U.S.A., ain't that right? An American would have to be charged; go to trial."

"But a non-American—a nobody—you can do whatever you want with him."

"That's right," said Griffin. "Anything at all. And you know what? We might even be able to let him go."

"You tell me something: Who's my enemy now? The assholes in the cages, or the assholes outside of them?"

"I'm your friend, Kurtovic."

"I'll remember that."

"You're damn straight you will." Without warning the back of his powerful right hand came across my face hard and blinding.

I tasted blood-salt inside my mouth. "You're gonna die, fucker," I said, spitting red.

"You think so, you uppity piece of shit. Well let me tell you something." He leaned in close to my face, his teeth bared in anger, but his voice a whisper. "It's you and me against the world right now," he said. "There's shit coming down inside and outside. And I *am* your friend. Your only friend."

I just nodded, feeling the tingle fade from my face and jaw and sensing fear in his whisper.

"You awake now, asshole?" he shouted.

I spit again.

"Listen to me, boy," said Griffin. "You want to get out of here—ever—you got to play the game." He spit on the floor. "Think it over."

After a long pause, all I said was "Move farther faster and fight harder."

Griffin smiled. "Now you got it, Ranger boy."

"If I get you what you want, you get me out of here. No more bullshit."

"Roger that."

"Yeah. Right." He was lying. But as far as I could see, the only way out of this place for weeks, maybe months or years, was his way. We could count up the lies and settle the scores later on. "Who do you want me talking to?"

"Who we want talking to you is already in a cell next to yours."

"The Sudanese? The Kuwaiti?"

"A Pakistani—a Baluchi, in fact."

"The Squatter," I said.

CHAPTER 25

"They're afraid, the Americans," the Kuwaiti whispered through the wire after lights out. "Afraid at last! That's why they broke your lip last week, Qibla. That's why they kept me for so long in the question house today. They are, how do they say, shitting in their shorts."

There was a long silence. Afraid at last. A twisted sentence echoed in my head: Afraid at last. Afraid at last. Great God Almighty, afraid at last. "They know about the weddings," I said.

"They know nothing."

"Enough to be afraid."

"*Hamdulillah,*" laughed the Kuwaiti.

"After the weddings, then the *real* jihad," I said.

"War everywhere," he said.

"'Are the people of the townships then secure from the coming of Our wrath upon them as a night-raid while they sleep?'" I quoted one of the verses I memorized long ago from the Qur'an, and that I'd read again from the copy of the Book left in my cage by the U.S. Marines. "'Or are the people of the townships then secure from the coming of Our wrath upon them in the day-time while they play? Are they then secure from Allah's plan?' The words spoken by the Prophet, peace be upon him."

"Peace be upon him," said the Kuwaiti.

"Soon Allah's plan will be revealed. But—"

"But?"

"I think one wedding was stopped," I said. "Maybe more."

The Kuwaiti was quiet.

"When they ask questions," I said, "then you learn things. You learn what it is they want to know."

"Yes."

"They are asking about boats. And I don't know anything about boats."

"Yes. They talk about ships." After a long silence in the next cage, the Kuwaiti said, "They are not so smart."

"Tell them nothing," I said. "Silence is jihad."

About an hour later, when he thought I was asleep, I heard the Kuwaiti at the corner of his cell whispering to the Squatter in a language I didn't recognize. But the tone, even in a whisper, was urgent.

The Kuwaiti kept away from me for most of the next day, and I didn't try to talk to him. Whatever he knew, whatever he found out from the Squatter, he'd have to come to me with it in his own time, and I figured he would. He liked to talk, this Kuwaiti kid. What had happened in September and since, I realized, was all kind of unreal to him. I wondered if he'd ever seen a man dead, and if he had, if he'd ever thought about what he saw. The real slaughter in the name of his imagined God was no more real to him than the video gore of a shoot-'em-up game. He talked about the attack on America like a teenager who's just typed in his name for the high score.

The Squatter was almost impossible for me to read. He sat for hours on his haunches looking around him slowly, really slowly, like a bird on a wire. His skin was black, his eyes were black—not like he was African, but like he was charred, like he was a devil who used to sit on some ledge in Hell. I watched him watching for hours at a time, a slime-black toad, a soot-covered carrion crow, and I could feel sometimes, starting to crawl under my skin again, the same ants I'd felt in the hole on the ship. Not until then would I look away, close my eyes, begin again to nail the shingles one by one on the roof of the house by the pond. As far as I could tell, the Squatter didn't speak any English at all, and in the weeks we'd been caged side by side he'd never even looked me in the eyes. But each morning when the chaplain made his rounds, the Squatter, at last, stood up to talk.

It must have been two or three nights after the session with Griffin that I heard the Kuwaiti whispering at me again after lights out.

"They say you are American," he said. "I told them no, you are Bosnian. But they say they are sure."

"How would they know?"

The kid was silent.

"Did the imam tell them?"

"No, no," he said too quickly.

"Listen," I said. "I am Bosnian and I have an American passport. Don't you?"

"My brother has one."

"And is he American or Kuwaiti?"

"Yes. You are right. But Ahmed does not trust you."

"Ahmed? Is he that man in the next cage? I do not trust Ahmed. He talks too much to the imam. But I do not want anything from him. So why do I care?"

Silence. "He says you are spying for the Americans."

"And the imam is not?"

"That is what he says."

"Then he's not very smart."

"You are wrong. He is very, very smart. He knows about the weddings. He knows very much about the weddings."

"Bless him, then. I am his friend whether he believes me or not. Now let's get some sleep while the night is a little cool."

The Kuwaiti was only quiet for a couple of minutes. "Only two weddings were canceled," he said.

"Hamdulillah," I said. "I can sleep better now."

Two weeks to the day after Griffin's first visit, thirty-two days after I arrived at Guantánamo, eighty-two days after I got shackled for the first time, Griffin had me strapped to the gurney and wheeled to the interrogation shed for our second meeting. He was leaning against the desk staring down at me as the guards started to strap me to the chair.

"Leave it," he told them.

"Sir?" said one of the guards.

"Leave it. The interrogator has the prerogative. I'm exercising that prerogative." Griffin looked at his watch, impatient. The guards left. The door closed behind them and we were sealed in the interrogation shed. I was standing but still shackled. "They'd have stayed if they took off the other shit," he said. "Can't leave me alone with a dangerous son of a bitch like you."

"I think I got some of what we need," I said.

"Yeah?"

"There are six more ships."

"We knew that."

"You mean you heard that. I'm confirming it. And there's more. But tell me about Miriam and Betsy."

"They're good," said Griffin, and a kind of sadness passed over his face like a shadow.

"What's wrong?"

"Your family is okay." The discipline snapped back in his voice. "Now tell me what you got."

"Griffin, man—what's *wrong?*"

"Tell me what you got." He looked at his watch again, a big steel Rolex. "You got the targets for the hits? How many ships?"

"Six."

He nodded.

"Port of departure."

"Somewhere in Indonesia, I think. Can't say what island. But that was a while ago. The idea was to lose them—change the ships' ID completely—on the long trip around the world."

"Targets?"

"In the United States, two new ones: Houston—because of oil and Bush."

Griffin nodded again.

"And Chicago, because it's in the middle of the country. 'The heart of the country' is what they say. But they could change that any time."

"Where else?"

"New York and Boston, like we knew before. And outside the U.S., Gibraltar and Panama."

"You're batting a thousand," said Griffin. "What else you got? Names? Dates? Methods?"

"The Squatter doesn't talk to me. He talks to the Kuwaiti. And the Squatter thinks I'm a spy. Somebody told him I was American. Who the fuck do you think did that?"

"Don't know. I'll check."

"Well check that fucking imam the Navy sent us."

"Will do," said Griffin, but his eyes weren't focused on mine.

"It's slow going," I said. "And I'm not sure how much the Squatter knows about whatever is happening now. The ships were put in motion in November. Now it's almost March. They're making long, slow trips with lots of stops in little ports. The names of the ships change. The papers get shuffled. But the real cargo stays the same—just like you found near England and Japan, a whole lot of nitrates, and enough radioactive stuff from industrial sources to panic the country when the dust cloud settles and the Geiger counters go off. You haven't caught the other ships yet 'cause they're hanging back. The first ones you got were almost like trial runs. The next six are just waiting for the order."

"When's that coming? Who's it coming from?"

"I don't know. I'm not sure anybody here knows. But I'll tell you what they think. They think the man with the plan is inside the United States."

Griffin looked at his watch. He looked into my eyes. "Yeah," he said, nodding his head gently. "A sleeper," he said.

"Maybe *the* sleeper," I said. "The brains. The guy who blends in and nobody notices, and who runs the whole show. Or maybe it's just some kind of story they made up in the Afghanistan camps."

Griffin looked at me. Waiting.

And then the lights went out.

The little interrogation shed didn't have any windows, so now we were in total darkness. The air conditioner stopped, too.

"Don't move," said Griffin. His voice echoed in the sudden silence. "The mikes and cameras are off as long as the power's out. But the power will be back in a couple of minutes. Right now we can talk straight."

I thought this might be some kind of show for me, a little psy-op to secure my trust. "So talk," I said.

"There's a war inside the government right now," he said. "A war about the future of the war. That's what I was trying to tell you when I saw you the last time."

"What do you mean 'war about the future of the war'?"

"You fight to win, right? That's my business. That's your business. You fight to win so you won't have to fight anymore—at least not the same enemy. Ain't that right?"

"Hell yes."

"Well, some people don't see things that way. They want the war to go on, and if this one ends, they want a new one."

"That's fucking crazy."

"Yeah, but it's a fact. I haven't really figured out why. Power? Money? A message from God? They live in their own weird inside-the-Beltway universe. But the fact is, the war-makers in Washington think they're going to cook up a whole new world. And to do that, they got to keep the fire burning."

The blackness closed in around me. "Why are you telling me this?"

"Because these assholes don't seem to care about the bad guys—the *real* bad guys. We're hunting them. We're catching some. You got the biggest prize so far. But the war lobby doesn't give a shit about Abu Zubayr. You know what I think?

I think if we caught Osama himself they'd be rip-shit because that might end support for their war."

"Go on."

"So the ones who know about you—"

"You said nobody knew I was here."

"Almost nobody. There ain't many, but the ones who do are powerful, and some of them don't want you out of here."

"You mean they don't want me hunting down the bad guys. Well I didn't do it for them anyway. And if it helps, I won't do it anymore. Send me home. I'll stay there."

"Kurt, listen, I am your friend. I got to tell you it's going to be hard as hell to get you out of here."

"Ah shit. Shit!"

"And there might be some big trouble on the way. They need some victories to keep up the appetite for war. They're looking for sleepers inside the U.S.A., people they can point to as 'the enemy within.' "

"There *are* sleepers, and they're dangerous as hell."

"But they can't find them."

"Okay, then I can find them."

"You don't understand. They can't seem to find the real ones, or maybe they don't want to—but they got to point the finger somewhere and fast. With your background, with some of the things you've done, I think they're going to point the finger at you. If that happens, you're going to be a public 'captured American,' some kind of 'American Taliban.' And you ain't ever going to be free."

There wasn't anything I could say. Griffin only knew part of the story, and what he didn't know—what I'd almost done—was far, far worse than he thought.

"Don't give up," said Griffin. "I've got a couple of ideas—things I set in motion. Let's hope they work."

"What?"

The lights went back on.

"This session is over," said Griffin.

The door to one of the bedrooms on the second floor of the house by the pond was kind of special to me. I'd given it simple inset panels, and at the top I'd jigsawed three little hearts. I thought that if this was a little girl's room, that would be a nice way to be able to check on her without crowding her too much. And I hoped that Miriam would like it when she saw it. But now the door wasn't hung right. When I tried to swing it closed, it stuck against the jamb. I took it off its hinges, put the wedges back in and reset it. But still it wasn't right. All that work. All that work! And still it wasn't right.

The scream from the next cage made the whole house disappear. The floodlights were out, so it must have been between two and four in the morning, but there was still enough glow from the watchtowers to see the Squatter writhing naked on the cement floor of his cage, holding his gut like he was trying to squeeze out the fire inside. Spit was foaming at the corners of his mouth, and diarrhea spread underneath him. I backed away from his cage and sat down, watching, from the other side of mine. The Squatter groaned now, in too much pain to scream, and the body jackknifed on the ground, then unbent, violently folding and unfolding in a terrible convulsion.

"Poison." The voice of the Sudanese was right next to my ear. "Must be poison." He shook the wire of the cage. "Murderers!" he shouted. The floodlights went on and a guard platoon charged down the alley in front of the cages. "Murderers!" shouted the Sudanese, and others started to join in the chant. Suddenly the loudspeakers erupted with the call to *fajr*, the morning prayer: "God is Great. Prayer is better than sleep . . ." drowning the shouts of the prisoners. Four of the guards threw open the door to the Squatter's cage and struggled to pin him down for the chains and shackles, but he writhed like a man possessed, the demon jinn more powerful than him or the men around him. The imam who had come to lead prayers now went inside the Squatter's cage, pacing at the edge of the struggle between the guards and the twisting, buckling man on the ground like a referee at a tag-team wrestling match. "Get out!" one of the guards shouted at him, but the imam kept working his way around the ring, stepping past the spilled slop bucket and the sleeping mat. The Squatter always left the plastic wrappers from the food lying around inside the cage. Now the imam-referee bent down and picked up an empty pack of raisins, slipping the Sun-Maid into the pocket of his BDUs. If I hadn't had my own ringside seat I wouldn't have known what he was doing. "Poison," I said so the Sudanese could hear. "They poisoned his food."

"It is true, Qibla," said the Sudanese. "Poison for talking."

"Talking?"

"Talking too much, talking too little," said the Sudanese. "Talking gets you killed."

There won't be any explanation, I thought. They'll take the Squatter away and he'll just be gone, maybe dead, maybe in a hospital, maybe in a cage on the other side of the camp, maybe in some hole for hard questioning. Nobody here would know. Did the imam poison him to shut him up? I looked at the Kuwaiti, who seemed, for once, to be completely speechless. The chains were on the Squatter now, and the gurney had arrived so he could be strapped down. No, we weren't going to know, and I wasn't going to learn anything more from the Squatter, not now, and not ever.

Soon after the sun came up full, the imam came back. He looked around the floor of the cage. There was nothing left but the spilled buckets, the worn foam pad, the filthy towels piled in a corner, junk-food trash, and the smeared pool of liquid shit. The imam was looking for something in particular. He bent down and picked up one raisin, then another, but he was still looking. Like someone in a silent movie saying "Aha!" he picked up a towel by its corner and shook out of it the Qur'an. Everybody who could see him was watching him as he wiped it off with his hand, held it to his chest, and left.

"Attention," barked a man's voice on the loudspeaker. "Collect your belongings. Today cells will be changed. Repeat: collect belongings. You will be taken out of your present cells and you will not be returned to them."

None of us had any belongings, but every fifteen minutes the message repeated until, slowly, some of the detainees rolled up their bedrolls and tied them with the towels. Others embraced their Qur'ans. Most, like me, did nothing. Just before noon, the transfers began, as one by one the prisoners were taken out of the cages, chained, and shuffled onto the buses that had brought us from the airport so many weeks before. They came for me about four in the afternoon. I was one of the last to be taken away. Eight or nine other prisoners and about the same number of guards were already on the bus. None were men I'd ever seen before.

They took us in full restraints to a large hangar near the airstrip that had been divided into crude plywood cubicles. Each of us was put in a separate box. I heard the doors closing on some, doors opening on the others. Some of the detainees shouted and complained. I didn't. I was still working on the heart-door of Miriam's room in my house by the pond.

Later, maybe a few hours later, the plywood entrance to the cubicle I was in swung open and two guards came for me. We shuffled out into the open and I saw it was night. Even with the runway lights around me I could see the sky was full of stars, and realized with a flash of pain how long it had been since I had seen a full nighttime horizon. We shuffled out onto the tarmac, and I looked around to see where the bus was. I was tired. I didn't want to have to shuffle too much farther in these fucking chains. But we stopped beside one of two executive jets parked on the apron.

One of the guards unlocked the chains on my feet and pulled them off. "Up," he said.

"What the fuck's going on?"

"Up," was all he said.

I stumbled up the steps into the unlit cabin and saw Griffin alone at the back, looking out the little round window at the guards below. "That's it," he shouted. The guard stepped back down. The stairs immediately rose up into the side of the fuselage. The lights went on. "Come here and let me take off the cuffs," said Griffin, holding up the key.

"What the hell's happening?"

"Right now?"

"Right now."

"You're going home, Kurt."

"Don't fuck with me."

"I ain't fucking with you."

"You said it was going to be just about impossible."

"Yeah. Unless somebody called the President."

"Yeah."

"Well, somebody did."

Kansas

APRIL–JUNE 2002

CHAPTER 26

"The President of the United States? What the hell are you talking about?"

Griffin was facing me in the narrow cabin of the plane, but if he reacted I couldn't tell. The only light was from the thin, dim thread that ran along the floor and the stroboscopic flash from the wingtips.

"Who called the President?" I asked again.

"Can't say. A friend of yours, I guess."

"I don't have any friends like that."

"Yeah, you don't have friends, do you? But it looks like you have an angel."

"Nobody knew where I was, unless you told them."

"Let's not go there," said Griffin. "Let's not worry about how you got out. Let's worry about keeping you out. And having you ready to move if we need you again."

I remembered the magazine in Kenya with the picture of the old Bush and the Aga Khan. I remembered those long nights with Cathleen, and the way she talked about her boss's friends in high places. "Faridoon," I said. "Faridoon got me out of the cage."

"Don't go there. Don't go back over any of this," said Griffin. "Don't talk about Guantánamo. Because damn it, you never were there."

"Yeah. Five months of never was. But you called Faridoon."

"Someday I'll tell you the whole story. But not tonight." Griffin turned his shadowy head to look out the window.

I slept, woke with a start, slept.

"That's the Mississippi down there," said Griffin. A couple of lit-up ships moved on its night-black water. We seemed to be following it upstream. "The Big Muddy," said Griffin.

I knew then that we really were on our way home. "The Big Muddy," I remember saying, and that was all. I fell into a sleep so deep I didn't wake up again until we were rolling to a stop on the runway apron.

"Kurt."

"Yeah."

"You're almost home."

The lights went on in the cabin and I blinked awake. "What?"

"Almost home. We're at McConnell."

"Good. Good God. Yeah!"

"And there's some folks here I think you want to see."

Both of them were standing in front of a big old Suburban—standing out in the headlights looking as bright as a USO show. I waved through the tiny window of the jet and Betsy said something to Miriam, picking her up and pointing. But Miriam looked around, a little lost, not seeing any face she knew.

The jet's stairs went down and Griffin put his hand under my arm like I needed help, which, to my surprise, I did. "I got it, I got it," I said, hunching over as I made my way out the cabin door. The air smelled like black fields fresh-turned. We must have been at the edge of the base, because it was all farm smells, earth and straw, and nothing ever smelled better to me in my life. And then Betsy ran toward me with Miriam. I took my child in my arms, and Betsy, too, all in one long hug that I wouldn't and couldn't stop, breathing them in, smelling Betsy's neck and hair—the perfume from the bottle with the crystal doves. And I guess I pulled back for a second because of the weird memory from the deck of the carrier. Betsy looked at me, then looked at me again real serious. "Is that you, Kurt, behind that beard?" Miriam was wiping the kisses off her face, and looked a little scared.

"Oh, Baby," I said. "I can't believe it's me either, and you, and Miriam. Come on, Miriam, give me an Eskimo kiss." She pulled back. "I can't—can't believe—oh, God, Baby let's go. Let's just get the hell out of here and go home."

"We have to stay in a motel tonight."

"If we're together," I said, "then that's home."

"We've got so much to talk about," she said.

"Yeah," I said. "I guess we do."

We didn't make love that night at the Ramada. Miriam was in the bed on Betsy's side, and restless in her sleep, but that wasn't the only reason why. We didn't fight, but that was closer to what happened in the long silences between us.

"Tell me what it was like for you all this time," I asked.

"Lonely," said Betsy. "About as lonely as a person can be. That's how it was."

"But Griffin took care of you."

"Was it Griffin? Somebody made sure we had a place to stay and something to eat and a little TV to watch. We were in Arlington, Virginia. But we might as well have been in prison. No friends. No work. No phone calls allowed unsupervised. God Almighty, Kurt. You go away and Miriam and I wind up hundreds of miles from home under some kind of house arrest, and to this day I have no damn idea what the hell you were doing or why."

"I want to tell you, but if I start, Baby, I won't stop. And I can't do that."

"Just tell me one thing then," said Betsy, and right then Miriam let out a long half-cry from deep in a nightmare. "Just tell me one thing," Betsy whispered again. "Did you save the world?"

"I stopped a few bad guys," I said.

We were lying side by side and I could feel the warmth from her body, but something like a force field kept us apart. Every so often a car would pull through the parking lot outside and send a beam through a crack in the curtains sweeping like a searchlight across the stucco on the ceiling. The little red standby light on the TV glared like a snake's eye. I tried to think of the house on the hill by the pond. But it wouldn't come together. It was just an idea now, not a place to be.

I thought of Guantánamo. I thought of the padded cell in the hold of the ship. I thought of the desert and the mud and the beehives, and of Nureddin moving through the night, and of Cathleen and her bottle of mother's milk, and Faridoon and the Ismailis and their friends, maybe some of them in the White House. And I wondered how I could have been so many places and done so many things that I couldn't begin to talk about with the woman I loved. I saw Waris in her father's arms and smelled again the smell of death that was around her in the hospital. I saw the video arcade in Granada, and felt the cold water rush over my half broken body on the floor of the bodega. I drove the blade into Abu Seif's bull-neck—

"What is it?" said Betsy.

"Nothing," I said. "A bad dream I guess."

The tape in my head kept rewinding, the images skipping by, each worse than the next, until I saw the people on the videotape in Granada, the woman I killed and the half-seen face of Al-Shami, whoever the hell he was. Al-Shami was in Granada. I was pretty sure he was in Somalia, too. Now he was with me in my sleep. He was every fucking place I turned.

Full awake, I lay still and looked at the roughness of the ceiling. "Betsy?"

"What is it, Kurt?" She was no more asleep than I was, and her whisper was uneasy. Miriam shifted in her dream and put her arms over her mother's neck.

"Why did you leave the house, Betsy? Griffin hasn't told me a damn thing."

"Forget it, Kurt."

"Please tell me—just—what happened."

"I wanted to tell you everything, Kurt. Everything. I was so scared. But you weren't there."

"I'm here now."

Another car pulled into a parking space not far from the curtains. The light froze above us. I heard the door of the next room opening and closing. Finally the headlights clicked off.

"Please try," I said, and I tried to get my voice under control. "Please."

"Somebody came to visit. Said he was a friend of yours."

"What did he look like?"

"Never saw him before. And he sure as hell didn't look like anybody you would know one way or the other. Not local. Not army. Dressed too well, sort of slick in spite of himself, like a rich man trying not to look too rich."

"I'm trying to figure—"

"Black hair with a little gray. Wolfy blue eyes. Average height. Maybe forty-five or fifty years old. A little like that actor Alec Baldwin, if you want to know. Pressed slacks and soft brown loafers, an ironed blue shirt and a blazer that fit like it was made for him. That give you an idea? He didn't look like anybody you'd know."

"He was American?"

"Near as I could tell. East Coast, I guess. Maybe New York."

"What did Griffin say about him?"

"Griffin showed me a bunch of pictures. A lot of guys with beards—or shaved by the computer, you know. Griffin didn't say much. He just asked a lot. Kept asking what the man said about this Zoo Bear guy."

"Yeah."

"The man only said the name once. Said he knew you were looking for him, and he thought he could help."

"Betsy, you sure there's no way the man was an Arab?"

"His eyes were as blue as yours, Kurt."

"There're Arabs—"

"You and Griffin sort it out."

"Did he have a limp?"

"A limp? No. Not as I recall."

"He scared you. He threatened you?"

"He scared me just 'cause he was at my front door. He was one stranger too many after all those men who dropped by in the middle of the night before you went away—and now you *were* away and here was another one. You know? And we had that break-in. Just kids, I guess. But, Kurt, I really love my home and I really don't want to have so goddamn many strangers knocking at the door. You know? But, no, he didn't threaten at all. Not like that. Not at all. He was real polite. Said he tried to call, but the phone didn't ring—and he was probably right. We should have replaced that goddamn phone years ago."

"And you remember his face."

"Hell yes."

"Did Griffin have somebody do a drawing?"

"Yeah."

"You have it?"

"No. Kurt?"

"Yeah?"

"I haven't seen the house in so long, I don't even want to think what it looks like."

"Yeah."

The silence was a real long one this time. Miriam quit fidgeting on the far side of Betsy and our little girl's breath slowed to the rhythm of sleep. But Betsy's breathing was silent, awake, and so was mine.

"Betsy?"

"Sleep, Kurt."

"What did he say he wanted?"

"He said he wanted to help you with Zoo Bear. And he said he loaned you something."

"What?"

"Money, I guess."

"Did he say money?"

"He said 'something.' "

"And you said?"

"I said, 'What the hell are you talking about?' And he laughed, and he said, 'I just want to see him before somebody lets the genie out of the bottle.' "

"And you called Griffin right after that?"

"Nope. He called me almost right away after that. And I didn't know who the hell *he* was either. You know? He calls and says he's working with the government and working with you, and he wants to talk to me—and then this black dude, 'Mr. Griffin,' comes to the house and says Miriam and I have got to move away for a while. Like we was in the witness protection or something. And of course I said no. Hell no. But he said we didn't have a choice. And he said he could make us come with him, but he didn't want to do it that way. And you know why? Because he was an old friend of yours, too, Kurt. You know, you've just got so goddamned many friends I just can't stand it."

CHAPTER 27

We started driving before light. Betsy rode shotgun, silent, her eyes closed. Miriam lolled asleep in the back. The mist was rising like breath out of the land and the sun came up warm against the side of my face until, twenty miles from home, I swung off the interstate and headed straight into the dawn. A little after six-thirty, we were in our driveway.

I guess I expected there would be old newspapers piled on the front step and brown leaves from the maple that were never cleared away and junk mail—and all the signs that there's nobody home and hasn't been for a while. And there was all of that. But what I wasn't ready for was the deadness of the house itself, like the soul of it was gone.

Betsy was awake now, just staring straight ahead, and she saw what I saw.

"You want to stay in the car until I have a look around?" I asked her.

She got out of the car. She handed me the keys to the house and I fumbled with them, but the front door pushed open, unlocked. The lights in the house didn't go on. The carpet in the living room was stained where water had come in from a broken window, now covered with a piece of cardboard, and the TV and the video that used to be up against the wall were gone. In the kitchen, the refrigerator door was wide open and the chicken pieces inside rotted so long ago they looked like fossils.

The little TV on the counter was gone. So were the TV and video in the family room, and my computer. The water was turned off. Upstairs, the sheets were turned back on our bed and on Miriam's just the way they must have been the morning they left. But all the drawers in all the dressers were open, clothes were thrown around. The toilet in the bathroom was dry. The medicine cabinet was open, and there were no medicines in it. Even our lousy bedroom phone was gone.

"We'll clean it up," I said. "We'll—"

"I can't do this," said Betsy. "I can't."

"Sure you can. *We* can. We can make it a great home, just like before."

"Nothing is just like before, Kurt. And it never will be."

What I should have said was, "We'll make something new that's even better than what we had before." But I didn't, because I didn't have the heart to say those words, and I didn't believe them.

"I'm going out to the car—to Miriam," said Betsy. "Maybe I can leave her with Ruth. Today's her day off. Or it used to be."

I let her go. I just let her go. Our life had been ransacked by strangers who came from nowhere Betsy had ever been and nowhere I wanted to remember anymore. The Feds. The muj. Griffin. Fuckers. Who was the man at the door? My instinct told me it was the Syrian, but there was no limp. Betsy would have had to notice that.

Betsy. God. She was so lost now. She was my compass in life, my whole Global Positioning System, and she was totally fucking lost and I didn't know how to begin to help her.

I backed against the wall in the front hall and slid down to the floor, my eyes wandering over the inside of the door. I looked up at the frame I'd built with my own hands. There was a big chip out of it near the upper right corner. I couldn't think at first why that would be there. I never saw it before. It looked like it was put there on purpose. There were little bits of putty on the edge of the hole. They'd pulled something out of this hole, probably a microphone they used to listen to everyone who stood in the doorway. If I looked I was sure there would be other holes like this. Maybe they wired the house during that break-in by "kids." That must be how Griffin was tipped to the visit by my unknown friend who warned about the genie in the bottle. I buried my head in my knees in the old Guantánamo position. My unknown goddamn friend.

I listened. Why hadn't I heard Betsy's car start? There was no engine noise. No—nothing. I ran outside. She hadn't moved. She was slumped forward in the front seat, and Miriam was crying in the back. I threw the door of the car open so hard it rocked on its wheels. And Betsy looked up at me, her honey-brown eyes pools of tears.

"I'm going," she said.

"Don't go."

"I'll be back, Kurt. I'll be back—soon. I'm sorry. I—I don't know. I'll be right back. I'm just going to drop off Miriam. Really."

"I love you," I said.

"You should," she said.

"Come back to me."

She just sort of smiled and closed the door of the car and backed out the driveway.

The house cleaned up faster than I thought possible. Ruth still had Tuesdays off, and she did take Miriam, and then Betsy and I bought what we needed with Betsy's credit card, which was still good, and not much used lately. We even bought a new TV and video. It was a much better day than I thought it could be. We weren't talking much. We were moving around each other, not toward each other. But by the time Ruth brought Miriam back about five in the evening, the house looked like someone could live in it. Maybe even us.

"Well Lord have mercy," said Ruth when I opened the door. "I just can't believe you all are still livin' and breathin'."

“Kind of hard for me to believe, too,” I said. “But, hey, I am happy as hell to see you, too, Ruth.”

“You going to tell me what you was doing all this time?”

“Reserve duty.”

“That’s what Betsy said. But, you know, that don’t say much. What kind of Reserve duty?”

“Usual. A waste of time. But somebody’s got to do it.”

“You in Afghanistan?”

“Nope. Nothing exciting.”

“You wasn’t? I told everybody you was in Afghanistan.”

“Well I won’t tell them any different.”

“Why, Ruth!” said Betsy, coming to my rescue. “You didn’t have to bring Miriam back. I was just about to come pick her up.”

“You got enough to do,” said Ruth. “I told you—I told her, Kurt—I used to come over here a couple of times a week, but I didn’t have no key or nothing and I just figured—well I don’t know what I figured. But I figured you all sort of gave up on the place. You know? I mean, like you—it was so strange the way you all disappeared. You, and then Betsy and Miriam.”

“I told you what happened,” said Betsy. “Kurt’s assignment was kind of dangerous—and don’t ask what, ’cause I don’t know either—and with all the strange things going on here and everywhere in the United States, they decided to have us protected for a while.”

“I know, I know. I mean I know now. But I didn’t know then. She coulda told me, couldn’t she, Kurt?”

“We were all under orders,” said Betsy.

“I didn’t know they could do that to wives,” said Ruth.

“Oh, yeah,” I said. “You’d be surprised.”

“Miriam says you all was in Washington, D.C.”

“I took her there a couple of times to get off the base,” said Betsy. “But, Ruth, you know, all we want to do now is think about the future.”

“I’m just dying of curiosity.”

“Well I’m just dying of hunger,” I said. “Maybe we could all go down to the Chuckwagon or something.”

"Oh, wait!" said Ruth. "Wait right here." Ruth ran over to her old Explorer and opened up the back. "I brung dinner for all of us."

"You are so sweet," said Betsy.

"Kurt, can you give me a little help with this ham?"

"That's a big one," I said.

"Nothing too good for you all."

"You shouldn'ta," said Betsy.

There's nothing like food to bring a little soul back into a house, and after a few minutes, even though we were eating off paper plates with plastic forks, the ham and the potato salad and the Coke and the deviled eggs made everything feel stable, maybe even hopeful.

"Is the war over, Kurt?" asked Ruth.

"Far as I'm concerned it is."

"Feels over from here," said Ruth.

"Does it?"

"Watch the news," she said. "It's all about other stuff these days. But I just wish they'd catch Bin Laden."

"Yeah."

"You think he's behind all that stuff?"

"I really don't know."

"If they'd catch Bin Laden, everything would be okay."

"Sure," I said.

"But that Saddam Hussein, he's bad news, too."

"Yeah," I said.

"You was in the Gulf War, right?"

Betsy rescued me again. "Where *did* you get this ham, Ruth?"

"Somebody gave it to me last Christmas and it's been hanging in the cellar, and I thought I'd cook it for Easter, but then I didn't do anything for Easter, and then, you know, I thought this was as good a time as any to celebrate. Tell you the truth, I was thinking I'd bring some pork chops or something from the Jump Start, but looks like we're out of them. I even squeezed into the back of the freezer—remember we used to have some back there?"

"What happened to them?" I said.

"Oh, they're still there. But the ice is so thick, I'm surprised the freezer's still working. I mean, you don't even want to know what's back there, you know?"

"Well, this ham's just delicious," I said.

CHAPTER 28

Betsy's Saturn was still in the garage and my pickup was out back, but neither one was running. So I spent early the next morning trying to get them cranked up. Finally at about ten, in the slow time between breakfast and lunch, I drove Betsy to the Jump Start to talk to Bill Tuninga about getting her job back.

"Betsy! Kurt! Hey there, Miriam, you look all growed up—great to see you all again," said Bill, who was fat and red-faced. Folks always thought he was jolly when they first met him. "You know, Betsy, we was kind of worried. You left me in a fix when you just disappeared like that. Where'd you take this girl, Kurt?"

"Bill," I said, "I want to let you all talk. Is Ruth around? I'd like to thank her for bringing supper yesterday."

"Back to the back," said Bill. In fact, Ruth was all the way out the back door smoking a cigarette.

"Hey, Ruth," I said. "While Betsy and Bill are talking, I thought I might help you free up some of those pork chops."

"They been there so long, I don't know if they're going to be worth eating. Bill swears he's going to defrost the whole damn thing and empty it out this weekend."

"Guess we better get stuff while the gettin's good," I said, and Ruth winked back at me.

"Well," she said, "you are about skinny enough to get back

there. Bill's too fat. That's why it's like that. You want a bag or something?"

The freezer was so full of frost it looked like an ice cave at the back. I used a big screwdriver to chip it away, making a racket, and then reached up to the shelf above the pork chops and old hamburger patties for the extinguisher I'd left there months before, when I thought I'd be gone a couple of weeks at most. The bag of ice was still there. I dug at it with the screwdriver. Prying, chipping, excavating. Despite the cold, I started to sweat. I reached. I touched. And for a second, just enough to make my pulse surge, I thought the extinguisher was gone. Then my fingers made out the shape under a last layer of frost. Somebody's watching out for us, I thought. I pushed it hard to free it, but the extinguisher wouldn't budge. I laid my hand on it and tried to rock it back and forth, but it wouldn't move.

"What you doing in there, Kurt?" Betsy's voice.

"Nothing, Baby. Just trying to get some of this old stuff out of the ice."

"Well hurry up. Bill wants me to work the afternoon shift today, and I want to go home first."

The warmth of my hand finally loosened the extinguisher and it pried free with a kind of sucking sound, like an ice cube from a tray. I slipped it into my daypack. I jostled a box of pork chops free, and a box of hamburger patties for good measure, threw them into paper bags, and handed them to Ruth as I squeezed back out of the freezer.

Betsy was smiling at me. "You look like Frosty the Snowman," she said, and Miriam laughed.

In the early afternoon I drove to the old waterworks, which was just on the northeast edge of Westfield. I remembered taking a school trip there when I was eight, and being really impressed that the waterworks had a big hot furnace. I couldn't tell you what it was for, but I hoped it was still there. I was just sort of reconnoitering, and then I saw the name on the manager's door was Sam Perkins; the same Sam Perkins who was my best friend in third grade, when we took the field trip. Then his folks moved and we went to different middle schools. It's strange how you can lose track of people, even in a small town. You just quit asking about them, and one day they're not in your life anymore.

Sam was a lot more serious as a grown-up than you ever would have guessed when he was a kid. In a town full of people who wanted to look straight as arrows, Sam had a real rage to be normal. I was away in the Rangers, but every so often I'd hear how he got married and had two kids, and now three kids, and four kids, and how he was going to church every Sunday, and then some. Not like my crazy dead Bible-banging nigger-and-Jew-hating brother-in-law. Sam wanted to be seen as a good Christian, a decent man. And maybe he was. I didn't really know him anymore.

"Kurt! Man! You're back!" said Sam when I was shown into his office. The clothes were just what I'd expected, a white short-sleeve shirt and a striped tie, but the face was a lot heavier, and maybe sadder than I thought it would be. "I hear you've been off defending our country," he said.

"Reserve duty, that's all," I said.

"The way you all disappeared caused a lot of talk around here."

"You know what the army's like," I said. "They want to do something quiet, they make a big noise about it. But there was nothing to it, really."

"Ranger stuff."

I was a little surprised he knew anything at all about what I used to do. But Sam made himself pay attention to other people. "Yeah, sort of," I said, "but I really can't talk—"

"If you told me about it you'd have to kill me, right?"

"Right." I laughed a little and shook my head.

"How's Betsy and Miriam?"

"Good. Yep, real good." I couldn't for the life of me remember the name of his wife or any of his kids. "And your family?"

"Caroline and the children are fine, thanks. Gosh, Kurt, it's good to see you."

"Good to see you, too. Real good."

"What can I do for you?" he said. I was about to ask him, just sort of by-the-by, for a tour of the plant—ask him to show me what he did. But then Sam asked me: "You looking for a job?"

"Not exactly."

"Well if you want one, I got one for you."

"Sam, I just came by to say hello, 'cause I was passing by and I thought it was a long time since I saw you."

"Yeah, and I'm glad you did," said Sam. "And I know you'll get your contracting business up and running again soon. But I was thinking—fact is, I could use your help around here."

"What do you have in mind?"

"Somebody with a little discipline is the first thing I've got in mind." He got up to close the door to his office. "You look at the people I get here and you'd want to cry. The smart ones think they're too smart for the job, and the others are just too stu—Well, not smart enough. And what none of them have is good old reliable discipline."

"What do they have to do?"

"It's mid-level supervisory stuff, watching the computer, monitoring equipment, checking charts. One of the main things you do is watch the chlorine supply to make sure there's no leaks. There's alarm systems and all, but you can't be too careful. I mean, we're not a nuclear reactor here, and you don't have to be an engineer, so don't worry about that. But we need somebody who's serious about the work, and smart. You got any plumbing background?"

"Putting in kitchens, I did some of the work myself."

"That's enough, least for short term. But there is a lot of responsibility. If we don't keep things working right, folks don't get clean water. Or worse, they get bad water. And that chlorine gas—whoa, boy, you got to treat that with respect. So when I heard you were right outside my office door I thought,

Sam, your prayers have been answered. I had to fire my last night-supervisor just last week. I've been doing double shifts myself since then. And I am just about beat."

Sam leaned forward over his desk. "Kurt, you'd be doing me a real favor if you'd come on board for a couple of months, just to tide me over until I can find somebody else. That is, if you decide you don't want to stay. And if you do want to stay, then I'll get the papers going to make you full time."

"Can I think it over?"

"Sure," he said. "Let me know tomorrow?"

I looked at my old friend, who was so different than he used to be, but still my old friend. "I've thought," I said. "I'll do it."

When I got back to the house, the TV was on in the family room and Miriam was planted in front of it. The dishwasher was running in the kitchen, filling the room with clean white noise. The message light was flashing on the new telephone by the bed, but I didn't see Betsy anywhere.

I went back to Miriam. "Where's Mommy?"

The *Scooby-Doo* rerun was just about over, and Miriam waited a second for the titles to roll. "Mommy's in the shower," she said, without taking her eyes off the screen.

Betsy was just wrapping a towel around her when I opened the bathroom door. "Oh, Baby," I said.

"No time," she said. "You're late and I've got to be on time at the Jump Start. I can't believe Bill was so nice."

"I got news for you, too."

"Yeah?"

"Sam Perkins over at the waterworks gave me a job to help us out. It's a night shift, but it's money."

Betsy tried to judge whether I was serious about the offer, and then whether I was serious about taking it. "That's real good," she said.

My second night on the job, I brought the Sword of the Angel with me. The waterworks furnace was fired up hotter than a steam engine's, and the yellow-red glare showed through the old mica port. All this equipment was going to be replaced in a few months. Sam said it was a miracle he'd been able to keep it operating so long with such a low budget, but it was on its last legs. I opened the small door and popped the extinguisher inside like a shell into a breech, then slammed and bolted the door. In a second I heard the pop as the bottle exploded and melted. The Sword of the Angel was no more. My old war, my holy war, was over at last. But I was the only one who knew.

CHAPTER 29

The first few weeks we were back in Kansas, every time the phone rang I expected Griffin to be on the line. But the little display on our phone never showed the 703 area code, or 202, and only once, from 917, was it actually Griffin calling on a mobile phone, a little before midnight in the second week of May.

"Just checking in," he said.

"Yeah," I said.

"Everything cool with you?"

"Yep. How about you?"

"Hang loose," is all he said. Then, "Got to go."

I tried to call the number back, but all that came up was a digital-voice answering machine. It wasn't easy to sleep on that conversation.

It wasn't easy to sleep at all. Betsy and I were in the same bed, but didn't touch, didn't spoon, didn't snuggle. Didn't talk.

What was Griffin doing? He took a personal risk trying to get me out of Guantánamo. He went to bat for a terrorist, as far as his bosses were concerned, and what was worse for him in the bureaucracy, he won. They'd make him pay for that if they could. And now he wasn't even using me. He was just letting me sit here, waiting for the world to blow up, or not. Waiting for the law to knock at my door again, or not. Waiting for my life to start again, or not.

He was waiting for something to happen here, I realized as I looked at the blankness of the ceiling. He wasn't going to tell me what it was. He probably wasn't going to warn me. Or my wife or my child.

I thought of a scratchy old film I was shown during a chemical warfare training session. A goat is tied up in an open space in some scrub-covered hills, like bait for a tiger. But there are no tigers here. There's only a small explosion upwind, and a thin cloud of smoke from the charge. The sarin gas that was in the shell is not visible. The goat doesn't see it or smell it. Then the symptoms begin—drooling, shitting, twitching. And the goat's dead in thirty-seven seconds.

I was staked out here. So was Betsy and so was Miriam. We were bait, or part of an experiment. I couldn't prove it, but I knew it.

"Betsy?"

"Mmmm—what is it?"

"Bad times are coming for us here."

"What?"

"Maybe we should leave. Maybe we should get in the car right now and just get the fuck out."

"I told you I was going to stay home."

"It's not safe."

"Where is safe?"

"Not here."

"Ah, Jesus, Kurt. Do you remember what you said to me the day you left in September? Do you? You said God himself couldn't keep you from coming back to our home. And now you're telling me you're leaving again? And because you're scared of you-don't-know-what, and you want us leaving again with you? Well, you go, Kurt—wherever you think you have to go. Do what you have to do. But what I have to do is stay here. And anybody who wants to make me leave this place again is going to die trying."

"We could be—"

"We could be what? Killed?"

"We could be bait in somebody else's trap."

"You know something that you're not telling me? Hey—what am I saying? You never tell me a damn thing anyway. But it doesn't matter."

"All I know is what I told you."

"I'll keep my eyes open," said Betsy. "I'll get a gun if I have to. My stepdad taught me how to shoot, and he taught me good."

"I know."

"So you do what you have to do. But I ain't going anywhere. You told me you'd come back to me. You did. I told you I'd stay. I have and I will stay at home, in my home, in my kitchen and my bed with my baby in the next room and my husband right here beside me—if he stays. And the rest of the world? They can go fuck themselves. You hear me, Kurt?"

"I hear you, Baby."

"You sound funny."

"I'm smiling," I said. "Whatever happens, it will happen here—or not. I ain't going nowhere. We ain't going nowhere."

I felt Betsy move across the bed. She kissed me gently on the cheek, then pulled back again.

"I love you, Kurt."

"Ah, God, Betsy, I love you, too."

"It's going to be okay, isn't it?"

"Someday, yeah. It's going to be okay. Soon." I wished I believed what I was saying. I didn't think Betsy did. But she kissed me again, then rolled over in the bed away from me, staring at the wall in the dark. "Let's sleep while we can," she said.

The next morning I went to Wal-Mart with Betsy's credit card and maxed it out. I bought a Mossberg twelve-gauge automatic with a pistol grip and buckshot loads, a Ruger Mini-14 with Remington .223 rounds, plus a new HP desktop and printer. The total bill was just shy of three thousand dollars.

CHAPTER 30

Months in the cage had worn down my endurance, and the running was harder now than I ever remembered it. The first time I set out on my old ten-mile course I made it about three miles, nowhere near to Jeffers' Rocks, and I was so winded that I decided to walk, limping, back to the house. After that, I set a different program for myself, and through most of May and early June I took fairly easy jogs around town.

Since I was on the night shift at the water company, I'd get off about six in the morning and that's when I'd run, just as Westfield was waking up. Instead of heading away from the center, like I would have done in the old days, I headed into it. I passed little brick houses where the lights were almost always on, and I could see through the kitchen windows that the families were finishing sleepy breakfasts. Or maybe their dad was just getting into his pickup to head for the farm where he worked. And he'd wave as I ran by.

In front of a lot of the houses, American flags were flying. Some hung from poles mounted over the front doors, some flew from poles put up in the yards. Small ones on sticks were tied to mailboxes. After September 11, every day was the Fourth of July in Westfield, I guess, and in a lot of the rest of America, too. There were flags on the sides of cars, and flags on the backs of cars, and lots of flags in the rear windows of pickup trucks, just behind the gun racks. And every morning that I ran by them, I thought they just weren't the same flags I saw at Guantánamo. The ones here in Westfield were about pride and about faith in our country, which is all about faith in ourselves. The flag of quiet pride, that was the one I loved now, and there were dozens of them flying in front of me every morning when I ran through town.

On a lot of those mornings, when I took the most direct route from the water company past the Super 8 Motel and along Coffey Road, I'd go by Kmart. It had a huge flagpole out front, but no flag flying on it. The Kmart had closed down while I was away. The entrance was all boarded up. The sign was gone. The company went bankrupt and it was shutting stores that weren't doing well, and most people went to Wal-Mart these days anyway. It was bigger, newer, cleaner. So the Kmart parking lot was empty except for a beat-up old Buick station wagon with four flats abandoned there. And somebody had taken down the flag.

You wouldn't think you'd mourn a Kmart, but I did, a little, every time I ran past it. I remembered when it opened, when I was ten and my father was still alive. And my mother got a job there at the checkout counter and we'd go visit her, pretending we were customers so she wouldn't get in trouble for talking to us her first few days on the job. And now my father and mother were gone, long dead, and even this place where we'd been, that had been so new, was boarded up.

I kept on running.

When I hit the center of town, near the courthouse and the Veterans' Memorial, I started to pass people on the street, and just about every one of them would wave or nod in my direction, and I'd wave back. It was first light, but a farm town opens early, and sometimes there were so many people around that I must have looked a little crazy, waving here, waving there, like I thought I was finishing up a long race and waving at the crowd. But it made me feel so damned good just to know all those folks were around, even the ones I didn't know well, or at all, and that they cared enough, just enough, to nod in my direction.

It's funny the way you take possession of a place by running through it. Not the same as when you just walk, when each little piece of the place—a newspaper on a doorstep, or something in a shop window—can grab your attention and hold it. When you run the details don't slow you down. The smell of bacon coming out of a diner gives way to a single headline on a newspaper, then a flock of crows are calling each other awake, and your eye falls on the out-of-state plates of a rented Impala. You run through bits and pieces of experience, some of them that you expect, and some that you don't, none of them really related to each other, but all of them coming together to make a whole town. And maybe because you've run for it, worked for it, and you're tired, you feel like you own the place; like you earned it.

Each day after I got a little sleep I sat down at the computer and tried to read up on all that happened in the world while I was on the ship and in the cage. It took some searching, but I finally found stories about the boat sunk off Japan and the freighter stopped in the English Channel. There was no hint in the articles about how dangerous those attacks could have been. And there was nothing at all to show what happened to the other boats I'd heard about.

I read through the old news I'd missed: how alert followed alert in America and around the world, and every so often an arrest was announced. Abu Zubaydah, who was under Abu Zubayr, was the big one for a long time. The papers said he was caught in Pakistan, and eventually he started telling a lot of stories. But whether they were true or not, no one seemed to know. Every so often there'd be an alert about banks, or about nuclear power stations. And word would go out that the threat was learned from Abu Zubaydah. But he never talked about ships, at least as far as anyone could learn from reading the papers. Then news leaked, on purpose I figured, that Abu Zubayr had been caught. The papers said he was picked up in

Pakistan, too, which was a lie of course, and that he was "critically injured."

Yeah.

I read about Israel and Palestine and about all the slaughter there. I was never in those places and that was a fight that never touched my soul, but I knew the muj would use it to fire up their hatred. If you looked at the world from a Muslim view, then Muslims were under attack everywhere. *Everywhere.* But the heart of the action was in Palestine. Just like if you looked at the world from a Jewish point of view, then Jews were under attack everywhere, but the center of the drama was in Israel. And you saw a lot about Christian victims on the Web, too, like they didn't want to be left out. One of the churches in Westfield took up collections for their brothers and sisters in Christ who were persecuted in Muslim Egypt.

I sat there in my house in Westfield looking at the computer screen and through it at the whole world full of dangers, and thinking about what people thought they knew and all that they really didn't know at all, and then I'd turn in my chair and look out the window at the lawn and the driveway and Miriam's Barbie bicycle and the neighbor's sprinkler fanning water back and forth and it all just seemed so far away, like we were back in the eye of the hurricane, and somehow we could stay there. And I wanted that. Much more than I wanted God and more than I wanted justice, I just wanted to keep the hurricane away. But if I closed my eyes and listened, I could hear the howling of the wind. And if I wasn't careful the darkness of the storm would settle in around me, until I could not move or think or talk, even to myself.

Al-Shami was still out there somewhere. Still a threat. Faridoon was out there, too, and whatever he was doing, and whoever he was doing it for, I figured I owed him a huge debt. Sometimes I wondered what Cathleen was up to. She'd been a great good friend. Would I ever see her again? Or hear from her? What happened to Nureddin? Did he survive? And Waris? No, I thought, I would never see any of them again. I was spent. My war was over. I had no more business in those places.

The alarm went off on the computer every weekday at about three-thirty and whatever I was doing, however I felt, I'd get up and I'd walk over to Miriam's summer playgroup, which was just about half a mile away, to pick her up. Then we'd walk back and she'd talk the whole time about the things she painted or made, and who her best friends were.

"How is Charlene today?" I would ask.

"I don't like Charlene. She's mean."

And then the next day I'd ask, "Did everything go okay with Charlene? She wasn't mean to you?"

"Daddy! Charlene and me, we're going to be best friends forever!"

I didn't try to figure this out.

Usually a little after Miriam and I got back to the house Betsy would get back from work. Sometimes we'd eat takeout from the Jump Start or the Chuckwagon. Betsy tried to avoid McDonald's. "Fat food," she called it. And sometimes I'd fire up the little grill in the backyard and cook us some hot dogs or hamburgers, and I thought they were pretty good. Then one day Betsy handed me a plastic bag from Wal-Mart. "Thought you'd like this," she said, and gave me a kiss on the cheek. It was a book called *Born to Grill: An American Celebration.* I read it, and I guess my cooking was a little better after that.

Betsy and I were going through the motions of being married and doing a better job all the time. But the motions didn't make us connect. We weren't accomplices anymore, and we weren't really lovers. If I touched her she pulled away, and those times when she touched me I felt like, suddenly, I didn't want her so close. And sometimes she'd just turn to me for no reason I could figure and say, "We've got problems, Kurt." And I wouldn't say anything, because that was a stone I just never wanted to turn over.

All we could do was keep trying, and we'd had more time to do that than I'd expected. It was mid-June and there were no more calls from Griffin, and no traps had been sprung, and I had learned what I needed in order to do the job at the waterworks, and I was starting to get a few carpentry jobs, too. Sometimes the howling still surrounded me. Sometimes the darkness settled in, especially when I was alone. But the world of Westfield started to look safer and safer, even so, and I started to let down my guard because—well, because you can't be on guard all the time.

CHAPTER 31

"Kurt, boy, sorry to bother you."

"Sam, it's midnight. What are you doing in the office at this hour?"

"Not business, I'll tell you."

"Thought maybe you came to help me change the chlorine cylinders."

"No," said Sam, a little surprised. "We don't usually do that at night. It's not a one-man operation."

"I know," I said. "But people have been using a lot of water, and the cylinders have got to be changed a little more often. And since you're here—"

"Can it wait until tomorrow?"

"Until the morning."

"Yeah." Sam wiped the back of his hand over his forehead. "Long as I been doing this, those cylinders always make me a little nervous. You're checked out on all the safety gear, right? The masks, the breathing stuff? Yeah. Let's leave it until tomorrow. There's something else I want to talk to you about."

"Shoot."

"The Fourth of July. We're looking for a flag bearer."

"Check down at the VFW. There's a lot of guys down there who'd love the job."

"Sure thing, Kurt. But when I talked to some of them, they

thought—you know, they wanted somebody who's been part of the War on Terror."

"You mean me?"

"None other."

"Sam, what I was doing, I can't talk about it, and I don't want people asking about it."

"We don't want to know what you did. All we know, and all we need to know, is that you did it."

"Sam—" I started, but I couldn't think what to say. It was just a little hometown parade, but I'd watched it every year I was growing up, and when I went to be a Ranger I probably had an idea in the back of my head that I'd lead it some day. But I hadn't thought about that for a long, long time. "I'd be honored." The words came out before I could stop them.

At the end of my shift I drove home and parked in my driveway. The lights were on inside the house, but I didn't go in because I didn't know what I wanted to tell Betsy, or even whether I wanted to talk to her. I had this good news, this funny news about the parade, but I couldn't seem to share it, and sadness surrounded me like someone had cast a spell. I forced myself to get out of the pickup's cab and put my two feet on the ground. I looked at my gym bag on the seat and my running shoes, my old Ranger technicals, on the floor of the cab. What was happening to me? Why was everything closing in like this? In the wars this didn't happen to me. Even when I was a prisoner this never happened. And now I was home, and happy to be home. And I was going to lead the goddamn Fourth of July parade. How about that? And some part of me kept saying it's just time to die, Kurt. *It's over.* And I didn't know *what* was over. I didn't know. I clutched my T-shirt and shorts, meaning to put them on, but holding them against me the way Miriam squeezed her raggedy doll.

"Kurt?" Betsy was calling out through the kitchen window.

"Yeah?"

"You okay?"

"Yeah, Baby. I thought I would go for a run."

"You're sure?"

"Yeah, Darlin'."

I stripped down right there in the driveway, put on my shorts and shoes, then started out on my old route, from so long ago, that followed Crookleg Creek toward Jeffers' Rocks. It was only after about three miles that I started to think I was going to make it. The movement helped to break the spell. I found the energy and the breath I needed. The silver morning on the stream gave me more of whatever it was I had to have. By the time I got to the little stand of cottonwoods around the rocks, which was five miles out, I felt like I could go on running forever.

A car was pulled up near the trees, a Chevy sedan, but I didn't look too close. I didn't want to see somebody fucking, or whatever they were doing that brought them to this place at this hour. So I just kept running along among the open fields and was amazed again, like so many times in my life, by the blessing of dawn.

Where to go? I wanted to make a big loop around toward the Route 70 junction. I figured that would give me about a twelve- or thirteen-mile run by the time I got back home. But I really wasn't sure of the way. I was exploring now, taking a farm road I'd never taken before through a shoulder-high stand of corn. The earth was just soft enough, and easy on my legs, a pleasure to touch, and on the far side of the field was a man-made pond reflecting the robin's egg blue of the sky. The lake must have been about an acre, and I skirted along the edge, then ran easily up the low hill on the other side.

It was fifty-two minutes since I left the house, which was about seven miles, and I had to figure which way to head back, so I jogged in a small circle on the top of the hill to get my bearings. There were no buildings visible in any direction, just fields and that pond with a big willow on the far edge of it. It was about as pretty and peaceable a scene as I ever remembered. It was, I realized, the place my mind had made.

The morning was bright and hot and I was breathing fire and soaked with sweat by the time I got back to the house. Betsy's car was in the drive. She'd already dropped Miriam off at the playgroup. I stripped off my T-shirt, my socks, my shorts, and threw everything in the washer. When I got to the bedroom I could hear the shower running.

"Betsy? You in there?"

"I'll be out in a minute."

I opened the door of the stall. Her hair was wet and pushed back off her face, her eyes were half closed, and her nipples were hard from the touch of the water. "I'll be out in a second," she said, but I stepped into the shower and put my arm around her, pulling her water-slick body next to mine. "No," she said. "No, Kurt, I've got to—" I covered her mouth with mine and felt her, suddenly, almost unexpectedly, opening herself, bending to me, *with* me, kissing my cheeks and neck and eyes, wrapping her arms around my shoulders, her legs around my hips, my hands on her ass holding her up from behind, my fingers gripping, massaging, entering, until, now, she was up on me and I leaned back against the sweating tile of the shower, lifting her and lowering her on me, rhythmically, my cock swelling inside her as she gripped and pulled me deeper, deeper. "You bastard," she said, half-biting my shoulder, her mouth open, raking her teeth over the hard-flexed muscle near my neck. "You bastard!" she said sobbing, screaming, biting, fucking, breathless, shivering on me, around me, over me. I carried her out of the shower and lowered her onto the bed, still inside her hard, framing her face with my hands, kissing her eyes, her lips, thrusting, swelling. "Enough," she said. "No, Baby," I said, "there's more," feeling the surge rising inside me, inside her, and the gush coming again, again, again. She screamed and shivered, and I thrust crying out some word from before words, so basic, so helpless, spent, and joined, and exhausted with joy.

When I opened my eyes, I saw the message light, but couldn't remember when the phone had rung. Maybe when we were in the shower. Never mind. I was not going to move from this bed, this moment lying naked and in love with my wife, to hear a recording of somebody who promised to improve my off-peak long-distance service.

"The message light," said Betsy, her voice groggy, her naked body spooning next to mine on top of the sheets.

"It can wait."

"Might be Miriam," she said. "Check it or I'll worry."

"All right. Yeah."

I rolled over and pushed the button. The message started with silence like a wrong number, then the empty clicks of switching circuits, and then a man's voice. I couldn't make out the first part of what he said, just the words "Go on." And then Miriam's voice, "Daddy?" I stopped breathing.

Another pause on the line, almost like it went dead, and then a man's voice—it sounded like a second man's voice—very clear, with no accent at all that I could tell. "You have something that belongs to me," he said. "We will call back in ten minutes to tell you where to find your angel, and where to bring our sword."

Betsy's jaw was clenched and her hands were trembling. "The voice. The goddamn voice! That's the man who was at the door," she said. "I'm going to check the school, find Miriam."

"We're both going."

"No! You are staying here, Kurt. You're taking that call, and you're going to give them whatever the hell they want."

I nodded and she was gone.

The second call came maybe five minutes later. I picked up on the first ring.

"Yeah," I said, writing down the number showing on the phone's display. The rush of adrenaline made my hand shake so badly I could barely read my own scrawl. A 207 area code. I had no idea where that was.

"You know the place they call Jeffers' Rocks?" The same voice with no accent, like a TV announcer.

"Yes," I said.

"Bring it there at noon exactly."

"And you will bring my little girl."

"We will make a trade."

The phone clicked off.

The front door slammed and Betsy was in front of me a second later, her face twisted between rage and grief. "She's not there. *Nobody's there!* What have you done?"

"This is the end of it," I said. "Today. Right here. Right now. But you got to do exactly what I say."

"Where's my baby?"

"There's a meeting."

"I'm going with you."

"Miriam won't be there."

"What the fuck do you mean?"

"They won't bring her. They'll try to take what they want and give up nothing."

Betsy pushed me back, punching, pounding like she wanted to drive me through the wall. "Who's got her, Kurt? Some of your fucking 'friends'? Some of those bad guys you can never tell me about?"

I grabbed her wrists. "You got to go right now to Sam Perkins and you got to get him to give you one of the cylinders. He won't want to do it. But he's got to. A chlorine cylinder. Get him to help you. Tell him whatever—do whatever. Whatever works. Then take it to the old Kmart and put it inside there—somewhere it's half-hidden."

"What the fuck are you talking about, Kurt?"

"I don't have what they want. But the cylinder will buy us time and—" I put my hands up on each side of Betsy's face and I smiled. "—and we're going to have Miriam back here in time to watch *Scooby-Doo*."

I ran for the hall closet, unlocking it, pulling out the shotgun and the Ruger.

"I'm taking one of those," said Betsy, her voice as cold as I ever heard it. She looked straight into my eyes. "You say Sam's not going to want to give me that cylinder? I might need a persuader," she said.

"You sure?"

"The Ruger." She grabbed the gun out of my hand, popped the clip, and opened the breech. "Ammo?"

"There," I said, pointing to the box of a hundred .223 rounds. Betsy loaded the clip like it was second nature, like stacking spoons in a drawer. She dumped everything out of her shoulder-strap purse and threw the cartridges in there, then picked up her cell phone and ran through the kitchen to the garage. "One cylinder. In the old Kmart," she said, slamming the door of the Saturn, burning rubber out of the garage and wheeling, tires screaming, out of the driveway.

I watched until she turned up toward Garth Road. As far as I could tell, nobody was following her. I put the Mossberg and a box of shells behind the seat of my pickup, and a boot knife under my jeans, then headed for the Route 70 culvert over Crookleg Creek.

Was Griffin watching? I wondered. Did he see the bad guys take my little girl? Or what happened to her playmates? Was he sitting in a van somewhere, or maybe in one of the empty new houses a couple of blocks away just watching it all on a little video screen, listening on earphones, sipping a cup of Chuckwagon coffee? Or maybe he gave up? Maybe he was nowhere near, and neither were his people. Maybe he had a grand plan that was vetoed by the bureaucracy, and then forgotten, along with me, and Betsy, and Miriam, and our lives.

There was no one in my rearview mirror; no sign of a tail. "Happy now, Griffin, you motherfucker?" I shouted. "They took the bait. Yes, indeed. Now you gonna help me get Miriam back?" The mirror was still empty.

The culvert where I parked was about a quarter mile from the stand of trees and Jeffers' Rocks, but on the far side of a low rise. The creek bed made a deep cut in the ground and gave pretty good cover up to within the last sixty yards or so. I crept forward, stalking the stalkers until I had a clear view of their positions. The Chevy Impala I'd seen at dawn was parked in the shade of the cottonwoods. No other cars were visible. Whoever was there had been there for at least four hours—and before Miriam was taken. It looked like one man was seated behind the wheel. Another was smoking a cigarette about fifteen feet away from the car, waiting.

There had to be at least one more, maybe two.

There—I saw a flash like a shiny coin in the sun and knew it was the lens of a telescopic sight down near the ground among the cornstalks, just about a hundred yards away from the trees. That shooter was in prone position with a good field of fire. And was there another? Where?

A pair of crows soared over the treetops, dancing angrily through the air, cawing and diving, then suddenly breaking away, then coming back on the attack, like they were protecting a nest. There—high in the biggest cottonwood, a man crouched easily in the branches like a frog on a stick, but with an AK at the ready. So the site was covered. And it didn't look like Miriam was anywhere near it.

The time was eleven forty-eight. I worked my way back to the truck. I left the shotgun and ammo behind the seat and put the knife in the glove compartment. Then I jogged out to Route 70 and walked up to the turnoff for Jeffers' Rocks. Unarmed and empty-handed I approached the trees.

The guy with the cigarette saw me coming a long way off. He was short and dark, wiry, maybe Indian or Pakistani, and clean-shaven with features a little like a weasel. When I got close enough to see his black eyes, he pulled an automatic pistol out of his belt and walked toward me. "You bring it?" he asked.

"No," I said. "Where is my little girl?"

"Did you bring the Sword?"

"No. *Did you bring my daughter?*"

"The Sword. *Now!*" He pulled a cell phone out of his pocket and held it up with his left hand. "I call and your child dies," he said through a veil of smoke.

"And innocent blood is on your hands," I said, "and hell shall be your portion." For a fraction of a second I saw the bloody living remains of Abu Zubayr, remembering what I had done to him when he threatened my baby. The vision gave me a grim sense of assurance.

"*Where* is the Sword?" said the guy with the cigarette.

"When my daughter is safe I'll take you to it."

He stared at me blank-eyed and spit the cigarette onto the ground. He looked around at the open fields, maybe realizing how visible we were, and motioned toward the trees with his pistol. As we walked he put the cell phone to his head, waiting for a number to go through, waiting for a connection to a connection, I thought, electronic cutouts rerouting the call so police couldn't track it. That was why I hadn't recognized the area code. It was probably just some coin phone in a filling station parking lot in some state far away from me and from the caller.

"Hands on your head," said the smoker as I walked in front of him. We were passing the car. The driver had a round, dark face and the untrimmed beard of a Salafi Muslim fundamentalist. I didn't look in the direction of the cornfield or up at the tops of the trees. No need. I knew both shooters had me in their sights.

CHAPTER 32

The wolf-eyed man Betsy saw at the door, the man whose voice she recognized on the answering machine—I didn't think he was here at Jeffers' Rocks. And he was the man I wanted to see. He was the one I figured was giving the orders. He was the one who was on the other end of this little chain-smoking Pakistani creep's cell phone, maybe just down the road, or maybe halfway around the world.

"Let me talk to him," I said. The smoker looked at me half annoyed, half puzzled, and kept jabbering in Arabic. Then he listened, his face twisting in an effort to hear and understand the phone.

"Let me talk to him," I said again. The smoker waved his gun to make me back away. "I know what you want," I said.

Still the smoker concentrated on the phone, but now his eyes focused more clearly on me, and the gun in his right hand was raised with more purpose, pointed straight at my face. Reflexively, I backed up against the tree—the same tree, I thought, where the AK shooter was up in the branches. He wouldn't be sitting so solidly if he was trying to keep me in his sights. Hard to aim past all those branches. And with us here in the trees, the sniper in the cornfield wouldn't have a clear shot either.

The smoker put the muzzle of his pistol right up against my heart, which was about at the level of his face, then stepped back, his arm straight out, sighting my chest. "*Tamam*," he said into the phone: "Okay . . ." He was following orders step by step. He didn't have to think. But something was bothering him. He kept turning his gun on its side, flicking it with a wrist motion, a kind of gangsta-rap thing that made a good macho gesture in a video, but made this guy look real nervous. He was losing control. If he kept that up, I thought, he was going to kill me before he meant to. Now his eyes settled on mine and he listened to the voice on the phone, but he couldn't quite make out what was said. He was rubbing the side of the pistol with his thumb and flexing his three outside fingers. I watched the trigger. And his eyes. He'd lost focus, like he was trying to see across the miles and read his boss's lips.

I sidestepped and caught the wrist of his gun hand, twisting it behind his back in a move as old as kung fu. Like wrenching a turkey leg, I popped his right arm out of its socket and he gasped, voiceless with pain, and dropped the pistol, but he held on to the phone in his left hand like he thought Motorola—or the man at the other end—was going to save his life.

Bullets blasted down from the branches above us, but the biggest branch protected me in that first second. The Pakistani creep wasn't so lucky. His face and skull seemed to melt from the top down. I wiped a chunk of brain off my face. Some of the blood seeped into my mouth and I could taste the salt. Leaves floated through the air like autumn, cut by the rain of lead. I stayed close to the trunk of the tree, shifting position. The man in the branches didn't have any discipline. He was going to use up all the rounds in that AK just about—now.

For a second the click of the clip release was the loudest noise in that stand of trees. I dove for the smoker's 9-millimeter pistol, rolled, aimed, and fired. The shooter fell part of the way down, but was stopped, half-crucified, by the branches, the empty AK dangling from a strap over his shoulder.

The bearded driver was starting the Chevy's engine. From a prone position I was able to send one round through the windshield. He slumped back. The engine coughed and jerked and died.

The sniper in the corn wouldn't be able to get a clear shot at me as long as I was in the trees and as long as he stayed where I knew he was. But he was going to move. Might be moving now. If I sprinted for Crookleg Creek, I might make it, but then he would come hunting me, and if he had any skills at all he could catch me easy before I got to the culvert.

I pried the little Motorola out of the smoker's tobacco- and bloodstained fingers. There was no one on the other end of the line. I pushed the call button, redialing the last number, and I waited. A minute must have passed. I stared out at the corn for any sign of movement, but there was a light breeze rustling the stalks. I couldn't see anything that would give the sniper away.

"Mr. Kurtovic," said the voice on the phone.

"That's right," I said, surprised, and then surprised again a fraction of a second later when my own voice echoed back, electronic and hollow, *"That's right."*

"What has happened, Mr. Kurtovic?"

"Your men—*your men*—are dead—*are dead,"* I said. The echo was enough to make you crazy.

"*Some* of my men," he said. "There are many left. And they will kill you, Mr. Kurtovic. And your daughter will have to die, too."

"I am ready to give you—*give you*—what you want— *you want."*

"You should have brought it with you."

"You don't get anything unless you give me my daughter—*daughter."*

"What do you propose?"

"Call off your man in the cornfield—*cornfield.* Call him off—*him off."*

"And then what?"

A big chunk of wood exploded off the tree beside my head and sent splinters into my cheek. I hit the dirt and crawled toward the Rocks, expecting a second shot and a third, but they didn't come. I tasted blood again, but this time it was my own.

"You sound out of breath," said the voice on the cell phone.

"Call him off," I said, trying to talk over the echo and ignore it. Through the gaps in the trees I could see the cornfield, but still no sign of movement.

"I would like to hear your plan first, Mr. Kurtovic."

I wondered if the voice and the sniper were the same. "It's now twelve-oh-nine," I said. "If Miriam walks into the lobby of the Super 8 Motel at one o'clock—*o'clock.* I will know, and I will tell you, then—*then*—where to find the Sword of the Angel—*the Angel.*"

"Why should we trust you?"

"What choice do you have?—*you have?*"

"To kill everyone you love, and then you."

"You'll always have that option, won't you?—*won't you?* But this is your one chance to get the weapon you want—*you want.*"

A single bullet ricocheted off the rocks a couple of feet away from my face.

"Was that one close?" asked the voice on the phone.

"Do you want the Sword—*the Sword?*"

"Yes. Keep the phone and call again from the motel."

When I got back to the truck I was shaking from adrenaline, shaking like I couldn't control it. The sniper was out there watching, tracking, waiting for orders. The creek water was cool on my face as I washed off the blood. I toweled off with my T-shirt and put on an old blue-jean jacket I kept stuffed behind the seat. I put the killers' phone in one pocket and used my own phone to call Betsy.

"Have you got Miriam?" she said as soon as she picked up.

"Not yet, but I will. Have you got everything?"

"Got it."

"Then meet me—"

"I got what you wanted and put it where you wanted. There's a room behind the old photo department. It's in there. But I don't want to see you again until you've got Miriam." She hung up, and she didn't pick up again.

The six screens in the security office at the Super 8 monitored twenty-four cameras that flashed video of just about every angle outside the building, the main hallways inside, and the kitchen and laundry areas, too. The hotel's deputy manager, Ira Jacobsen, went to school with Betsy. I told him I was thinking of putting in a video security system at my house, and asked if I could watch how this one worked. Ira was friendly enough. "Sure," he said. "You look like you could use some security. You're pretty beat up." I just smiled and pulled up a chair, looking at the screens.

The portico was empty in the front of the hotel. There were only a half dozen cars in the lot behind. The hallways all looked pretty much the same. In one, a maid pushed a service cart. The front drive was still empty. I could see cars racing by on Route 70. None slowed or turned into the motel driveway.

I was so fixed on the front of the hotel that at first I didn't see the little kids walking through the parking lot in the back, walking in line, almost like a parade, just the way they learned to do for field trips at school. Now I saw them more clearly, and they looked frightened. Some of them were crying. They were the kids from Miriam's playgroup. But I didn't see the teacher, Mrs. Watkins. And I didn't see Miriam.

"Ira," I called to the manager. "Ira, where is this camera pointed?"

"North parking lot," he said. "Out the back."

The kids were already inside the hotel, looking around, lost. One of them with long red pigtails, Charlene, was carrying a rolled-up piece of paper, like some painting she'd made at school.

"Where is Miriam?" I asked her.

Charlene shook her head. "She went away."

"Where?"

Charlene started to cry, waving the paper. "Mrs. Watkins said to give this." I picked her up, holding her against my chest while I unrolled it. "CALL NOW," it said. The words were written in big crude letters like fingerpaint, but the color was reddish brown, like dried blood.

I punched the redial button on the killers' phone and waited, desperate for someone to pick up. "Mr. Kurtovic?" The man's voice.

"Yeah."

"The service road. Now."

I sprinted across the lot behind the hotel, vaulted the split-rail fence, and ran toward the only vehicle there, an old crew-cab Dodge pickup with a cap on the back. It was parked facing away from the motel, the engine running.

In the backseat was a gaunt, fair-skinned man with a shaved head, hollow-looking eyes, and barbed-wire tattoos that wrapped around his neck and the biceps on his arms. The driver in front had dark skin. I would have said he was Mexican or Central American. And he had three teardrop tattoos on his cheek. These men didn't look like pious Muslims to me, they looked like gang members. Then the one in the back looked down at his groin. Miriam was lying across his lap, and he held her down easily with one hand while he put the barrel of a .357 Magnum against the back of her head, pushing her face toward the seat.

I felt that kind of calm, almost like a trance, that comes with extreme anger. It's a different plane of hatred. Real quiet.

The driver made a gesture with his hand like he was talking on the phone. I put the Motorola to my ear.

"Get in the truck," said the voice. "You and the little girl will get us what we want. And then we will be finished with you."

"For good?"

"For good, Mr. Kurtovic."

CHAPTER 33

"Listen," I said. But the driver with the teardrop tattoos wasn't listening. He looked ahead at the traffic on Route 70, as uninterested in what I was saying as he was in the passing cars. "Listen to me," I said. "You can't handle this shit we're getting unless you've got special equipment. Understand?"

"If we don't get what we want, we're going to kill you and your fucking little girl."

"You got to be careful with it."

"Shut up and tell me where we go."

"This stuff is more dangerous—you have no fucking idea how dangerous, do you? . . . Straight through the light then make your next right . . .Do you? There's smallpox virus in the canister I'm giving you," I lied. "If it gets out, all of us will die. The fever is like burning to death. Your skin bleeds and starts to come off—"

"Shut up!"

Miriam moaned in the back. *"Cállate!"* shouted the son of a bitch holding her down. He slapped her on the back of the head with his free hand. She cried out for a second and was quiet.

Miriam, my little girl, would never forget this. She would never forget the fear, and she would never forget the things she had seen and what she was about to see, and there was nothing I could do to prevent any of what was going to happen—any of what I was going to make happen—right in front of her eyes. "Don't touch her," I whispered.

"Which *way?*" said the driver.

"Straight ahead until you see the Kmart on the right."

"Kmart?"

"It's empty. But the stuff is there."

"That where we're going?"

"It is."

The driver punched a button on his cell phone. *"Hay un Kmart. Dice que tiene la cosa allí."* He listened for a second. *"Bueno. Okay."*

"There it is on the right," I said. The front doors were still covered with plywood and the parking lot was still empty except for the old station wagon sitting on its rims. But a big American flag was flying from the pole.

"Around back," I said.

He pulled the truck to a stop in front of the shuttered loading platform. "It's in there?"

"Yes."

"We wait here," said the driver.

"Why?"

He said nothing, and I heard Miriam groan again in the backseat. "Shut up," said the man with the barbed-wire tattoos, and he slapped her again. "That's twice," I whispered. "Give her to me."

"She's so sweet and soft. Maybe I keep her."

"Shut the fuck up," said the driver.

A Chrysler van pulled next to us, followed by another rented Chevy sedan. Five men got out of the van, three from the Chevy. Most looked like gang members, but one had the scraggly beard and short haircut of the Salafis, who think they look like the first followers of Muhammad. They all pulled assault rifles out of the backs of the cars except for one. His dark brown face could have been Mexican and he had a sniper rifle with a telescopic sight. I looked at his black eyes. He might have been the man shooting at me from the cornfield. But he wasn't the man I wanted.

The cell phone in my hand rang out. "Yes."

"You are there," said the voice.

"Where are you?"

"The brothers will go with you to get the Sword."

"I'm not going anywhere without my little girl."

"You get her when I get the Sword."

The gunmen were deploying on the loading dock and the corners of the building. One of the Salafis pressed an earphone into his ear. He looked like he was waiting for orders.

"I take her now," I said.

The line went silent and I couldn't tell from the electric emptiness if it was dead or not. Then the voice came back. "Hand the phone to the brother in the backseat."

The man with the barbed-wire tattoos listened to the voice. He pulled back the hammer of the .357 and smiled, then raised the barrel and pointed it straight at my face. He handed the phone to me.

"Get out of the car," said the voice. "Take the girl. But move slow."

I watched the barrel of the pistol as I got out and opened the rear door of the truck. The son of a bitch with the barbed-wire tattoos grabbed Miriam's hair and jerked her head off the seat. "Go to Daddy," he said, and I saw for the first time that her face was bruised. I picked her up and held her to me, and it was like I was holding my whole life, the whole future of my world in my arms. She cried softly, breathless, beyond screaming. "Let's go inside," I said.

One of the Salafis kicked through a piece of plywood over the old entrance and three others went into the opening. They moved like men who'd been trained for urban combat, sure of their footing and their aim. The lead Salafi held up his hand, listening on his earphone, then motioned me to enter. The man with the barbed-wire tattoos came after me.

The inside of the Kmart was dark and hot and the stale air smelled like dust. Some light came in through the hole where we entered and some through cracks around the plywood at the front, but it wasn't much and my eyes adjusted slowly. All the merchandise was gone except for bits and pieces of boxes on the floor. But the high steel shelves were still there in the middle of the store, row after row of them, and at the back and around the side walls the big shelves for heavy merchandise climbed like scaffolding toward the steel rafters beneath the aluminum roof.

The barrel of the .357 pressed up against the base of my skull. I hugged Miriam to me and heard the voice on the phone in my hand. "You are inside the building?"

"Yes."

"Get us what we want. Now!"

With two gunmen on each side of me and the barbed-wire tattoos just behind, I walked as fast as I could through the dark. The other gunmen came into the building and spread out around the floor, searching for anyone who might be there before them, setting up an ambush for anyone who came after them. The photo section was near the front. The developing machines had been hauled away, but the counters were still there. At the back was a door into a windowless room where the chemicals used to be stored.

"Anybody got a flashlight?" I asked. "It's in here."

The Salafi pulled a Bic lighter out of his pocket. The large cylinder was upright at the back of the little room with a heavy chain wrapped around it several times that attached it to a vertical water pipe on the wall. On the floor was a mostly empty garbage bag that looked like it had just been tossed there, except there was no dust on it. "The lock's down at the bottom," I said.

"Unlock it," said the man with the barbed-wire tattoos and the pistol to my head, the man who had beaten my baby daughter. I knelt down, holding her close, and pushed the garbage bag to one side. I could feel rubber and straps inside and one, maybe two, canisters.

"I need more light. I can't see the combination," I said.

The barbed-wire tattoos stepped forward to shoot the chain with his .357.

"No!" I shouted. "You crack the cylinder and we're all dead."

He stepped back.

I fumbled with the lock, studying the chains, the garbage bag, trying to figure what had been left here for me. The combination on the lock ought to be zeros, or my father's birthday, 8-31-20. Betsy would know that. Zeros didn't work. One of the Salafis behind me was talking in Arabic into his earphone. The birthday didn't work. Maybe the left-right sequence was wrong. Miriam shifted in her exhausted sleep, thinking she was safe now that she was in Daddy's arms.

The phone in my hand rang. "The cylinder is too big," said the voice.

"That's for extra protection," I said.

"What have you done with the Sword? This is not it."

"Yes it is."

"Step out of the little room," said the voice on the phone.

"Damn it, where are you?" I shouted, kicking the garbage bag out through the door. "Can you see me? Can you see it?" I was well clear of the room now, holding Miriam, turning as if I was trying to find my persecutor. Two of the Salafis were still inside, fooling with the chain and the canister. "Look at the thing for yourself," I shouted. "It's a high-pressure cylinder. The Sword is inside."

The Salafi near me with the earpiece listened intently, looking back and forth between me and the man with the barbed-wire tattoo. Then he made a simple gesture: the pulling of a trigger. I looked into the barrel of the .357.

The pistol exploded, flying out of the tattooed-man's hand, sliding across the floor, and taking some of his fingers with it. He looked at me like I'd done this, too stunned even to cry out in pain.

A fraction of a second later, there was a quick series of shots and metal pinging noises and the gas canister inside the little room exploded. Shrapnel blasted into the guts and faces of the two Salafis still in there. A thick fog of chlorine billowed out through the door. I grabbed for the garbage bag, my eyes closed, my breath held, pushing Miriam's face into my sweat-damp blue-jean jacket. My right hand felt the mask, the straps. I put it on and cleared it with an explosion of breath. I inhaled. The air was clean. There was another canister in the bag about the size of a Coke can—one of the emergency hoods from the waterworks. Miriam was struggling, desperate and terrified in my arms. I shook out the plastic smoke hood and put it over her face, then pulled the drawstring tight around her neck. For a second the plastic smothered her, sticking to her nose and lips, stopping her screaming breath, and she wrenched in my grip, but a second later the little can filled the bag with air. Now she could breathe, too. But she wouldn't and couldn't calm down.

There were other shots, other sounds like exploding tanks of gas. From every corner of the building came the strangled shouts of the gunmen in the thickening cloud. Bursts of gunshots cut through the air, making starlight patterns in the aluminum roof.

I hit the concrete floor with Miriam hugged close. Someone was choking screams right in front of me and making a strange thudding noise against the floor. Still I couldn't see him. Then the barbed-wire tattoo on his bare arm loomed through the chlorine mist. His body twisted and writhed like a snake run over on the road. He beat his head against the floor, trying to smash the pain out of it. His eyes rolled back, his mouth foamed pink with his dissolving lungs and his blown-apart hand oozed red bubbles as the chlorine mixed with blood to make hydrochloric acid in his bare veins.

"There is justice," I said.

Somewhere the mobile phone rang, but I had dropped it when I was fumbling with the mask, and there was no way I could look for it now.

I figured everyone had headed for the hole in the plywood. Maybe some made it. Maybe they were waiting outside. With Miriam in my arms I didn't want to take that risk, but she was using up the oxygen in her emergency hood real fast. I had to get her out of the poison cloud. Chlorine is heavy. If I could climb into the scaffolding on the walls, I might be able to get above it. My throat and nose were burning and I was coughing from the little bit of gas I inhaled before I got the mask on. Miriam was still struggling, mucus running down her face, tears pouring from her eyes. I had to keep her arms pinned so she wouldn't rip off her hood, holding her tight. So tight.

The scaffolding was right in front of me. I climbed toward clearer air, balancing and grabbing handholds, and about fifteen feet up looked down on the poison like it was mist in a mountain valley. My eyes were used to the shadows now. I could see all the way across the inside of the building. On the top level of the scaffolding near the door somebody was moving. A small figure. A slip of a thing. Betsy. It had to be Betsy. She wore a gas mask and she was prone. Beside her was a high-powered hunting rifle with a telescopic scope, but she had the Ruger shouldered. She was watching for movement in the gas billowing below. She didn't see Miriam and me. Then a tiny tremor shook the scaffolding under my feet. Somebody else was up here.

"Miriam, Sugar, I'm going to put you down. Please, please, don't take this bag off your face. Please, Sugar. Just stay here. Please."

Her eyes were wide and red, her jaw clenched and her body rigid as she looked at the masked monster in front of her, her father.

I swung up onto the next level of scaffolding, the one just below the roof and in that second saw the Mexican sniper leveling his rifle at Betsy. He was wiping his eyes, trying to focus through his scope, but he was in control of his body. He was steady. He'd have her in a second.

Sirens wailed outside.

The only weapon I had was the knife in my boot, and I couldn't slow down to reach for it. I screamed from deep inside me but heard my voice muffled by the mask. The sniper wiped his eye again, and refocused. I tore off the mask as I ran, letting loose a yell of rage and fear that echoed under that huge metal roof like a banshee wail as I sprinted with everything in me across the top of the scaffolding. The sniper put his eye back to his scope and pulled the trigger. I made a dive for him that nearly carried both of us over the edge. He twisted and tried to break free, but now I had him pinned flat on his belly beneath me, his arms over the edge so he couldn't push up. Now my boot knife was an easy reach. Now I brought it clean through his carotid artery. Now a gush of blood, almost black in the shadows, sprayed down into the gray-green gas.

A thunder of guns sounded outside the back of the store, and new streams of daylight cut through the fog of chlorine as bullets blasted more holes in the plywood, holes in the sheet-metal side of the building, and holes in the roof.

Betsy was sitting up on the scaffolding opposite me. She waved and pointed at the level below me, at Miriam. I was gasping, taking in a little more poison with every breath. Part of the sniper's corpse beneath me started to vibrate. Then it stopped. Then it vibrated again. A telephone. A much bigger one than most people carried, almost the size of a brick. I didn't answer it, but I took it.

Betsy was holding her arm and it looked like a black stain covered her fingers. She leaned on her side, trying to see what was going on, but with no strength left.

The gunfire outside ended and a splintering of wood brought an explosion of light, then through it shadows of men dressed in black, masked in rubber, armored and armed for war. I tried to shout to them, but my throat was raw with chlorine and blood. I left the corpse of the sniper where it was and struggled down to Miriam. Somebody below shouted at me with an electronic voice. But I didn't hear. Couldn't listen. My little girl was lying on the platform so still; still as death. Her tiny hands were next to her face. But she hadn't taken the mask off. She did what Daddy told her. And then she quit breathing.

CHAPTER 34

Glimpses of Westfield and the sky flashed by through the window on the back of the speeding ambulance—a church steeple, a stoplight, the sign in front of the Kansas Inn, which was the last motel on the edge of town—then Westfield grew smaller, farther away, and disappeared.

A hand over my face held down the respirator. My throat and lungs ached and I sucked every breath like it was my last. "My daughter," I said. "My wife."

"They've gone up ahead to Ark City," said the attendant. "Betsy and—your little girl's name is Miriam, right?" I recognized him now as Jack Whitten, the owner of Whitten's jewelry shop, where I'd bought Betsy her ring. He was a hard-drinking old bachelor most of the time, but he spent part of his week as a real sober, real dedicated rescue volunteer.

"They're alive," I said.

Jack hesitated for just a second. "Yes," he said. "Yes. Don't try to talk. They're gonna be just fine."

I tried to sit up and he pushed me back down, his hand still over the respirator mask. "I heard Miriam is responding to CPR. And Betsy—Kurt, Betsy is going to be fine, but she did take a bullet in her shoulder."

The siren moaned around us.

"That was a hell of a thing you all did back there," Jack said.

I opened my mouth, then closed it, silent and aching.

"Who'd have thought those bastards would come to Westfield? Attacking our children! Kurt, God only knows what they'd have done with that poison gas if you hadn't stopped them."

He was convinced and proud of this half-made-up story about "their" poison gas. Maybe it would do as the truth.

"Deputy Nichols was mad as hell, I can tell you. He said Betsy warned him and then he called the FBI and that was the biggest mistake he ever made. They told him to wait until they got to the scene. Do nothing. Can you believe it? Hell, if Nichols had kept waiting, you might still be in there."

I put my hand on my bare chest, feeling for the pocket of the blue jean jacket, but it wasn't on me any more, there were just thin rubber tubes all over me.

"What do you need?" Jack asked.

"Phone."

"That's going to have to wait." He took his hand off my face and picked up the jacket from the bench beside him and reached into the pocket. "I haven't seen a phone this big since I don't know when," he said. "'Iridium.' What kind of phone is that?"

"Satellite."

"Whoa. Serious stuff. How do you turn it off? Interferes with things in an ambulance just like in an airplane."

I reached for it, then hugged it to me. My heart pounded and the monitors in the ambulance beeped like a slot-machine jackpot.

"What the hell you doing, Kurt?"

If he turned it off, I might not be able to turn it back on. I pushed the menu button.

"Come on, Kurt."

I scrolled up and down looking for "Recent Calls." There were six, all from the same number, 212-555-3728. I showed it to Jack. "Please write down," I said.

The light in the hospital room was dim and the only sound I heard at first was the faint whoosh of the oxygen machine. I tried to look at my watch, but on my wrist I read my name on a plastic band with a bar code.

"I'm sorry, Kurt." The voice in the chair beside me was familiar.

"Griffin?"

"I'm really sorry."

"Where's Betsy? Where's Miriam?"

"I should never have let them get dragged into this."

"Where the fuck are they?"

"Down the hall."

"I want to see them."

"As soon as you can walk."

I ripped the oxygen tube out from under my nose and stood up, bracing on the side of the bed.

"Hold on," said Griffin.

The saline drip was on a rolling stand. I used it as a kind of crutch. "Let's go," I said.

There were two beds in the dim room down where they had my family. Miriam was on the near one. Betsy on the far one. Both of my girls had oxygen tubes in their noses and pain and fear had drained all the color from their faces. Miriam's open eyes stared straight at the ceiling. I wanted to kiss her and hug her, but I was afraid I'd hurt her somehow. She saw me and started thrashing in the bed. I stepped back. She froze again, looking at me in horror.

"She'll get better," said Betsy.

"You are the bravest woman in the world," I said.

"Woman?"

"Life-saving Angel," I said.

She smiled, and then the smile faded. "Angel of Death," she said.

"Oh, Darlin'," I said, trying not to unplug anything as I hugged her. "You saved so many lives today. Mine and Miriam's, and all the thousands of people those assholes wanted to kill."

"We stopped a few bad guys."

"We sure did."

"But we didn't save the world." She looked at me, and then at Griffin.

"We've done all we can do," I said. "We've done all we're going to do."

"Let's end it somehow, Kurt."

"We will," I said.

I held her as tight as I could and we stayed that way for a long time that wanted to be forever.

About halfway down the night-empty hall between my family's hospital room and mine, I turned on Griffin and threw him against the wall. He didn't fight back, but waited until, seconds later, I had no breath in my body and I stood before him red-faced and helpless.

"Don't bother killing me, Kurt. I'm leaving the Agency," he said. "I'm AWOL right now, as far as they're concerned."

"Who gives a shit which agency you work for."

"I'm leaving the government."

"Why don't you just get out of here and leave me—leave *us*—alone?"

"I'm leaving the government because I saw you betrayed, and I couldn't do anything about it. I'm leaving because when you got back here and you were waiting—we should have watched you twenty-four/seven, just to protect you."

"Go on."

"But we didn't. The Agency had to stand back and the FBI wouldn't pick up. I tried to check in on you. But—"

"You're telling me that I was here as bait, me and my family like some rotten pieces of meat in a crab trap, and there was nobody interested enough to haul it in."

"Worse. Not *allowed* to bring you in."

"Reason?"

"A jurisdiction thing. They said I couldn't make a case for why anyone would come after you."

"What did you tell them?"

"I told them you had some unfinished business with the bad guys, something about a genie in a bottle. I told them some of the bad guys had already come sniffing around here."

"And they said—"

"Said it wasn't enough to go on. And if we didn't get it out of you at Gitmo, we weren't going to."

"You should have warned me."

"Wasn't allowed. That's why I'm quitting."

"When was all this decided."

"Weeks ago. Then again yesterday, when we picked up some intel about people on their way here. Then again today, when we knew they got here. Every time, the word that came down was to leave you alone."

"All alone."

"Yeah."

"Even when the shooting started, nobody was going to send in the cavalry?"

He nodded. I opened the door to my hospital room."None of this makes sense." I didn't know what to say. "I still don't understand why."

"Maybe the Evil Doers were supposed to get what they came for."

A weight of emotion like a slab of lead pushed down on me. "I got to rest now," I said. "But if you think you owe me something, do me one favor."

"What's that?"

I pulled the Iridium phone out of my jacket on the door. It was dead. I unfolded the little paper with the number scrawled by Jack Whitten in the ambulance. And I handed the phone and the number to Griffin.

"Stay in the Agency," I said. "At least for a few more weeks."

Ground Zero

JUNE 29–JULY 4, 2002

CHAPTER 35

The sun was just coming up and half of America lay behind me in the night. Filling-station coffee sat in my gut like battery acid and my lungs were still raw from the chlorine. My eyes in the rearview mirror were red as dawn. But I was wide awake as I headed toward the Holland Tunnel and saw the emptiness where the Twin Towers used to be. I heard my voice as if it belonged to somebody else saying, "My God," and then again, "My God," and I was glad for all that I had done, and what I had not done, in my life. And for what I was about to do.

I didn't dare think anymore that I could end this war. I wasn't sure that anyone I loved would ever be safe. But today or tomorrow would get us closer to the end, closer to safety—a lot closer than we'd been since those two towers disappeared. That's what I believed as my pickup inched into the tunnel under the Hudson.

Griffin was waiting for me in Manhattan. He'd traced the satellite phone to a company registered in the Bahamas. Through the Agency databases he peeled away layer after layer of corporate fronts until he focused on a financial consultant in New York. That was as much as he would tell me on the phone. "This is really a strange one," he said. "I think this could be the sleeper of all sleepers. We need—I need you here, and I need you now."

It was hard to leave Betsy and Miriam. Real hard. They

were feeling better but they were still in Ark City Hospital. Folks were protecting us. The doctors. The sheriff's office. Everybody. And we all figured it was better for them to stay there, stay safe, stay away from the reporters who came nosing around about the "gang war in Westfield" story that went out on TV.

As Deputy Nichols told it to the press, a bunch of criminals from Wichita tried to take over our town. They pistol-whipped Sam Perkins and tied him up and stole the chlorine—and nobody knew what they were going to use it for. Nobody was sure, either, why they took some children hostage and killed the teacher. "Crazy violent crackheads," is what Deputy Nichols called them. "They must have thought Westfield was easy pickings, but they was wrong. All six was killed in the shoot-out."

The deputy didn't count the Salafis or the men killed at Jeffers' Rocks. He didn't mention them at all. He didn't have to. Bodies disappear in America these days, especially the bodies of foreigners. No one asked. No one told. So no one knew they were ever there. The FBI said it was still looking into the case, but had no comment on "what appeared to be a matter of state jurisdiction."

"Was this terrorism?" one of the reporters on Channel 2 asked Deputy Nichols. "They was terrorizing," he told her. "But this wasn't nothing to do with terrorism." Westfield was happy to live with that story, and after a couple of days so was the rest of the country.

I wished that it could all be secret. I wished that we could protect our people, our families, our babies without them ever needing to know. I wished my baby girl had never had to see what she saw, or feel what she felt.

And now I was in Manhattan, where the early-morning air smelled of garbage, sick-sweet and rotten, like day-old corpses on a battlefield. Rush hour hadn't really started yet. Eighth Avenue was wide open. By six-thirty I was at Columbus Circle and parked the truck in a lot and walked into Central Park. The roads and paths there were full of runners. It was like the city had poured all its restless flesh onto the pavement. Young men and women loped along at measured speeds, checking their watches and sucking on water bottles. Old men shuffled and bicyclers rushed by like kamikazes. Some joggers listened to rock and roll running cadences, others to the morning news. Dogs trotted beside their masters. Mothers ran behind their three-wheeled strollers, their babies braving the wind like little Red Barons.

It was a scene I'd seen more times than I remembered in those months when I lived here in 1992 and 1993. I used to run by the reservoir. But I never saw it quite like this before, knowing for sure how easy it would be for all this life to end. Didn't they see what happened here on September 11? Didn't they know the danger? Didn't they care that it could happen again right now? Or tomorrow? Any time at all? They were beyond caring. They were blessed by forgetfulness, protected by ignorance, which is maybe, just maybe, the greatest blessing.

In the narrow paths, across the little wooden bridges, in the part of the park called the Ramble, I found Griffin on a bench above the pond, just where he said he'd be. He wore a white short-sleeve shirt with a loose tie; his jacket was beside him and he had a Starbucks cup in his hand. He held another cup out for me.

"You look like shit," he said.

"I'm here," I said.

"You got a change of clothes? Something besides that T-shirt?"

"In the backpack. You got something to tell me?"

"A lot," he said, watching and waiting while some tourists in Bermuda shorts strolled by speaking Italian. "That sat phone was registered to a Bahamas holding company owned by a Cayman Island company—"

"Give me the name of the man."

Griffin nodded. "Uh-hunh. Ryan Handal. Mean anything to you?"

"Nothing. Who the fuck is he? Where is he?"

"You can look him up in *The New York Times.* There's an interesting article about him."

"Does it give his address?"

"Yeah. It does."

"Where is he now?"

"Where are any of them? Gone. Dust. Nothing but bits of jewelry and teeth."

"What the fuck are you talking about?"

"I'm saying that Ryan Handal is one of the three thousand."

"One of the three thousand killed in the Trade Center?"

Griffin nodded.

I sat back on the bench and watched an old man throwing a stick into the pond so his black Labrador would swim out and retrieve it. "Is that why I drove twenty-one hours to get here? Is that the end of the story?"

"It's a start," said Griffin. "Just a start. There's more but we don't know for sure what it means. And there's none of it that you're supposed to hear, not from me, not from anybody." Griffin took a sip of his coffee and watched the Labrador shaking the pond off his back. Griffin pulled a printed page from the *Times* Web site out of his pocket. There was no picture, just a headline: ALWAYS READY TO HELP.

> "Some men are known for what they say, and some for what they do," says Victoria Bernstein, who worked as Ryan Handal's assistant at Nova Ventures for six months. "Mr. Handal was a doer. He loved his work, but more than that, he loved to help people."
>
> Handal, 53, was born in El Salvador and immigrated to the United States in 1989. "He told me he lost all his family, and almost everything he had in the civil war in his country," said Ms. Bernstein. Like many immigrants, he saw the United States as a land where he could build a new life, and through hard

work and shrewd investments, he did. In the early 1990s, Handal established himself as one of New York's most successful, if least known, investors in advanced medical technologies.

One of the first to recognize the potential demand for magnetic resonance imaging (MRI) and other capital-intensive diagnostic equipment, Handal established a leasing company, ScanTech, in 1990 and took it public two years later. By the end of the decade he was a major investor, through his offshore holding company, Nova Enterprises, in the health and biotech areas. According to Ms. Bernstein, he was also a generous donor to medical charities. "He gave for research on multiple sclerosis and bone diseases. He was always ready to help, always ready to send a check," said Ms. Bernstein, "but he never wanted his name on any of it. 'The point is to do good for the people who need it,' he would say, 'not to do good for my ego.' "

On the morning of Sept. 11, Ms. Bernstein remembers, Mr. Handal had just returned to New York after a business trip to Las Vegas. "He called me on Monday and told me he was back in the city, and that he would be in the office early." Ms. Bernstein said she had a dental appointment and wouldn't be in until the afternoon. "He said not to worry, and to take the day off. He was just going to make a few calls. I got out of the dentist's about 9:30. We knew by then what had happened, but I couldn't get near the Trade Center. I tried to call, but there was no answer. When I got home, I had a message on my machine."

Like so many messages that were left that morning, this one was brief and poignant. "It's over," said Mr. Handal. "I think it's over. God save us. And God Bless America."

I handed the page back to Griffin. "The sniper's phone belonged to this guy?"

"To his company. Yeah."

"And the number I gave you?"

Griffin smiled. "To the cell phone of a V. Bernstein."

"What does she have to say?"

"Not much. She was in her sixties and after last September she decided to retire up in Maine. Last month she slipped on some rocks at the beach—hit her head and drowned."

"You're kidding."

"No." Griffin tossed his unfinished coffee out on the ground and put the empty cup back in the sack. "No, I'm not kidding."

"We're close, ain't we?"

Griffin nodded his head real slowly, like he was afraid to be too sure. "And you haven't heard the best yet," he said. "The obit makes it sound like Handal bet on a growing industry and won, but that's only one of the ways he made money. Some of his biggest hits came from shorting stocks."

"Which means . . ."

"Basically it means he bet on stocks going down. And if they did, the difference between the loan he got to pay for the stock and the price it actually sold for went into his pocket. A bank was left holding the stock, which he had put up as collateral, and he was left holding the money. He did that for most of the last ten years, and won real big on a couple of health and insurance stocks. All told, about fifty million dollars."

"Sounds big to me."

"Nothing compared to what he would have made if he'd lived. A little over a year ago he started shorting a lot of insurance stocks, and even stocks in areas where he never was active before, like airlines. And all of the stocks bottomed after September eleventh. Just dropped through the floor. If he'd cashed in at the end of September and early October, like he was supposed to, he would have collected about three hundred and fifty million dollars."

"But he was dead."

"Yeah. He was dead."

"So, what are you saying?"

"Some of those trades drew attention after September eleven. Do you remember the stories?"

"I saw a couple of headlines, but I was busy with other things."

"Yeah, well, there were calls for an investigation because it looked like somebody made a hell of a lot of money out of the tragedy—somebody who might have known what was coming. Then they found out the biggest investor was Handal and he was killed in his office on the ninety-third floor of the north tower, and that was the end of their investigation."

"But not yours."

"No. Handal's estate collected on most of those trades. The charity he set up, the La Merced Foundation, pulled in almost three hundred million dollars. And when you look at it closely, La Merced is kind of a strange thing. It's really a one-man show run by Handal's executor, a lawyer named José Oriente."

"So Handal's dead. What do we do?"

"We do Oriente. He came to the United States from Panama about the same time as Handal, and he was just about as successful. Oriente is real low profile in public, but high profile with the people who count. He's been invited to Kennebunkport by the President's father."

"Maybe I'm just more tired than I thought, Griffin. Where's the Qaeda connection? Where's the jihad connection? I don't get it."

"I don't know. But there's something here. Can't you smell it? All that money that went into the second-wave attacks—the ones you helped us stop—where did it come from? I think a lot of it came from La Merced's pot of gold. But the more I look into it, the more stone walls I run into. This Oriente has so many friends you wouldn't believe it. He's a big campaign contributor. Both parties. Nobody in the government wants to touch him. Nobody even wants him talked to. You go through channels and every channel is blocked."

"So here I am."

"Uh-hunh."

"To get around the channels."

"That's right. Who better?" Griffin smiled and shook his head. "The Agency knows I'm thinking about leaving; they don't like that, and they don't trust me. I'm not supposed to be here. I'm sure as hell not supposed to be talking to you. But I know one thing: there were eleven men in Kansas who snatched your daughter and would have killed her—and killed you—and killed Betsy if they could—and they wanted to kill hundreds of thousands of Americans. There was a voice that guided them, and it came to them over a phone from Handal's company and the number belonged to Handal's assistant. Since there's nothing left of Mr. Handal but the dust at Ground Zero and nothing left of Ms. Bernstein but the ashes at her crematorium, it seems to me that Oriente—the head of the foundation and the executor of the Handal estate—is the guy to talk to. But nobody wants me to do that, and nobody will do it for me. What do we do? What do *you* do?" He stared at the pond for inspiration. "The first thing you can do is change your shirt and put on a tie if you've got one." Griffin looked at his watch. "Oriente is supposed to be at a breakfast over at Sixty-sixth and Park this morning. I figure he'll be coming out of the building in about thirty minutes. Just about enough time for us to walk there."

"A breakfast at the Council?"

"You know the place. You worked there as a gofer in 1992 when you were banging that woman researcher, right?"

"I know the place," I said.

"Yeah, well, we're not going inside. We're going to stand back and watch."

The morning got warmer by the minute as we walked through the park past the rowboats and the pavilion and halfway down through the mall under the enormous elms.

"Where does the money go?"

"From La Merced?"

"Yeah."

"Medical research and soup kitchens and summer camps for inner-city kids, that sort of thing."

"A one-man United Way."

"Except for the religious part. All the groups that get money from La Merced are religious groups."

"What kind of religion?"

"Christian, Jewish, Muslim. They're what you call faith-based charities. Doesn't seem to make much difference which faiths."

"Big ones?"

Griffin smiled. "Not so big you've ever heard of them. And every one pretty fundamentalist."

"What's the thing you're not telling me?"

"Rehab centers. La Merced gives a lot of money to rehab centers for drug addicts and small-time dealers. There's one group called Resurrection House that's pretty big in the Midwest. It starts working with inmates in state prisons, then brings them together in halfway houses when they get out. And it gets most of its money from La Merced."

"It works with gang members?"

"You could say that. Six of them are lying unclaimed in the Ark City morgue right now."

CHAPTER 36

Black limousines lined up on Park Avenue and around the block on Sixty-sixth. Drivers waited beside them, or on the corner, many of them with their jackets off and their ties loosened.

"No Secret Service," said Griffin. "No government heavies here today."

Men in suits and women in business clothes started coming out the front door. I recognized Tom Brokaw from the Nightly News, and a couple of other faces I'd seen on TV. I saw Jeb Carlton, who was at the Council when I worked there, but I didn't think he'd see me, and didn't think he'd recognize me if he did. And then I saw Chantal. She was still tall and graceful and as alone-looking as a little girl with no friends on a playground. She was more than ten years older than me, and almost ten years had passed since I'd seen her. She walked right by me and I don't think she knew I was there. Maybe she thought I was just another one of the drivers. She had some other place to go.

"That's him," said Griffin.

A slender man with salt-and-pepper hair, a mostly gray beard, and a suit as elegant as Fred Astaire's shook hands with a couple of other Council members, then looked over the line of cars and the clusters of chauffeurs. For just a second, he looked straight at me. His eyes were such a pale blue they were almost white. I thought I read recognition in them, but then he turned and went down the line of cars on Park, walking normally away from us until, just on the last couple of steps, he dragged his left foot behind him like he'd had polio, or like the bone in his foot had been broken—like the metatarsal had been cracked with an iron rod, and never been allowed to heal.

The man's uniformed driver opened the back door of the big black Mercedes for him to get in, but he put his hands on the roof of the car like he needed to brace himself, or was about to be searched, and he just stood there for a second with his head bent down, thinking. Heat gushed off the hoods of the cars, making a mirage out of the air between us. Then he turned full toward me again, looking straight through the rippling light into my eyes, and he waited.

I walked down Park along the line of limos until we were close enough to shake hands, but neither of us reached out. "It is time for us to talk in cooler, more civilized surroundings," he said. He stepped back from the door of the car and gestured toward the leather seats. "Will you join me?"

"I'll get in on the other side," I said, glancing back through the haze of engine-heat toward Griffin, but he was gone.

"Fulton and Broadway," Oriente told the driver. "Take us right down the middle of the island." He turned to me. "We ought to appreciate the full grandeur of this city," he said.

"Before you destroy it."

"Hah! Is that what you think?"

"Yes."

"No. Destruction is so easy. Salvation is what's hard. And this is a city, this is a country, this is a world that needs to be saved. Surely you agree. Look up ahead of us, and all around us now." We were rolling toward the Met Life building. "God made mountains, but men made this skyline. When the clouds roll in and the tops of these buildings disappear, you know, Kurt, there's no way to know where the hand of man ends and the kingdom of heaven begins. The Tower of Babel was nothing compared to this. But this is not—" He shook his head. "Like Babel, this is not the way of the Lord."

We moved from sunlight to dark shadow as we followed the upward swerving tunnel that runs around the side of Grand Central Station.

"Who are you?" I asked.

"A pious man."

"In Granada you were a Syrian doctor disguised as a spice merchant. Here you're a Panamanian lawyer. Who the fuck are you?"

"Ah, that long afternoon and evening in Granada, when we got to know each other so well. Poor Pilar. She did not understand you as well as I did. And are you forgetting Kenya? You know, I think Cathleen was really quite fond of you. She was such a kind woman, for a spy. Didn't you think so? I believe she and Mr. Faridoon have gone back to the big hive in London now. Don't look surprised. You must certainly have guessed. But, you know, bureaucracies are so conservative, they would never have done anything in Somalia, in the end, if you hadn't—what should I say?—forced the issue? You are a surprising catalyst, Kurt, for so many things."

The late-morning sun burst bright through the windshield and lower Manhattan stretched in front of us. We rode in silence for a while before I said, "Yes, we do know each other."

He looked straight ahead and nodded. His face didn't show emotion, really, just quiet purpose. His expression was efficient. "Of course we do," he said.

"So where do we go from here?"

"To my favorite place in all of New York."

"Ground Zero."

"Not quite," he said.

"And then?"

"And then we shall see."

"We're just about to end this thing," I said. "You know it. I know it. Whatever your plans were, they're finished. You've been ID'd. You'll be arrested. It's over."

"Kurt, maybe you know me. But you don't know your country. You don't know this world you live in. Do you hear sirens? Do you see police?"

"You are never going to threaten me or my family again."

"That's right, Kurt. You know that and I know that, too."

"I destroyed the Sword a long time ago."

"Yes, I thought that was probably the case. But of course I had to be sure. That clumsy business in your hometown with all the gas—you couldn't have given me better proof. I knew you would trade me what I wanted if you had it. You wouldn't have played tricks. You worship your family. You would betray your country for them, your government. Even God. You would have let a hundred thousand children die to save your baby girl, and not think twice, I think. Once, you loved God. Now you love—is it Betsy? Miriam? Tell me something, Kurt, do you love one more than the other? Would you let yourself dare to think about that? But of course if you live long enough, that will change, too. Maybe you'll come back to God. I think you will."

"How long have you been working for Bin Laden? Or is it Saddam? He's the one who gave us the Sword, isn't he?"

We were passing from Soho along the fringes of Chinatown. Oriente watched the crowds of shoppers and tourists and delivery boys and bums and schoolgirls elbowing around each other on the sidewalks. "So many people work with me, and for me, and for the cause of righteousness. Some of them know their roles, some don't," he said. "Bin Laden is one player on the board. One player. Saddam is another player. But just one player. And what is so—I want to say sad, but I am not going to patronize you—what is so—frustrating is that you don't see the big picture, Kurt. Thousands and thousands of people are working for one purpose, and others are helping without knowing it, and one hand guides them all."

I looked at the empty sky high above Wall Street. "All part of some vast conspiracy, some huge plot. Is that what you're telling me?"

"Part of a huge purpose. Working toward one goal. The Final Act. The script was written before they were born. Before any of us were born. All we have to do is play it out. But—we're almost there. Look at the name of the street: Canyon of

Heroes. You always wanted to be a hero, didn't you? Well, here you are. This is the place you want to be. Someday maybe they'll throw ticker tape at you."

The sudden bitterness in Oriente's voice made me feel better. "I fucked you up," I said. "You know it and I know it."

"We're here," said Oriente. The car stopped in front of stone columns at the entrance to a brick church. "There are answers here to questions you never asked. You will see here what I know—and what you know."

We walked up the steps to a glass door with a sign on it: "St. Paul's Chapel is temporarily closed for refurbishment." Oriente knocked on the glass.

"You're Muslim," I said. "Why are we coming to a church?"

"There is only one God," said Oriente.

A young black man with gray plaster dust in his hair and a painter's mask over his face came to the door. When he saw it was Oriente, he opened up and said something in Spanish that I didn't understand, gesturing for us to enter. Painters and sanders were hard at work from floor to ceiling. "There is a lot of cleaning up to do," said Oriente. "And I've donated a lot of the money for it." He cast an eye over the workmen and the work. "There is a lot of history here," he said. "George Washington used to pray here." He smiled. "This is where the Founding Father came to meet with the Creator."

Oriente turned his wolf eyes toward me. "But we will leave the tourism for another time. Up there in front of the windows, the altar, that is what I wanted you to see. We'll have to get them to take off the canvas covering." Oriente shouted in Spanish to the workmen on the scaffolding in other parts of the chapel. One shouted back and a couple of them started climbing down. "This will take a minute," he said. "Let's have a seat on the front row."

Hot as it was, a cold shiver of superstitious fear ran through me.

"Do you remember," he asked, "exactly where you were when you saw the Towers hit?" I thought of the kitchen in my house in Westfield, and of Miriam drinking milk out of the carton. I said nothing. "Of course you do," said Oriente. "Everybody does. They remember watching TV over their morning coffee, or turning on the set in the boss's office, or frantically pushing the buttons on their car radios, changing stations to make sure they hadn't heard wrong. Everybody remembers. Everybody will always remember."

"Where were you?"

"Sitting right here." He looked over his shoulder for the workmen and saw they were bringing ladders up to the sides of the altar. They climbed almost to the second-story ceiling and untied the upper part of the canvas covering, then walked it down and pulled it away. I expected to see a crucifix, or at least a cross. But the image behind the altar was not quite like anything I'd seen in a church before. A thunderous white cloud was carved from wood, and golden shafts, half lightning and half light, exploded downward from it. In the center of the cloud, in the center of the explosion, was a single word written in an alphabet I didn't know. At the base of the cloud, delivered by the blast of lightning and shafts of light, were two black stone tablets with the Ten Commandments etched on them in gold.

"The flash of fire, the downward rush of the clouds—the altar has been like that since the days of George Washington. It has been here—waiting," said Oriente. "Do you see the Hebrew letters? YHWH. Yahweh. Jehovah. 'I AM THAT I AM.' The name before all the other names of God, the first name of Allah, Lord of the Worlds, the Beneficent, the Merciful, Master of the Day of Judgment. Oh yes. 'I am Alpha and Omega, the beginning and the ending, which is, and which was, and which is to come, the Almighty.' You feel it, don't you? You look at that and you know what it is and you feel it. 'Behold, He cometh with clouds and every eye shall see Him.' "

I looked at the altar, and at the sun coming from behind the windows, living rays lighting shafts through the plaster dust that hung in the air.

"I heard the first explosion," he said, "and the pews trembled, but I didn't move. I bowed my head, and I waited. Eighteen minutes later, the second explosion. And that was when I went to the back of the church. Come. Come with me now." We walked straight down the aisle behind us to the steel door, which was already half open for air. Oriente pushed it the rest of the way. "I will show you a beautiful thing," he said. "Look at the altar, and now look out this door."

In front of us was an old churchyard with crumbling headstones tilted by the roots of ancient trees. Around the graveyard was an iron fence draped with banners and posters too far away for me to read, and in the far distance, a few tall buildings.

"Beyond these graves, and beyond this fence, just there, filling your eyes with its enormity—from here to there—was the World Trade Center." He looked at me to make sure I understood. "I stood here," he said, "and watched the flames and the people falling. I listened to the screams of sirens and the screams of men. I smelled the brimstone of the buildings burning and the stinking pitch of jet fuel, and I was covered with the ashes of Hell as I watched one by one the buildings coming down. Not just two buildings, but all seven. Like the seven candles, the seven churches, the seven seals of Revelation. '*Behold, He cometh with clouds and every eye shall see Him.*' "

I resisted the horror and the beauty of the emptiness beyond the iron fence. But every image I had seen on television and in photographs and in my waking and sleeping nightmares was there in front of me. I resisted. But I saw it all.

"There is no God," I said.

"You do not believe that," he said, without surprise or anger. A simple statement of fact.

"And your client Ryan Handal, what did he believe up there on the ninety-third floor burning to death?"

The executor of the Handal estate and director of the La Merced Foundation weighed his words and decided not to use them. "Let's go across the street," he said.

"Are there many more like you?" I asked as we waited for the light to change at the corner of Vesey and Church. The smell of hot pretzels filled the air, and Oriente bought a bottle of Snapple from the street vendor.

"More what?" he said, offering me a drink, then shrugging and putting it back when I refused. "There are many pious men and women in this country and around the world."

"And if I was pious, what would you want from me?"

The light changed and we crossed, walking down Vesey to the entrance of the excavations. The guard at the gate, like the workman in the church, seemed to be an old acquaintance of José Oriente. He handed us each a hard hat, and we walked down the ramp under the office trailers to what must have been, once, part of a lower parking level. There was no one around us, and nothing to see in front of us but that huge hole and beyond it a mural painted on the side of a half-shattered building: a big heart in the colors of the American flag with the legend beneath it, "The human spirit is not increased by the size of the act but by the size of the heart."

"What would I want from you?" There were a couple of big industrial spools that used to hold electrical cable and he pointed at them like they were easy chairs. "My leg is acting up," he said. "Let's sit and talk. Sure you don't want a sip? No. Well. Kurt, what do I want from you? Just to listen—in here." He tapped his heart. "There's no question of giving you orders, or bringing you into an organization. There are no orders. There is no organization. There is inspiration, and God's will. There is the guiding hand. I just want you to let yourself be guided. I want you to be saved."

"You want to be my savior?"

"I want God to be your savior. But, yes, I suppose I want to play my part."

"Tell me who you are."

He shrugged. "I am who I am. I am the man talking to your wife at your door in Westfield. I am the voice on the phone the other day."

"The voice ordering me and my child to be killed."

"Not like that."

"You are José Oriente from Panama."

"Yes. And I am Ryan Handal from El Salvador." He let me think about that for a second. "I thought you guessed," he said.

"And who else?"

"A man with a lot of friends."

"Was it you that called the White House to get me out of Guantánamo?"

The man with friends smiled and shook his head, but I couldn't tell for sure what that meant. "I didn't know who you were in Granada, Kurt, but by the time I found you in Africa I did. And I knew what a gift you had."

"Did you call the White House?"

"Do you want me to trace a diagram in the dust here?" he said. "It would be a lie. It would be useless. It would teach you nothing and it wouldn't convince you of anything. What is true is that, just as I told you, I was a doctor who spent ten years in Tadmor prison. The pain is still in my bones, although sometimes I can control it. But mainly the pain is inside my soul. I have suffered for my belief in God. Suffered long and terribly. And from that suffering I have learned. When I was in prison, two things kept me alive: one was my faith, the other was a kind of strange dream. You know what it is like to dream, don't you? Prison dreams? I dreamed that when I was free, I could be whoever and whatever I wanted to be. Why limit yourself to one life if you can have many? And in America you can invent yourself again and again, even at the same time. And so I did, while I and the brothers prepared for Judgment Day."

"With terror."

"We're so close to the time. The lessons need to be learned quickly. The End of Days is near."

I looked out over the destroyed pit where so many people died. "All this for some bullshit vision of the Apocalypse. Is that it?"

"Listen to me. Listen. The clash is coming between Believers and Unbelievers. But that's nothing to what will come after. What you see here has created believers all over the world. Muslims, Jews, Christians—they witnessed the horror, they felt the fear, they've suffered the wars since, and they turn to God for help."

"God Almighty," I said.

"You have to understand, Kurt. And I think you do. We have entered the last age of man, when God has given us the power to work His Divine Will. We can build mountains, and we can tear them down. We can create human life in a glass tube and we can use the same science to devastate life across the entire face of the planet. Now what does that mean? It means we have waited thousands of years for Judgment Day, never knowing when it would come. But now we can put it on the calendar. We can fix a date."

I saw on his face the look of a man who is quietly content, and absolutely sure of himself. "When the Sword of the Angel came into our hands in 1992, we thought we had the key. When you stole it—you, Kurtovic—we thought we were lost." He looked at me and smiled charitably. "Then we learned better. God showed us the way. He brought us the four winged beasts with many eyes." He craned his neck to look up at the sky, as if he were following the flight paths of two airliners.

"When?"

"What?"

"When is the End of Days?"

He shook his head. "You aren't ready to know. There is more work to be done. More spreading of the word. More fire. More plagues." He gestured like an actor onstage, moving his hands through the air. "So much more. But with every horror on earth, more souls will find their way to Heaven. You know that. I know you do. Ah. Look."

There was a red dot of light on the palm of his left hand as he held it up. He looked at his other hand, and there was another red dot of light. No, two. He moved his hands in front of him, and the light didn't quite follow. Then he looked at his chest. More red dots danced across it, the pinpoints of laser gun sights. Somewhere in a tall shrouded building across the way, or from windows behind the all-American heart, people we couldn't see were taking aim.

"They won't shoot unless I make a move toward you, or I try to run," said Oriente. "There is too much they want to know. And I have so many friends. We can keep talking. This will be taken care of." He looked down at his chest and counted the quivering red dots as if he were looking for stains. "One, two, three, four, five, six, seven. Seven points of light," he said and twisted his mouth in an odd smile.

"You are so reasonable now," he went on. "When you thought you were Allah's man on earth, Kurt, you were not so useful. You were a child. You heard the wrong message. But now you reason. Now you'll see. All of this"—he swept his hand over the sanitized destruction of Ground Zero—"all of this opens the door to salvation."

He flinched. One of the red dots on his chest erupted dark red and liquid. "My friends," he said, suddenly short of breath. Now another of the dots exploded. "My brothers!" And another and another. Seven silent shots ripped through him, heavy-caliber bullets tearing his elegant suit and shirt and tie and flesh and bone and guts to shreds until he was left lying on the concrete floor of the ruin like a dog mangled by a thresher, his pale eyes staring out at the empty sky.

When Griffin walked down the ramp a few minutes later, a group of men in the uniforms of sanitation workers came with him. They brought white plastic garbage bags to pick up the last little pieces.

"Your shooters?" I said.

"FBI," he said. "And they weren't supposed to shoot."

CHAPTER 37

I kissed Betsy good night in the soft blue light of the hospital room. "We'll be there," she whispered. I moved as silently as I could past Miriam's bed, afraid to wake her, and afraid to see the fear on her face again if I did, then I drove the rest of the way home from Ark City to Westfield.

The house was completely dark, and dead quiet. The top of the washing machine was still open with my sweaty running clothes still in it. The bed where Betsy and I made love that morning so long ago was still covered with twisted sheets. On the answering machine, the light was flashing like crazy. I threw the phone across the room and went back to the truck.

"Sam?" I called out, knocking on his front door. "Sam? Are you home?"

His wife, Caroline, opened the door. His youngest daughter stood beside her and Caroline twirled a finger in the little girl's hair. "Hey, Kurt, you're back," said Caroline. "Thank God. Oh, thank God. How are Betsy and Miriam?" The little girl looked up. "Miriam?" she repeated. and now the other kids gathered around behind their mom, curious.

"They're good," I said. "Just resting."

"God bless," she said.

"I wanted to talk to Sam about Thursday."

"He's still counting on you."

"Yeah. Is he here?"

"No, Kurt, he's back to doing double shifts right now. Go on down to the waterworks. He's gonna be mighty happy to see you."

When I pulled the truck into the parking lot I saw Sam sitting outside on the back step. "Boy, am I happy to see you," he said. He put out his hand and I put out mine, but that didn't seem like enough. He threw his arms around me and hugged me like a brother.

"Thanks, Sam."

"It worked, didn't it, Kurt?"

"It did," I said. "You and Betsy—I don't know how you did it."

"All she had to tell me was the bad guys had come to town."

"I know."

"She had the plan. I wish I could have been there, you know, when it happened. I helped her move the canisters, and I wanted to stay. But she said I had to be back here to make it look right, like I was beat up." He rubbed his jaw. "She swung that butt pretty good."

We were both silent for a second. "Right," I said, and we broke out laughing.

"She okay? And Miriam?"

"They'll be okay."

"Ah, Kurt, man, who'd have thought it could happen here?"

"Yeah. . . . Sam?"

"Yeah?"

"You don't have anything to drink, do you?" I didn't really expect that he did. The county is dry, and nobody in his church drank, or admitted to it.

"Let's check the safe," he said. He got a couple of cups from the watercooler and from far back in the back of the safe he pulled a blue velvet bag. "You won't find better bourbon than this," he said. "It's so expensive, a bottle lasts me a couple of years." He filled both cups to the brim.

"About Thursday," I said.

"Everybody's looking forward to it, Kurt."

"You still want me then."

"Hell yeah," he said. "*Hell* yeah."

"After everything that's happened, I feel like, you know, a lot of people got fucked up because of this. Because of me."

He looked at me and nodded and drank a little more deeply into his cup.

"They were after me," I said.

"Well they learned a lesson, didn't they?"

"I'm thinking maybe we should go someplace else, me and Betsy and Miriam."

"No, Boy. No way." He looked at me through eyes watering from the whiskey. "This here's your home, and a man's only ever got one of those, you know? I mean, you can spend your whole damn life wandering around, and there's just gonna be one place—I mean not maybe where you was born—or school—that's not it." He took another sip. "It's a place you feel like you can be. You know? Where you can *be.* Like, it *is* who you *are.* You know any other place in the whole wide world where you can *be* like that? You? No. Westfield, Kurt. Here. You. Here." He put his arms out and hugged me again and was a little off balance. I helped him lean back on his desk. He finished his cup. "Good stuff," he said.

Betsy and Miriam got out of the hospital on Tuesday, but they didn't come back to the house. They went to Ruth's because Betsy thought our baby wasn't ready to spend a lot of time with her daddy just yet. Betsy said she'd talked to the doctors at the hospital and that was what they told her. They said we'd have to take it in stages, real gentle. In the late afternoon I drove by Ruth's house slow, hoping I'd see Miriam in the yard or maybe just get a glimpse of her through the window, but I didn't, and I didn't stop.

I wanted to go back to work right away, but Sam said he could handle it until next week and he wanted me to take the time off. I couldn't just stay in the house. I couldn't sit there and think. I didn't turn on the computer. I didn't watch TV. There was all this talk on the news about a coming war with Iraq. I didn't want to know. So I ran. But whatever was there for me on the old run along Crookleg Creek was gone now. There was no mystery I wanted answered at Jeffers' Rocks. I ran on through the fields and tried, without much heart, to find the hill above the pond, but I must have gone wrong in the high stands of corn, and I couldn't find that place at all anymore.

On Tuesday afternoon, I drove over to my sister Selma's trailer. It had been a long, long time since I did that, and when she came to the door I was surprised by how old she looked. Her hair was a weird brown with a streak of gray along the part. Her skin was gray, too, and leathery from smoking.

"Well if it ain't the hometown hero," she said.

"No, it's just me," I said.

"Nice of you to remember your big sister. What do you want?"

"I wanted to see you, because it's been too long."

"Well here we are." She looked down at her jogging suit, which looked like it hadn't been washed for a while. "Want some coffee?" She poured some cold stuff from that morning into a chipped mug and put it in the microwave. "Your wife okay? And little Miriam?"

"They'll be okay."

"So what do you want, Kurt?"

"I want to look in Mom's cedar chest."

Selma's eyes narrowed and there was something animal in them. "What are you looking for?"

I was walking toward the bedroom in the trailer, where I knew she kept the chest. It took up about a third of the space in those cramped quarters, but she maneuvered around me and stood in the way.

"The uniform," I said. "Is it still in there?"

Selma ran her tongue under her upper lip, making a show of thinking. She knew every little piece of memory that was in that trunk, big or small. Every so often she took all the clothes out and folded and refolded them, and put them all back in. And the uniform, which my mother kept for me, used to be at the bottom. What I didn't know was if she'd thrown it away.

"Yes," she said at last. "Yes, I guess it's still there."

On Wednesday I was lying naked in bed awake before dawn with the windows open to catch whatever cool there was, and whatever noise there was. The lawn sprinkler across the street hissed and sputtered for a while, then went off a little before sunrise. A couple of lonely birds sang. A car rolled down our street, and then slowed, and then drove back. The engine roared softly in front of our house, then shut down. There was nobody I wanted or expected to see today, not at this time of the morning anyway. My left hand felt the barrel of the Mossberg twelve-gauge on the floor beside the bed. I pumped a shell into the chamber, rolled off the bed, and stepped into the hall. The doorbell rang. I leveled the barrel at the door and waited for whoever it was to go away.

"Kurt?"

"Griffin? That you?"

"None other."

"You alone?"

"Yeah, sure."

"Good," I said, opening the door. "I'll put some clothes on. Why don't you go on into the kitchen."

"That gun for me?"

"Nope. The dick's not either."

"Fuck you."

When I joined him he was sitting at our little table with two big cups of Chuckwagon coffee, a box of Krispy Kremes, and a big thick manila envelope.

"So?" I said. "How goes the war in Washington?"

"It's going to be long and hard," he said. "You want to stay as far away as you can."

"I'm trying," I said. "But there's this asshole from Langley who keeps knocking on my door."

"This is the last time."

"You're not telling me this is good-bye."

"Could be."

"Well *hamdulillah*."

"This is for you," he said, pushing one of the coffees toward me. "And this too." The envelope.

"Court papers?" I didn't want to touch them if they were. He shook his head. "Take a look," he said

There were little bundles of hundred-dollar bills. A bunch of them. I sat down. "What the fuck is all this, Griffin?"

"That's a hundred fucking thousand dollars."

"Yeah. And?"

"For Betsy and Miriam."

"In cash?"

"From the DCI himself."

There was something wrong here. Real wrong. "You want me to sign a receipt?"

"Nope."

I spread the sheaves of bills on the table. "Whoa. It sure is pretty," I said. "Never seen that much money in one place, in cash like this."

"Yep. Mighty pretty."

"But, Griffin, where's it from?"

"Who it's for is you."

"Griffin, what's happening to all that money from La Merced?"

"I don't know. Gonna be tied up in the courts for a long time, I guess."

"This ain't part of it?"

"No. Shit no. The Director himself signed off on this."

"You're that tight with him? And he knows that much about me?"

"He knows enough."

"Right," I said. "Right. Thanks for the coffee."

"Sure."

"Keep the money."

"Kurt, what's the matter with you? This is enough to build a new house, at least. Betsy wants this. Miriam needs it. Man, it could be her college education."

"Uh-hunh. It's like a commission."

"What the fuck are you talking about?"

"I'm talking about three hundred million dollars in blood money."

"Fuck no. And anyway, you earned it, man. Who more than you?"

"Not like this. Not with you coming here like a bagman."

"You want me to get it out of an ATM like in London? That make you happier?"

"Forget that, Griffin. It's different. I can't take it."

Griffin put his big hands flat on top of the money. "Don't take it now. Okay. I thought it would be good for you. Maybe you'll think about it a little longer and you'll think so, too."

I took a deep breath. "Yeah." I took another couple of breaths for Miriam and Betsy. "Yeah. I'll let you know." I put the money back in the envelope. "Everything okay with you? Still leaving the Agency?"

"Not yet."

"That's what I figured."

"Yeah, the lines are drawn more clear since last week. The folks that count—they understand we got to do our own thing. The FBI's being cut out of the picture."

"You mean now that their shooters took Oriente out of the picture."

"Yeah. The Fucked-up Bureau of Investigation."

"But you were with them when that happened."

"I told them not to shoot unless he went for you or he tried to run. But you know, they don't listen, least not to the Agency."

"Right. Got it. That's why he got seven rounds in the gut while he was sitting still right next to me."

"I don't know what happened," said Griffin. "I haven't got to the bottom of it. But I will."

"Glad to hear it." We sat there drinking the coffee a couple of minutes. "I think you better go," I said.

We shook hands at the door. "Thanks for everything, Griffin. I mean it." I handed him the envelope. He took it without a word. "And—don't come back," I said.

Griffin walked toward his car, and I rested my hand on the barrel of the Mossberg leaning against the door frame. He turned quickly and looked over his shoulder, suddenly tense. I held up my empty hands. He smiled. With a wave that was half a salute, Griffin got into his rent-a-car and drove away.

A big storm was moving in from the northwest, and the air was real heavy at sundown. The bedroom was almost completely dark when I started to pay attention to the flickering in the vacant lot behind our house. "Lightning bugs," I said out loud. They floated like sparks over an invisible fire, cool and magic. "Look at that, Sugar," I said to the empty room. "Lightning bugs."

A second later the storm broke with a huge flash and a loud low rumble of thunder. I went to the window listening for the rain and smelling it on the wind. It came on fast and hard, beating the insects into the grass and stealing their glow. The jagged lightning cut across the sky. The white fire shot down into the fields, searching out trees and fence posts, and a sound like God's own war echoed across the land.

"Kurt."

I turned around and Betsy was standing just behind me. "Ah, Darlin'," I said.

Her clothes and hair and face were wet from the rain. I pulled her toward me. "Careful," she said. "The bandage." As I hugged her I could feel the chill leave her body and the warm begin.

"I've got to go back to Miriam in a little while," she whispered. "But I didn't want you to be all alone tonight."

The parade was due to start at ten in the morning. Most folks were out milling around in the parking lot of Westfield High a little after nine. The marching band tuned up a ragged version of "Over There." The majorettes threw batons in the air and caught them, or not. There were six or seven floats, one of them with a big papier-mâché face of Bin Laden peering out of a cave while a huge American eagle looked down at him. Another celebrated the cowboy heritage with a pretty collection of cowgirls from the class of 2003. There were kids all over the place on tricycles and bicycles with red, white, and blue crepe paper threaded through the spokes and streamers on the handlebars. And this year there was also something I'd never seen before: a roller blade routine put together by some of the regulars at the Genesis Health Club. One of the skaters was Ruth, decked out in red satin shorts, a red-white-and-blue shirt, and a gold glittery bicycle helmet.

"I'll be damned," I said as she rolled up to me.

"You look grand," she said, a little winded already. "If I'd have known you looked like that in a uniform, oh boy—"

"I never saw this side of you, Ruth."

"Oh there's lots of sides you ain't seen. Didn't Betsy tell you about all this?" She struck a pose.

"No."

"That girl. Only thing she ever thinks about is you, like you was going to break or something. You, the toughest bravest man—and just about the handsomest—that little ol' Westfield ever saw."

"Is she here? Did she bring Miriam?"

"They're waiting up at the Veterans' Memorial. Gotta go," Ruth said, and rolled away.

The VFW contingent was the biggest single group, some of them in dress blues like mine, but most in their old BDUs, or at least the jackets. There were maybe fifty who served in Vietnam, and almost as many who'd been in the Gulf War, one way or another. A couple dozen of the marchers were from World War II and Korea. I looked around to see if there might be one or two real old men left from World War I, but the ones I remembered from the parade when I was a kid were all gone now. At ten o'clock exactly they formed up in loose ranks. I took the cover off the flag and walked to the front. Winfield's little fife and drum corps struck up the march and we set off down Main Street.

There was a story that folks used to tell when I was a little kid, whenever there was a parade in town. I always thought it was just kind of an urban legend until one year somebody wrote a long letter to the *Westfield Dispatch* that gave a lot of the details. It happened in 1903. People said it was on July 4, but really it was in August. There was a town band then that used to give concerts on summer nights in the park across from the courthouse, where the Veterans' Memorial is now. It must have been the most peaceful kind of scene, like something out of Main Street in Disneyland. But there was a young man named Welbourne who'd been away in the wars, in Cuba and in the Philippines, and who came back changed. Everybody liked him. He was a good worker at the mill, and a kind of a hero just for having gone to war. And nobody saw how much he distrusted this place he called home, how much danger he saw around him. And nobody thought anything about it when Welbourne bought himself a twelve-gauge double-barreled shotgun at the hardware store, and eight boxes of buckshot.

The main thing I remembered from the article when I read it, when I was about fourteen I guess, was the description of Welbourne firing from Ninth Street, just off Main. He went down on one knee and let off both barrels, blasting through the man selling popcorn and the ladies in their big white bonnets and the band members who were suddenly desperately out of tune. And then he fell back a few steps like he was trained to do, reloading, and going down on one knee and firing again, and falling back, reloading, and firing again, until finally he pulled a six-shooter out of his belt and killed himself. And I remembered thinking that nobody in America knew that story except folks here in Westfield, and wondering if other towns in America had a Welbourne to forget.

I hadn't thought about the 1903 massacre for a long time, but as I led the parade up Main toward the corner of Ninth Street, I tightened my grip on the flag staff. There were just a bunch of little boys there waving little flags, and shouting and cheering. Then I heard an explosion. And another. A staccato like automatic weapons fire. I kept marching. The boys laughed and ran away from the string of firecrackers.

At Tenth Street I stopped, marking time, and the parade stopped behind me. The fifes and drums beat out a solemn march. I faced left, then walked past the low bleachers to the base of the granite column with the names of Westfield's war dead on it. I put the flag in its place. I stepped back and saluted. The fifes and drums stopped. A loudspeaker scratched and popped, and then a woman's voice sang out, "Oh say can you see—" Eyes straight. Head high. "—O'er the land of the free, and the home of the brave."

"Daddy!" Miriam was running toward me across the grass, with Betsy walking fast behind her. "Daddy! You're back!"

I picked her up. The parade was over for me.

"Where were you, Daddy?" It was like she'd forgotten the gas, the suffocation, the terror. Buried it. Erased it. At least for now.

"I went off to fight the Old Man of the Mountain," I said.

"Oh, Daddy, Aunt Ruth says that story's not true. Do you believe it?"

"Sure I do, Sugar," I said.

But the truth is, I've about given up on believing. It's enough just to be.

ACKNOWLEDGMENTS

The writing of this book relied, in ways that may not always be obvious, on the inspiration of two great friends. One was the novelist and essayist John Gregory Dunne, whose passion for American life and whose sure sense of patriotism impressed me and moved me for as long as I knew him. The other was Sadruddin Aga Khan, a tremendous fighter for the cause of humanity, sanity, and moderation in a brutal and disordered world. Sadly, both of them passed away in 2003. Neither of them ever had a chance to read this book, and I wish they had.

Most of *The Sleeper* was written in the months immediately after the tragedy that struck New York, Washington, and the world on September 11, 2001. Although the characters are fictitious, as are the precise circumstances in which they find themselves, the story was informed by ongoing developments and the facts that surrounded them. As I had done with *Innocent Blood* in the mid-1990s, I used fiction to game out the possibilities inherent in horrific events, based on my reporting about terrorist organizations, guerrilla wars, and government conspiracies since 1980. So, without implicating them in any way in this work of the imagination, I'd like to thank the editors of *Newsweek* for all their support in my pursuit of the truth, and among those editors, I'd like to single out my old friend Jeffrey Bartholet, whose critical eye for political and social nuance, along with his ear for good writing, have made the magazine's foreign news coverage consistently distinctive and distinguished.

I'd also like to thank both my editor at Simon & Schuster, Alice Mayhew, and my agent, Kathy Robbins, for their great and enthusiastic support through difficult and dangerous times. Without them, this book might never have been finished.

The larger story, as we know, goes on.

ABOUT THE AUTHOR

CHRISTOPHER DICKEY, *Newsweek*'s award-winning Paris bureau chief and Middle East editor, reports regularly from Baghdad, Cairo, and Jerusalem, and writes the weekly "Shadowland" column—an inside look at the world of spies and soldiers, guerrillas and suicide bombers—for *Newsweek* Online. He is the author of *Summer of Deliverance, Expats, With the Contras,* and the novel *Innocent Blood.* He lives in Paris.